PRAISE FOR
D. R. MEREDITH'S
MURDER BY IMPULSE

"John Lloyd Branson is a marvelous cross between Lord Peter Wimsey and Sherlock Holmes—bright, eccentric, and almost always in total control. But D. R. Meredith proves that mysteries don't need foggy London settings to be intriguing; the arid plains of West Texas do as nicely for murder and suspense. As a spinner of yarns about murder, Meredith has it all: fascinating crimes, marvelous characters, and a sense of humor to tie the whole together into a page-turning mystery that holds the reader until the final chapter."

Clay Reynolds,
author of *Vigil* and *Agatite*

"D. R. Meredith's High Plains mysteries started great and got better. MURDER BY IMPULSE is the best yet—delightful characters in a dandy story."

Tony Hillerman,
author of *Skinwalkers*

MURDER BY IMPULSE

D. R. Meredith

BALLANTINE BOOKS • NEW YORK

ISBN 0-345-34671-8

Manufactured in the United States of America

First Edition: January 1988

To Mike and Matt and Megan,
who fixed the meals,
did the wash,
and walked the dog,
so Mom could finish on time.

Canadian, Texas, is a very real, very charming town with red brick streets, huge cottonwoods, and many beautiful old homes. And for as long as you believe in John Lloyd Branson, he is real, too.

PROLOGUE

October

HE SHOULD HAVE STOPPED IN AMARILLO AND CAUGHT A nap instead of just having a cup of coffee. There was a truck stop just past the airport cutoff on I-40 where a man could get a shower, have a chicken-fried steak, and rent a bed. And if he had the urge he could always pick up a hooker and a dose of the clap for the same twenty-five bucks—sort of a buy-one, get-one-free offer. Prostitutes were always as thick around a truck stop as flies around an outhouse. Not that he was interested; it hurt his pride to have to pay for it, but he could've used a couple hours of sleep. He could've left at three and still arrived in Albuquerque by eight in the morning. It was an easy five-hour drive. Didn't even have to push the rig very hard to make it.

He blinked his eyes but the burning tiredness resisted so easy a cure. He was going to have to stop. Or take another pill and he didn't want to do that. A lot of good truck drivers ended up in trouble because of pills. Sometimes they ended up dead. You had to stay alert when you drove a rig weighing several thousand pounds. Particularly when your load was gasoline.

1

Glancing in the side mirror, he noticed the weaving headlights behind him. "Goddamn it!" he swore in the flat, slightly nasal accent common to the Midwest. "A stinking drunk. Or some kid high on something."

He hit his turn signal and swung into the right lane and began to shift down to slow the heavy rig. "Now get on around me," he said under his breath, glancing in the side mirror again.

"What the hell?" he exclaimed as the car swerved to the right as if attached to the truck by an invisible string. He tightened his grip on the big steering wheel. "Son-of-a-bitching kids! Must be drunk to play games with a truck—and in the middle of I-40! Wish to hell I was out of town where I could pull over onto the shoulder. Then we'd see how they'd like a lug wrench across the mouth."

He peered through the windshield. This stretch of interstate was like a concrete canal running through a residential area, all embankments and underpasses. No place to go if the car got too close. He laughed. Hell of a funny thing to be thinking: looking for a place to run when his rig was a lot heavier and bigger. Except he was hauling gasoline. Tank trucks were well built and supposed to withstand a few bumps.

He felt the sweat break out on his forehead. What was supposed to happen and what he'd seen happen were two different things. It hadn't been too long ago that a buddy of his had been rammed by a car and his rig had blown up. He wiped his forehead on his sleeve. He might die in a wreck. It was a risk for any trucker when you considered how many miles a man drove in a year; but he'd be damned if he was going to be trapped in the cab of his truck and burned to death like his buddy.

He hit his turn signal again. He was taking the next exit and getting off this damn interstate. There was a filling station just up ahead. He'd pull in and if the car followed, he'd get out and call the cops. He didn't generally like the cops. They were too quick to give a ticket or check his manifest, but by God this time he'd be glad to see one.

He shifted down, gritting his teeth at the sound of the gears squealing in protest, but there was an exit and he had to slow his speed or he'd risk coming off the interstate too fast. "Easy now," he said, unconsciously talking to his truck.

He glanced in the mirror. "Holy shit!" he screamed and stomped his foot on the accelerator.

The autopsy determined that he didn't burn to death; rather, he died of a broken neck.

The police were lucky in one respect: traffic was light on I-40 West at one o'clock on a Wednesday morning in early October. It was a little early in the season for skiers driving all night from Dallas and Fort Worth in order to be on the slopes of New Mexico by morning.

On the other hand it was too late in the season for the tourists. It was also too early in the morning. Tourists were either bedded down in a motel or cramped into a motor home or camper parked in a campground. Tourists had to be on their frantic way by eight o'clock in the morning.

So nobody was inconvenienced by the wreck except the ambulance squad, the fire department, the wrecking crews, the justice of the peace who was hauled out of bed to pronounce two charred bodies dead, and, of course, the police. But they were paid to be inconvenienced.

They were not ordinarily paid to lose their midnight lunch on the concrete median, but it was Patrolman Lewis Brown's first night as a rookie. It was also his first wreck and he'd discovered he didn't like looking at dead bodies.

"You gonna throw up your toenails, son?" Sergeant Larry Jenner was ten years older and had seen every variety of mutilated body. He could never decide whether he'd rather see one before he ate or after. Either way it soured his stomach.

"God, Sergeant, did you see those bodies? I mean,

God, there wasn't nothin' left 'cept black leather and teeth." He choked and whirled around to relieve himself of whatever remained in his stomach.

It was a rhetorical question so the sergeant didn't answer. "Get your flashlight and walk down the road a piece and check for skid marks."

"There aren't any," said a deep, hoarse voice.

The sergeant felt an instant's resentment, quickly followed by guilt which made him feel even more resentful. He didn't have any reason to feel guilty; he was doing his job. But Schroder could make God feel guilty.

"Things a little slow down at the Special Crimes Unit, Schroder? You checking out car accidents now?"

The burly man took a puff of his cigarette and the sergeant watched the red smoldering end creep to within a hair of the filter. One of these days Schroder was going to set the filter on fire and burn his upper lip. Or the end of his nose. Then he'd think twice about sticking it in everybody's business.

Ed Schroder ground the cigarette under his heel, then picked up the filter and put it in his pocket. "I was in the neighborhood," he said as he handed the sergeant an oblong piece of metal. "License tag," he explained briefly. "Impact must have knocked it off. Personalized, too. I've already run a check on it. The car belongs to a James Steele in Canadian, Texas."

The sergeant vowed to himself that whichever of his men had missed that license tag was going to wish he'd never been born. "Damn it, Schroder, I wish you'd let me do my job. You're a detective; go detect something."

Pale blue eyes ringed with sparse sandy lashes focused on the sergeant's face. "I am," he replied. "I'm trying to detect why there aren't any skid marks. Doesn't seem likely anybody'd drive up a truck's tailpipe without at least trying to stop."

The sergeant noticed he had a death grip on the license tag and consciously loosened his hands. He wondered what kind of departmental reprimand he'd get if he bent the tag over Schroder's head. "Maybe the driver went to sleep, or was drunk. Maybe the trucker slowed down to turn onto an access road and didn't signal; maybe he went to sleep and swerved over in front of the car. I sure as hell can't ask, can I? They're both charred meat. What I'm trying to say is there's no way to tell. No witnesses, not enough left of the bodies to do blood tests. It's a no-fault accident as far as I'm concerned, and if the insurance companies want to sue each other, they're damn sure not going to get me to testify one way or the other 'cause I can't.''

He touched the detective's shoulder. ''Unless the lab finds what's left of a bomb, it ain't murder, Schroder, so why don't you go on home and let me do what I'm supposed to do.''

Schroder's eyes blinked once. ''Let me know if you find out anything.'' He waved one stubby-fingered hand and ambled off, his barrel-shaped body reminding the sergeant of a bear in clothes.

''Who the hell was that fat slob?'' asked Patrolman Brown, his curiosity overcoming his nausea.

''He's not fat, son; he's stocky. And he's not really a slob. He just buys his shirts prefrayed.'' The sergeant rubbed his chin. ''He's an investigator at the Special Crimes Unit; you know, the ones that check out all the murders and suspicious deaths. He's the best they've got, and if I'd killed somebody, I wouldn't want him sniffin' my tracks. He's wrong this time though; this is just another damn fool accident.''

CHAPTER
ONE

L. A. FAIRCHILD WAS ON THE VERGE OF A NERVOUS headache, and she prided herself on never having headaches, nervous or otherwise. She'd found in the course of her twenty-four years that diligent study of a situation, careful preparation, and intelligent anticipation of all eventualities prevented nervousness—and thus headaches. Diligence, preparation, and anticipation had all failed this time. The exceedingly tall, thin man with graying blond hair unfolding himself from a high-backed leather chair in this ridiculously nineteenth-century office had simply refused to be reduced to three-by-five index cards, filed alphabetically, and studied at leisure.

Eccentrics always resisted being presorted and John Lloyd Branson was reputed to be the Texas Panhandle's most eccentric lawyer since Temple Houston had defended the innocent, the defenseless, and a few soiled doves in Old Mobeetie more than a hundred years before. He certainly dressed eccentrically. His beautifully tailored three-piece suit looked as if it were imported from Savile Row. The turquoise bolero he wore in place of a tie was a domestic bit of fashion from a Navajo reservation. A gold watch chain stretched across his vest. From it dangled a Phi Beta Kappa key and a tiny bear made of polished black pottery. His boots were black and handcrafted, polished to a mirror-like shine that reflected the silver-headed cane hooked over the arm of his chair. He should have looked mismatched. He didn't.

Looking up, L.A. received another shock. Eyes as black as obsidian were examining her, seemingly piercing her skull to analyze her thoughts. She stood motionless, aware she was in the presence of a will stronger than any she had ever known, directed by an intelligence greater than her own.

An unconscious sigh escaped her lips when eyelids closed over his piercing stare. His eyes opened again to express a watchfulness mixed with a mild curiosity. She blinked, wondering if her mind was playing tricks on her. She must have mistaken his expression because his eyes were such a shock. The blond hair and fair skin led her to expect blue eyes. Those eyes with irises dark brown enough to appear black were so unusual and so unexpected she had seen more force of personality than was actually there.

"So you are L. A. Fairchild." A slow drawl that was almost more a caricature than a natural voice startled her. A deaf person could go to sleep trying to read those lips was her first irreverent thought.

"How do you do," she said, slowing uncrossing her fingers but not offering to shake hands. Imagine shaking hands with John Lloyd Branson and leaving a wet palm print. Why at all the important times in her life did her palms have to sweat?

The black eyes blinked slowly in the thin, austere face. "What is your name?" he asked.

She swallowed and her headache went beyond verging and into completion. "L. A. . . ."

"L.A. is a city, young lady, where people occasionally spit on the sidewalks. You are a woman, and I refuse to address you by those ridiculous initials." The drawl had been replaced by a distinct voice that clipped each word with the precision of a sharp knife.

Her first instinct was to slap hell out of him, her second to call him a nineteenth-century male chauvinist pig and a twenty-four-carat bastard. Self-preservation stopped her first impulse; John Lloyd Branson didn't impress her as the type to turn the other cheek. As for name-calling, her gut instinct told her that he was better at it than she, and since she hated to lose, she satisfied herself by politely inclining her head. "Then you may call me Miss Fairchild."

She caught a sudden glint of respect in his eyes. He waved his hand toward a wooden armchair conveniently placed at one end of an enormous rolltop desk. "Sit down, Lydia Ann, and tell me why you decided to come to Canadian, Texas."

"W-what?"

He glanced at an open folder on his desk, then looked up. "Having aspirations toward being a gentleman, I'd appreciate it very much if you'd sit down so I can. Gentlemen never sit while ladies are standing, and you are a lady, I believe." His drawl was back, slower than ever.

Lydia took two steps and sank into the chair. "You already know my name?"

John Lloyd sat down and smiled at her. "Do you think I would consent to hire a law student just finishing his"— he cocked one eyebrow in amusement—"or *her* second year to clerk for me without knowing everything?"

He lifted the folder off his desk and quoted from it, his black eyes never leaving her face. "Lydia Ann Fairchild: twenty-four years old ; five feet, ten and one-half inches tall with blonde hair and blue eyes; daughter of an auto mechanic and a librarian . . ." He interrupted himself to smile again. "I presume your father was the auto mechanic?"

"Yes!"

"Don't be so defensive, Miss Fairchild; I wasn't denigrating his profession. I was merely ascertaining if it was indeed your father and not your mother who was the mechanic. These days one can't be sure.'' He glanced at the folder again. ''To continue, you graduated with honors from The University of Texas, entered Southern Methodist University School of Law, and at the end of two years have the highest grade point in your class. An admirable academic record,'' he said, placing the folder back on his desk. ''But to repeat, why did you come to Canadian, Texas?''

She considered lying but discarded the idea. She wasn't good enough at it to fool John Lloyd Branson. ''I needed a job. The dean recommended you as the best lawyer in Texas. You sounded interesting''—she avoided his eyes— ''so I came.''

''Miss Fairchild,'' he asked, stroking the little pottery bear with with one long finger. ''What exactly did the dean tell you?''

Those black eyes were disconcerting at such close range, and Lydia swallowed. ''He said John Lloyd Branson could climb into a pen full of Brahma bulls, climb out again, dust himself off, and call the vet to come treat the survivors.''

He laughed, a laugh as slow and deep as his voice. ''He might have exaggerated a little,'' he murmured. ''And what else did he say?''

''That Lawyer Branson was eccentric, but brilliant, and that he attended Harvard Law School and clerked for one of the justices of the Supreme Court in Washington.''

''Did he mention why I moved to Canadian? ''

''You were born here. You came roaring back into town one day cursing Washington, the Supreme Court, and judges in general. You said everybody east of the Mississippi was a goddamn crook, and that you weren't leaving Texas again. You said you preferred the home-grown variety of crook to the sleazy, sneaky kind around Washington.''

John Lloyd cocked one eyebrow. ''That is an approximation of my comments.''

"You also always vote for yourself in presidential elections."

"I prefer to vote for a trustworthy candidate."

Lydia leaned back in her chair and crossed her legs. She found herself enjoying telling him what the dean had said. She would enjoy it even more if John Lloyd Branson had the decency to act uncomfortable at hearing himself described as an egotistical, arrogant son of a bitch.

John Lloyd smiled and she suddenly became disconcerted. "Did he also tell you I'm a very dangerous man to cross? That I'm a good friend and a bad enemy?"

She sat up straight. "Vengeance is mine, saith the Lord, and Lawyer Branson sees himself as the Lord's right-hand man."

John Lloyd leaned back in his chair and hooked his thumbs in his vest. "I believe I'm known around the Panhandle as a God-fearing man."

"I'm certain you are. God makes sure he stays on the right side of Lawyer Branson."

She sat back again, feeling as though she'd finally won a point—several in fact—in this verbal confrontation. Until she noticed the expression in John Lloyd's eyes. He was amused.

"My dear Miss Fairchild, I'm certain your last two comments are not direct quotes from the dean."

"I'm capable of drawing my own conclusions," she retorted.

"So am I, Miss Fairchild," he replied blandly. "And I conclude that you are worth saving."

"Saving!"

He nodded. "The dean, who is a close friend of mine, tells me you are quite brilliant, always well prepared in class, but you show a marked proclivity for unsuitable relationships. This flaw demonstrates a lack of discrimination and objectivity."

She gasped. "I don't believe Dean Johnson said that!"

John Lloyd placed the folder on his desk. "You're quite right, Miss Fairchild; he didn't. What he said was that you were a sucker for a worthless man and you were going to ruin your . . . I believe his words were 'God-damned career if somebody didn't teach her to look for nettles among the roses.' So far you've managed to extricate yourself from these relationships with your reputation, if not your virtue, intact, but . . .''

"You leave my virtue out of this discussion!"

He cocked an eyebrow again and she felt an almost overwhelming impulse to find the nearest razor and shave it off. "I intend to, Miss Fairchild. Although you are beautiful, quite desirable in fact, I have no designs on your body. It is your mind I plan to seduce."

"You're not seducing either one," she said as she rose with as much dignity as she could muster. "I'm going back to Dallas. And I'm going to tell the dean exactly what I think of him."

John Lloyd pushed himself to his feet with an awkward motion. He caught Lydia by the shoulders. She found herself gently but firmly sitting down again. "I don't think that would be wise, Miss Fairchild."

In her opinion she had three choices: she could kick him in what her rape prevention instructor had indicated was a man's most vulnerable area; she could turn her head and bite his wrist; or she could behave in a civilized manner. Since open-toed sandals are not ideal kicking shoes, and her dentist had warned against endangering her caps by biting down on something hard, like a wrist, she opted for civilized behavior. It was probably safer anyway. "Unhand me, Mr. Branson, or I'll scream. You don't want your secretary to catch you in the act of man-handling me. She seemed like such a nice old lady."

John Lloyd's grip tightened. "My secretary was indicted for chopping up her husband with an ax. You may have heard about it; there was some little notoriety at the time. I succeeded in obtaining a suspended sentence for her and as a result she's quite fond of me. So you see, my dear, Mrs. Dinwittie wouldn't come to your rescue if I were disemboweling you."

"Chopped up her husband?" she asked, positive she'd misunderstood.

"Actually she was justified. He had several nasty habits, one being his enthusiasm for target shooting. Unfortunately, under the influence of alcoholic beverages he sometimes would discharge his pistol in the house. Mostly at Mrs. Dinwittie."

"Oh, God," said Lydia with as close to a gasp as she was capable.

"I didn't mean to frighten you, Miss Fairchild."

"Frighten me? First you tell me Lizzie Borden is your secretary—"

"I believe some unimaginative journalist so dubbed her," John Lloyd interrupted softly.

"Then you physically prevent me from leaving your office, and now you have the gall to tell me you don't mean to frighten me? "

"I told you about Mrs. Dinwittie to indicate that an emotional scene would prove more embarrassing to you than to me. As for my physically restraining you, I apologize."

He grinned, which shocked her almost as much as discovering Mrs. Dinwittie was an ax murderer. She didn't equate John Lloyd Branson with so plebeian an expression as a grin.

"I distrusted the expression in your eyes. To be quite frank, Miss Fairchild, I expected physical retaliation."

She smiled, or at least her lips stretched. She wasn't sure if the action was a smile or a grimace. "I never dreamed of kicking you, Mr. Branson."

"In that case"—he released her and sat down, again with a barely perceptible awkwardness—"we'll continue our discussion." His drawl was gone, his tone as sharp and quick as a whip.

"I don't think we have anything else to discuss. You made very unprofessional comments about my personal life."

"But necessary," he interrupted. "You see, Miss Fairchild, in additional to everything else I know about you, I also know your taste in reading material. You enjoy romances. Nothing wrong with that *except* I don't want you casting me as a romantic hero. I also am"—he hesitated—"unsuitable."

John Lloyd settled back in his chair and crossed one elegantly clad leg over the other. "Nothing to say, Miss Fairchild? No rebuttal? No discussion of my character?"

She took a deep breath, something she realized she'd been doing frequently since meeting John Lloyd Branson. "Let me see if I understand you, Mr. Branson. You're going to *save* me from my evil companions and, being above the sins of the flesh, you promise not to seduce me as part of my salvation. In return, I'm to control my romantic tendencies and not fall in love with you." She batted her lashes. "Did I leave anything out, Mr. Branson, sir?"

John Lloyd chuckled. "With a summation like that, Miss Fairchild, I predict a great future for you arguing before juries filled with religious fundamentalists." He studied her, then sighed. "However, you're wrong on several points. I'm not in the business of saving people; I leave that to God."

"I'm sure He's most appreciative," remarked Lydia dryly.

Other than a raised eyebrow and a sharp look John Lloyd ignored her. "Secondly, I'm not above the sins of the flesh. I merely don't indulge during office hours. Nor do I seduce my employees."

"In other words, you don't mess in your nest," remarked Lydia.

John Lloyd responded with another sharp look and continued. "Thirdly, your companions are not evil, merely inappropriate. A football player on academic probation is not your intellectual equal. Nor is the gentleman who flunked out of four universities while trying to find himself."

"He hasn't decided in what direction he's intended to go," Lydia protested.

John Lloyd's voice was without a trace of a drawl. "Then I suggest he buy a road map. As for your most recent swain, the less said the better."

Lydia felt like squirming. Her judgment had been a little poor in that particular case. "He had a legitimate grievance against the English Department."

"Nailing a protest sign to the office door of the president of the university was not the way to handle it, Miss Fairchild. Besides, the dean tells me four out of the ten words on the sign were misspelled, leading me to believe it was the English Department with the legitimate grievance. Your defending him by referring to the president of Southern Methodist University as"—he glanced at her file—"a *tyrant* was very foolish. Your exile to Canadian and my office was the dean's equivalent of getting you out of town until the heat's off. In other words, until the president's desire for a pound of flesh has passed, yours being the flesh in question, of course."

John Lloyd's voice slowed and deepened to its country drawl. "To sum up . . ."

"Don't bother," said Lydia sharply. "I don't think I'm up to any more character analysis."

John Lloyd ignored her and she wondered why she hadn't saved her breath. Stopping John Lloyd Branson from speaking his mind was comparable to stopping a landslide: both were forces of nature and would flatten anyone who got in their way.

He touched the tips of his fingers together as if he were a Chinese philosopher. "To sum up," he continued. "While it is an American tradition to help the defenseless, it is wise to first determine if they are defenseless only because someone took away their switchblades."

"Just a minute! None of my, uh, companions were violent," interrupted Lydia.

"You misunderstand me, Miss Fairchild. I was speaking metaphorically."

"Then try speaking plainly."

"You form these unsuitable attachments because you cannot recognize a lie when your emotions are involved, Miss Fairchild, and that is a skill you must develop. Otherwise . . ."

"Otherwise what?"

"You will fail in your chosen profession." John Lloyd leaned forward, his black eyes intent. "Your clients will lie, opposing attorneys will lie, the police will lie, witnesses will lie. You can believe no one."

"No one but John Lloyd Branson?"

He tapped a thick file lying on the corner of his desk. "Study this. I'll pick you up around seven and we'll have dinner with the people involved in this little legal action." He frowned at her. "And do something with your hair. Although I'm not a connoisseur of ladies' hair styles, I believe the bun is as out of date as old maid schoolteachers and spinster librarians. To use the vernacular, you resemble a peeled onion."

He handed her the file. "Enjoy your beauty, Miss Fairchild; it is a fleeting thing."

He abruptly turned his chair toward his desk. "Seven o'clock," he said in dismissal.

She was standing in the middle of the tiny bedroom of her garage apartment before she realized he'd never denied that he, too, would lie. She glanced in the dresser mirror. He didn't lie about one thing: she did look like a peeled onion.

CHAPTER
TWO

SERGEANT JENNER SWORE THE COFFEE SHOP IN THE basement of the Amarillo Police Department served the best submarine sandwiches west of New York City. He also swore they were responsible for half the weight gain of the entire force between departmental physicals. But what the hell, he thought as he surreptitiously loosened his belt another notch. He could eat rabbit food the rest of the month, take off ten pounds, and pass the physical with no sweat. He bit into his sandwich, savored the spicy blend of flavors, and swallowed with regret. That first bite was almost as good as sex. Which was another reason he was glad he was on the day shift: night duty played hell with his sex life. He took another bite, chewed happily, and contemplated his life. Submarine sandwiches at lunch, sex at night; a man could die content.

"Thought I might catch you here."

Jenner swallowed his bite half-chewed. "Damn it, Schroder, don't sneak up on a guy."

Ed Schroder pulled a chair out and sat down, a half-smoked cigarette already in his hand. ''Remember that wreck last October?''

''What wreck?'' Jenner asked, although he knew exactly which wreck Schroder meant. Jesus, he'd had a bellyful of that wreck. Both insurance companies had hammered at him for weeks until he wished he'd flipped a coin and blamed one dead driver or the other.

Schroder looked at him with all the patience of a grizzly who just treed a hunter in a sapling. Sooner or later the hunter had to come down. ''The gasoline truck and the Continental.''

''Oh, yeah, that one. You must have read the accident report to know it was a Continental. I mean, it was burned up pretty good.''

An inch of ash from Schroder's cigarette fell on the table. He shed cigarette ash like dogs shed hair in the summer, thought Jenner with the irritation of a nonsmoker. ''There wasn't much in the lab report or the autopsy,'' said the investigator.

''Hell, Schroder, the vehicles were burned, the bodies were burned. What kind of lab report did you want? There wasn't enough left of the Continental to determine if the brakes failed or the steering. As for the bodies, it's damn hard to do blood tests for drugs on overdone meat, or check for heart attacks. Besides, the families said neither driver took drugs or drank, and both were healthy, particularly the woman. There weren't even any dental X-rays for her. Her husband said she had perfect teeth, never had braces.''

''That was James Steele?''

''Huh? Oh, yeah, that was the guy's name. He was real shook up, sick as a dog after he saw the body.''

''How did he identify it?''

''Height, weight, right age, and it was female, of course. The Continental was his, and his wife backed it out of his garage and drove off in it three hours before the wreck. It was Mrs. Amy Steele all right.'' He bit into his sandwich again and wished to hell Schroder would go away so he could enjoy it.

Schroder pulled a folded magazine out of one sagging coat pocket. "You seen this?"

Jenner swallowed. Hell, by the time he finished playing twenty questions with Schroder, his submarine would be stale. "No, I don't read a lot of magazines. Or books either. I don't have much time between the job and the family."

Schroder opened the magazine, brushed a gray smudge of cigarette ash off a page, and pushed it across the table. "Jim Steele"—pointing a thick square-tipped finger at a photograph—"and his wife." The finger moved to another figure.

With all the resignation of a martyr, Jenner laid his sandwich down and studied the photograph. "She was a good-looking woman. No wonder he got sick to his stomach when he identified her body. She sure didn't look like that in the morgue."

"She wouldn't have looked like that anyway. This is the second Mrs. Steele."

Jenner scratched his head. "What are you getting at, Schroder? So the guy gets married again. That's not against the law."

Schroder looked at him and the sergeant flinched, then covered himself by pushing his chair back and turning it sideways so he could cross his legs. Schroder looked like an ill-humored bear hunting for somebody to swat. Jenner was almost sure he wasn't the somebody, but better to move out of range just in case.

Schroder's voice grated like coarse sandpaper. "The grass hasn't covered the first wife's grave yet."

Jenner rubbed the back of his neck where tiny hairs were standing at attention. Schroder's voice could give a sweating man a case of the chills. "Maybe he was lonely, maybe he met this lady and got a case of the hots, maybe she wasn't giving any away without a wedding ring first. Beside, people don't bury themselves with the first wife anymore . . ." His voice trailed off and he gulped. He'd forgotten. Schroder's wife died about three years ago and gossip around the department was that he still took flowers to her grave every week.

"Jesus, I'm sorry, Schroder; I forgot. But not everybody's like you. I mean"—he stumbled for words and wished he'd never started apologizing —"everybody knows how close you and your wife were. You took care of her like she was . . ."

"Was what, Sergeant?" asked Schroder, motionless unless one noticed his thick fingers curling into a fist. Jenner noticed.

". . . something special," finished Jenner in a rush of breath. She was, too. She'd been a lush for years, but he'd seen Schroder deck a rookie cop for saying so.

Schroder relaxed back in his chair, his fingers uncurling. "I've been to Canadian."

"Huh?" said Jenner. It was hard to hear over the pounding of his heart.

"You ever lived in a small town, Sergeant?"

"Uh, no. I grew up right here in Amarillo."

Schroder lit another cigarette, took a deep drag that produced a quarter-inch of ash, and exhaled as he spoke. "Funny things about small towns. Everybody knows everything about everybody else and generally their favorite subject to talk about is each other. Mostly they get some of their facts right, and sometimes they get most of their facts right, but they don't ever agree on all the facts. Except in Canadian. About Amy Steele."

"Wait a minute, Schroder. Special Crimes has jurisdiction in Potter, Randall, and Armstrong counties. You don't have any authority in Canadian; that's Hemphill County. And even so, you don't have any right to ask questions about Amy Steele. That wreck was an accident, and you're running around acting like it was murder. You ever heard of harassment, Schroder? You mess around asking questions and bothering people and the widower's gonna complain. Then what do you think'll happen? The Chief'll kick your butt around the police station if he doesn't kick you off the force instead."

Schroder's faded blue eyes didn't change expression.

"There weren't any skid marks, Sergeant; that makes the wreck suspicious."

Jenner felt a trickle of sweat run down the side of his face and wondered why he was sweating. Schroder always had that effect on people. "There could've been a hundred reasons why she didn't try to stop."

"But no good one, Sergeant, and that's why I've been spending my spare time poking around Canadian."

Schroder stubbed out the fraction of an inch left of his cigarette and rested both broad hands on the table. "When a body's found, I don't hang around looking over the lab boys' shoulders while they check for fingerprints, or vacuum up the dust in the room to see if there're foreign particles that don't belong. The lab's got their job and I got mine. Our lab's good, maybe better than most, but physical evidence is worth less than warm spit if I can't tie it to a person. So you know how I investigate a murder?"

"No, and I don't care because . . ." Jenner began.

"I look for motive. I poke around until I find somebody who hates the victim." He leaned over the table. "Do you know the kind of hate I mean? The kind that makes your voice shake when you talk about the person you hate. The kind that wakes you up at night with your belly hurting. The kind that grows and grows until your whole life is hating. The kind that ends in murder."

He whispered the last word and Jenner shivered. He wished he were out investigating some six-car pileup complete with victims. That kind of death seemed so much cleaner than the kind Schroder was talking about.

"But I can understand hate; I've hated people myself. To my mind it doesn't excuse murder, but at least it's understandable. There's something worse than killing somebody because you hate them, and that's killing somebody because they're in your way. That's treating people like they're garbage, just something to throw out like potato peelings. That kind of murderer is the worst kind there is. Half the time he doesn't hate his victim; he doesn't think of them as people. Be careful of standing between a man like that and his heart's desire, Sergeant. He'd as soon kill you as look at you."

"So which is Jim Steele? That's who this is all about, isn't it?"

Schroder nodded approvingly and Jenner snapped his teeth together in frustration. Damn it, don't ask any questions; questions just encourage a man like Schroder.

The detective lit another cigarette. "I haven't decided yet, maybe both. He and Amy Steele didn't sleep together and he's the one who moved out. Had a new wing built onto his ranch house and told her to stay out unless she was invited."

"Living in a small town must be like taking off your clothes with the curtains open: everybody sees the wart on your behind you been meaning to have burned off and haven't gotten around to yet. But, Jesus, do they have to describe it to every stranger that comes to town?"

"Listen to me, son, and maybe learn something. The good folk of Canadian hated the first Mrs. Steele too much to keep from talking about her, but they like Jim Steele too much to talk about him at all. What I found out, I learned from the people you don't notice: the carpenters, the plumbers, the painters, the carpet layers, the lady who hung the drapes, everybody that worked on that new wing, most of them from Amarillo. They saw plenty and heard more because the people in the house got used to having them around, forgot them even. In the old days, you talked to the maid. Now you talk to the plumber and the garbage collector. I think maybe Jim Steele hated his first wife."

Schroder puffed at his cigarette and exhaled a cloud of smoke that added to the layers of gray vapors over the table. "And that wife stood between him and what he wanted—which was the second wife."

Jenner waved his hands, trying to find enough unpolluted air to breathe. "Hell, Schroder, he could've divorced her; he didn't have to kill her."

One thick forefinger tapped the open magazine, scattering cigarette ash over the pages. "Didn't you read the title? 'The New Texas Rich,' and Jim Steele is one of the newest and richest. Oil in Hemphill County, barrels and barrels of it, all discovered in the last six months, and most of it on Jim Steele's ranch. Community property, Sergeant. What's mine is yours, share and share alike, split down the middle. Half of everything, millions for a divorce, or murder. What do you think?''

"You've already decided the poor son of a bitch is guilty. Why are you asking me what I think?''

"Because you're a good cop,'' he answered, dropping his cigarette into his half-empty coffee cup. "You had both vehicles examined and had the pathologist check for drugs and alcohol. You didn't like that wreck and you still don't. It keeps wiggling around in your mind like something you can't exactly remember. Your instincts are good, but your technique is all wrong. Motive first, always motive.''

The detective shifted and the plastic chair creaked under his weight. "So what's my next step after I find somebody or maybe two somebodys with a reason to want the victim dead? That's when I go to the lab and check over the physical evidence. Then I can interpret it. If my suspect works in a cement plant, I check the dust the lab vacuumed to see if there are traces of cement. If he's a mechanic, I can check to see if grease was found on the carpet. I've isolated my suspect and I can build a wall of evidence around him. Because a murderer always leaves tracks, Sergeant. The only perfect crime is the one where the detective isn't patient enough to keep looking.''

Schroder lit another cigarette and smiled. "I'm very patient.''

"But damn it, Schroder, there's no physical evidence. That car looked like it was the main course at an all-day barbecue. We tore it apart, or at least what was left, and if anybody booby-trapped it, the evidence was broiled away.''

Schroder added another layer of smoke to the already hazy air. "You looked at it from the wrong direction.''

"Wrong direction? The hell we did! We looked at it

upside down, right side up, backwards, forwards. Are you telling me I don't know how to do my job?''

"You looked at the car; I looked at the driver. You figured the car'd been tampered with; I figured the driver'd been tampered with." He paused, rubbing the rim of his coffee cup with two fingers so stained by nicotine they looked as if he'd dipped them in yellow dye.

"You still got nothing, Schroder. Just in case you didn't notice, the driver was broiled, too. If her husband slipped her a Mickey Finn, there's no way to prove it . . ."

"Yet."

". . . and we can't use rubber hoses or our fists to get a confession either. Remember that suspect last year that tripped over a door jamb, blacked his eye, said the jailer hit him, and threatened to sue? If his attorney hadn't tripped over the same door jamb, the department would've been up the creek without a paddle. So now we got to make sure they don't catch a hangnail or bump their shins. I tell you, Schroder, sometimes it ain't worth . . . What do you mean *yet*?''

Schroder shoved the magazine toward Jenner, dropped his cigarette into a coffee cup, and pushed his chair back. "Read that," he ordered.

"What do you mean *yet*?'' Jenner demanded again, watching the detective tuck his shirt back inside his pants. Shirts always crawled toward Schroder's armpits the minute he sat down. The Chief said the Army ought to study the phenomenon, maybe synthesize it, and sprinkle it on Russian Army underwear; the U.S. could win the Cold War before it got hot. A man sure as hell can't fight when his underwear's creeping up on him.

"Just want to keep you up to date, Sergeant. May want your help a little later on." Schroder raised his hand and ambled toward the door with his usual side-to-side gait.

"My help!'' yelled Jenner. "Hell, no, Schroder! I'm not in Special Crimes; I'm a traffic cop. You get your own ass in a crack, but you're not putting mine there. You're up to something, you crazy bastard.''

The door closed behind Schroder, and Jenner flung himself around and pounded his fist on the table. The sound would have echoed if the small coffee shop had been big enough, and if it hadn't been so full of people; other uniformed cops, a few city employees, and a couple of guests, all staring at Jenner. He felt his skin growing hot and knew damn well his face was red. He grabbed his coffee cup, wishing it were three times as big so he could hide his whole head behind it. He had it almost to his mouth when he saw Schroder's cigarette butt floating among a few sodden flakes of tobacco.

"Goddamn it," said Sergeant Jenner.

CHAPTER THREE

"ABOUT MY APARTMENT . . ." BEGAN LYDIA, JERKING open the door before John Lloyd had a chance to knock.

"It isn't satisfactory?" he asked, brushing past her into the small living room, swinging his silver-headed cane. "Insufficient hot water, perhaps?"

"There's plenty of hot water."

"You dislike the color scheme? Although it was recently remodeled, I'm certain the landlord would be amenable to your repainting the walls."

"The walls are fine . . ."

"You're displeased with the furniture? Not everyone is fond of antiques, but I assure you they were selected for both comfort and beauty. No horsehair sofas." He smiled as if pleased with himself.

"I like the furniture . . ."

"Then the kitchen displeases you? I was assured that all the modern conveniences possible were installed."

"Why didn't you tell me *my* apartment was over *your* garage?" demanded Lydia.

"You didn't ask," replied John Lloyd, cocking his eyebrow in surprise.

He was calm, solicitous, irritatingly logical, and she slammed the door in frustration. "You're not my father, and you have no right to interfere in my personal life after business hours."

"Miss Fairchild, you may be sure that I have no fatherly instincts in regard to you. I also fail to see how your living on my property has anything to do with your personal life. Provided, of course, you're discreet. Canadian is a small town and its citizens won't condone . . ."

"You're already doing it," she interrupted, stalking toward him like a tawny lioness intent on making a meal of an antelope.

John Lloyd backed up and sat down on a comfortably overstuffed chair, resting his hands on his cane. "Pardon my lack of manners to sit while you're still standing, but it's been a long day and I'm tired. Now just what is it I'm already doing?"

Lydia stopped in front of him. "Telling me how to live my life," she shouted. "Insinuating that I'm planning on crawling into bed with every man that walks up those stairs."

John Lloyd applauded. "I can almost hear you in front of a jury. 'Ladies and gentleman, my client is the kindest, most patient woman in the world. She visits the sick, takes food to the elderly, bakes cookies for the neighbor children. She can hardly bear to kill cockroaches in her own kitchen. Never, for any reason, no matter what the provocation, would this wife, this mother, ever even think of stabbing her husband with a bread knife.' You will be magnificent, Miss Fairchild, but until you pass the bar I suggest you curb your propensity for exaggeration. It's an admirable skill for a trial lawyer, whether for prosecution or defense, but it's rather wearing on a daily basis. Add to that your distressing habit of jumping to conclusions, and you become a rather stressful person with whom to associate. Fortunately," he added, grasping his cane and levering himself out of the chair, "I've had sufficient experience in handling stress to cope with you."

Lydia clenched her hands into fists. "I won't be treated like a child."

"I believe that is my point, Miss Fairchild . . ."

"Point! You wouldn't know a point if you sat on it. You compliment me, insult me, insinuate you plan to manipulate me—all in one breath."

John Lloyd smiled. "Manipulate you? On the basis of our short acquaintance, Miss Fairchild, I would say that the man who could manipulate you hasn't yet been born. I suspect that even your unfortunate association with the illiterate English major was not manipulation as much as a heroine in search of a cause. In other words, you're suffering from a Joan of Arc complex. Kindly remember her ultimate fate." He grasped her elbow and gently turned her toward the door. "Shall we go? I don't wish to be late."

Lydia considered her options. She always seemed to be considering her options when dealing with John Lloyd Branson. It didn't help that her behavior had been childish. It helped even less that he found something admirable about that behavior. And it helped not at all that he had been right on target about the English major. She hoped he never discovered that nailing the sign on the president's door had been her idea. She only wished she'd checked the spelling.

She looked up to find him studying her. If he were anyone else, she'd think it was regret in his eyes. Except she would bet John Lloyd Branson never regretted any action in his life. He was far too sure of himself. "We haven't finished our fight," she reminded him, and stepping away, took a classic boxer's stance: one foot forward, arms close to her body, fists up.

John Lloyd looked startled for a moment, then tilted his head back and laughed. "Like all women you have to have the last word, don't you, Miss Fairchild?"

Lydia straightened her shoulders and rested her hands on her hips. "That's a chauvinistic statement, Mr. Branson. Haven't you ever heard of women's lib? Of course, you haven't. You don't even live in the twentieth century. I'll bet you still shave with a straight razor, and wear a nightshirt to bed. Why, you probably think it's a sin to make love with the lights on.''

John Lloyd's face was blank and she saw him take a deep breath as he reached past her to open the door. ''Shall we go, Miss Fairchild? We can discuss the file on the way. I presume you've read it?''

She knew she was blushing; she could feel it. She could also feel John Lloyd's disapproval like an arctic chill. She picked up her purse and the file and, slipping past him, hurried down the stairs. At the bottom she grasped the banister. Perhaps her reference to his sex life was a little personal, but she hadn't committed the faux pas of the year, for God's sake! Just because he was a throwback to the Victorian era didn't mean she was.

She whirled around, the adrenaline beginning to flood her body at the prospect of another verbal battle. ''John Lloyd!'' she began. ''I'll have you know . . . John Lloyd! What's wrong with your leg?''

He lurched down the last few steps, hanging on tightly to the banister with one hand and his cane with the other. Reaching the bottom, he took a step toward her, his limp almost imperceptible on the level ground. His eyes were as gleaming as the obsidian they resembled. ''Get into the car, Miss Fairchild.''

Lydia scrambled into the black Lincoln and turned to face the tall figure awkwardly sliding into the driver's seat. ''Why didn't you tell me you were handicapped? I wouldn't have expected you to climb those stairs.''

''Miss Fairchild!'' His voice lacked any trace of a drawl and cut like a razor. ''If I am not your father, then the reverse is also true. You are not my mother, and I can do without your nurturing. My person is not a subject for conversation or an object for your concern.''

She could have called down upon his head all the accusations that women have been hurling at men since human reproduction began: obstinate, foolish, childishly proud—finishing up with that catchall phrase of ''isn't that just like a man?'' Except John Lloyd Branson couldn't be reduced to a cliché. She cleared her throat to loosen the obstruction that felt very much like a sob, except she never cried, having learned long ago that blondes look terrible when they cry. "I'm sorry," she said, and was horrified to hear her voice wobble.

John Lloyd muttered what sounded to Lydia like a particular four-letter word she wouldn't have thought he would admit knowing, much less using. "Did you read the file, Miss Fairchild?" he asked in his drawl as he backed the big Lincoln out of the driveway.

"I—I glanced through it," she stuttered. Damn him anyway. He wasn't gracious enough to acknowledge her apology and now he had her stuttering. John Lloyd Branson gave the word *stress* new meaning.

"That is an imprecise answer. Did you read it?"

"Yes! But I didn't memorize it."

"That isn't necessary on your first day of employment," said John Lloyd wryly, turning onto the main street.

"Well?"

"You're being imprecise again, Miss Fairchild."

"Aren't you going to quiz me?"

"I'm not a schoolmaster. If there is a legal instrument you are unfamiliar with, I'll be happy to enlighten you; otherwise, enjoy the scenery. The Steele ranch is some seven miles from Canadian."

"A real ranch? With real cowboys?"

"Don't let your romantic nature get the better of you, Miss Fairchild. It is a real ranch; we don't have any other kind in the Texas Panhandle. As for cowboys"—he hesitated—"they're real. But it isn't always a romantic profession. Shoveling horse manure out of a barn is hardly anyone's idea of a good life, particularly when it isn't even your barn."

Lydia sighed dramatically. "Aren't you going to leave me any illusions?"

John Lloyd glanced at her. "I hope to. Your romantic illusions are part of your charm."

She was so astonished she couldn't think of a reply.

Even John Lloyd's compliments were stressful. She looked out the window at the scenery.

The two-story house of native stone seemed to spring from the ground as if Nature had piled golden-beige rocks one on top of another, added long narrow windows and doors, and tacked on a covered porch that ran the length of the building. Lydia looked closely and noticed that two wings had been added to what was obviously the original structure, and added so skillfully that old and new blended together into an imposing whole. Situated on a slight rise, the house seemed an integral part of the harsh prairie. Huge trees shaded the house and added a gentle rustling that circulated the pungent scent of wildflowers, the tangy scent of sage and mesquite.

John Lloyd parked in front of the house. "Ranch headquarters of the Steele ranch. If Canadian might be said to have landed gentry, then the Steeles are that gentry." He inclined his head as if paying homage.

Lydia immediately felt her palms become damp. The whole house screamed old wealth and she'd grown up on new middle-class paychecks. The only thing she'd have in common with the Steeles was the number of fingers and toes. She surreptitiously wiped her palms on the upholstery, and waited for John Lloyd to stop staring at the house as if he'd never seen it before. Finally, she cleared her throat. "Are we getting out, or does the family offer curb service?"

"Jocularity is out of place, Miss Fairchild," he said without drawling and she knew she'd stepped over some invisible line—again. Unfortunately he had more lines than graph paper, she thought as she watched him circle the front of the car and open her door. "Do you want me to bring the file, Mr. Branson?" she asked sweetly, ignoring his outstretched hand and slipping gracefully from the car.

"What?"

"The file, John Lloyd. Isn't that why we came out here? The lease agreement? You wanted the Steeles to look over the lease agreement?"

He pinched the bridge of his nose. "By all means bring the file, Miss Fairchild. And if you find it within your capabilities to observe without jumping to conclusions, I shall be interested in your opinions."

"My opinions of who?"

"Whom, Miss Fairchild," he corrected.

"All right, whom?"

He hesitated. "Of all those who live here." He took her arm to escort her, both of them studiously ignoring his awkwardness climbing the few steps onto the porch.

CHAPTER
FOUR

"SCHRODER, THIS IS FRIDAY NIGHT. IT'S MY DAY OFF. My kid has a T-ball game. I'm not on the Special Crimes Unit. I'm not a trained investigator. Schroder, goddamn it, are you listening to me?"

The burly older man squinted at a key and shifted his cigarette with its half-inch-long ash to the other side of his mouth. "Five," he said out of one side of his mouth. Schroder was an expert at speaking out of one side of his mouth. He had to be; the other side was always occupied with holding a cigarette.

"Five what?"

Schroder unlocked the padlock, dropped the key in his coat pocket, the one that had a folded magazine sticking over the top, and with a powerful jerk, sent the overhead door crashing up. ". . . not to work," he said.

"What did you say?" yelled Jenner, watching the door rock violently along its grooves, slam against the metal stop, and bounce back, quivering like a nervous virgin. Probably afraid Schroder would kick it in its seams.

"You got five excuses not to work," repeated Schro-

32

der. His cigarette ash was now an inch long and curving gently downward. As Jenner watched, it obeyed the force of gravity and showered the lapel of Schroder's coat—to be lost among the lint, cat hair, and other unidentifiable flotsam that Jenner didn't care to examine too closely.

"Well, then?"

"You got one good reason to work. That's enough." Schroder entered the storage building and squinted at the walls. "See a light switch? Supposed to be one."

Jenner impatiently flipped on the light. "What reason, Schroder? Just name it," he said to the back of Schroder's head as the square-bodied man lumbered out of the building and over to a car that looked at least as disreputable as its owner. "You're just dragging me out because you're pissed. That's it, isn't it? You're pissed because I'm not getting wired up over this wreck." He grabbed the flashlight Schroder tossed him. "You know what I feel like doing? I feel like amending my report. I'll say the lack of skid marks strongly suggests that Mrs. Amy Steele fell asleep or was otherwise incapable of controlling her vehicle when the truck driven by Mr. Leroy Sadler slowed to turn without giving a proper signal. How's that sound, huh? Gets both insurance companies *and* you off my ass."

"You won't," grunted Schroder, heaving a battered leather satchel out of his truck. "You're a good cop. You got commitment. Grab that camera, Jenner."

Jenner eyed the contents of the trunk with distaste and gingerly lifted out the camera. Did that wadded-up blanket tucked behind the spare tire move? No? It could have. Most likely there were whole colonies of undiscovered animal life residing in Schroder's trunk.

"So what's the reason, Schroder?" Jenner asked, following the older man back into the building. "Tell me why I'm standing in a rented storage building looking at a cremated Continental."

Schroder set the satchel down, extracted the last quarter

inch of his cigarette from his lips, ground it out on the cement floor, and dropped it into the pocket with the magazine and door key. "I used your name when I called the insurance company and demanded to reexamine the car. You tied down the scene, so technically it's your case."

"Son of a bitch! And they wanted to know why, didn't they? So what did you tell them? That I'd changed my mind? Well, I haven't. There's no evidence of mechanical failure and there's no evidence of tampering. That doesn't mean there wasn't both. It just means that evidence, if any, burned up. But I'm not writing up an incident report on what might have been, or could have happened. I'm not about to sit in a witness box and have some smart-ass cocky lawyer accuse me of speculation. Cops aren't supposed to speculate, at least not until there's evidence. Then it's called reconstruction, as in crime scene reconstruction. Besides, the damn case is closed. C-L-O-S-E-D."

Schroder's faded blue eyes held the long-suffering, impatient expression of a mother bear just before she cuffed an impudent cub. "And that's just what we're fixing to do: reconstruct the crime scene . . ."

"It wasn't a crime scene! It was an accident scene."

". . . Amy Steele left the Bar-S Ranch just before eleven P.M. An unexpected whim is what her husband called it in his statement. Announced she was going for a drive and left. Now this is where things start getting interesting. There were a couple of metal hinges and some melted plastic in the trunk—like maybe you'd find if a suitcase burned."

"So what, Schroder? Maybe she was going to spend the night in Amarillo and go shopping. Maybe they had a fight and she was going to scare him by not going home. It's irrelevant anyway."

Schroder held up a broad hand with thick stubby fingers. "It proves Jim Steele was lying. That's relevant. You got one dead wife that he hated. That's relevant."

"Do you know you're crazy, Schroder? You better take

some medical leave and consult a psychiatrist. Talk about
building a mountain out of a mole hill. You're down on
this Jim Steele character because you think he remarried
too soon. He didn't crawl into that coffin with his dead
wife. I'll tell you something. I don't want anything to do
with this crusade of yours. I'm taking my ass out of here
if I have to walk.''

Jenner set the camera on the floor of the storage building and headed toward the door. Schroder was totally,
completely crazy, around the bend, off the rails. He
couldn't figure out why he'd let the old bastard talk him
into coming out in the first place.

''Jenner!'' Schroder's hoarse voice seemed to reach
out and punch him in the back. ''You never closed this
case. It's still in the active file. You can't let go of it.
Your gut instinct tells you something's wrong. You gonna
walk out before you know if your gut is right?''

Jenner stopped outside and leaned against the building.
The metal was still blistering hot from the day's high
temperatures. Nearly a hundred and it was only June. He
couldn't remember it being this hot this early. It was
going to be a bastard of a summer: hot and dry and windy.
Be some grass fires out on some of the ranches. One
cigarette thrown out the window and you could have a
hell of a weenie roast. God, couldn't he think of anything
but fires? He ought to start walking. Maybe he could
make it to the ball park in time to catch the last inning
of Timmy's game. He drew circles in the dirt with his
foot. Hell, he might as well admit it. He wasn't going
anywhere except back in the storage building because
Schroder was right: he couldn't let go of that damn
wreck. But he didn't intend to admit it.

''I don't want you to get the wrong idea, Schroder.
I'm just staying to keep you out of trouble,'' he said as
he walked back inside.

Schroder continued as if Jenner had never left. ''They
have a fight and she throws some clothes into a suitcase
and takes off. No opportunity to tamper with the car before she left. It had been inspected and a new safety

sticker issued two days before according to the insurance investigator. No reason to suspect mechanical failure . . ."

"I know all that!" interrupted Jenner. "Any time you think an insurance investigator can outinvestigate me . . ."

"How many towns between here and Canadian?"

"What the hell does that have to do with anything?"

"How many?"

Jenner scratched his head. "It depends on her route. The quickest is by way of Pampa straight to Amarillo and pick up I-40 at the east edge of town."

"A lot of open country, straight roads, no traffic?"

"Well, yeah, for the most part. What's your point, Schroder? Practically the whole damn Panhandle's nothing but open country and straight roads. Hell, there's nothing to go around. Why put a curve in a road running through flat prairie?"

"When do most drivers go to sleep and have a wreck?"

"At night on the open highway where's there little or no traffic. The driver gets sort of hypnotized by the monotony of that little lighted patch of concrete in front of him. There's no distractions to keep him alert, keep the adrenaline pumping."

"Exactly," said Schroder, nodding his large, square head in approval. "So why did Amy Steele stay awake driving through quiet open country, then suddenly fall asleep in the middle of Amarillo with all the lights and traffic and noise?"

"I don't know! That's why I didn't cite her going to sleep as a possible cause of the wreck."

"How fast was the Steele car traveling?"

"I don't know exactly, but the force of the impact says at least the speed limit, maybe more."

"Had the car tried to swerve? Was it pointed toward the center median or toward the side embankment?"

"No," said Jenner slowly. "It hit that truck square in its license plate. Bang! Instant bonfire. "

"How fast was the truck going?"

"Again it's hard to tell. I *think* about forty. The driver was gearing down. We know that much from what was left of the cab. And the right-turn signal was on; at least, the turn indicator was in that position. There was an exit lane about a hundred yards beyond the point of impact. He could've been going to get off I-40. Or he could've swerved in front of her; she couldn't stop, and boom.''

"No skid marks," Schroder pointed out.

"All right, so she didn't try to stop.''

"Why leave I-40?''

"Who? The truck driver?'' Jenner wished Schroder would use complete sentences. Actually he wished Schroder would shut up. No wonder the man was the best investigator Special Crimes had; the Ayatollah would confess to being a Christian if it meant getting Schroder off his back. "I don't know. Maybe he needed to gas up or take a leak. There was a filling station just off the exit ramp.''

Schroder fumbled a cigarette out of his shirt pocket and lit it with the most battered lighter Jenner had ever seen. The old bastard must have bought it from a survivor after the fall of Troy, he thought. Schroder spoke through a cloud of tobacco smoke. "He did that at the truck stop twenty minutes before.''

"How the hell do you know that?'' demanded Jenner. "And if you know all the answers, why are you asking me? You're grilling me like I'm a suspect in a multiple homicide.''

"You're looking at this wreck from the wrong end. You're looking at the evidence and trying to reconstruct what happened, just like you're supposed to. You're trying to work from the facts to the suspect . . .''

"There isn't any suspect! We don't even know if there's a crime.''

". . . instead of starting with the suspect and working back to the facts.''

Jenner felt an urge to scream. Schroder was nothing but a scruffy, overrated, out-of-date slob. Modern police

work was a science. It was blood tests, saliva tests, soil
samples, fingerprints, plaster casts of shoe prints, weights
and measures. It was test tubes and microscopes, argon
lasers and computers, for God's sake. Solving a murder
by deduction based on instinct and a detective's seat-of-
the-pants knowledge of human psychology was only done
in mystery novels. Detectives weren't detectives anymore; they were scientists and accountants and forensic
pathologists.

Schroder evidently didn't realize—or care—that he had
been displaced by technology, thought Jenner as he listened to the deep hoarse voice expounding his theory
with the enthusiasm of a voyeur on a nudist beach. What
was worse, he was beginning to make sense.

"We start with the victims. Was anyone richer or
happier with them dead? Not Leroy Sadler, the truck
driver. In fact, it's gonna be hard on his family with him
gone. But Mrs. Amy Steele is different. Her husband gets
rid of a wife he hates without paying through the nose to
do it. Now we got a suspect, but do we have a crime?"

He stopped to light a cigarette and take a few deep,
lung-destroying puffs. If nothing else, the old man knows
how to tell a story, thought Jenner. "I give up, Schroder.
How did he do it?"

The burly detective rolled his cigarette over to one corner of his mouth. "Let's not get the cart before the horse.
Let's consider the facts."

"Jesus Christ! I've been considering the facts for eight
months! The facts don't tell me anything one way or the
other. The facts say the wreck couldn't have happened at
all."

Schroder's lips stretched over his teeth, his cheeks
bunched into round pouches, and his eyes narrowed into
slits. Jenner thought at first he might be having a fit until
he heard the rumbling sound work its way from the barrel
chest, past the inevitable cigarette, and into the open air.
God, if there was anything worse than Schroder frowning, it was Schroder smiling.

"Exactly," he said. "Dry roads, no excessive speed,

no mechanical failure, no bomb. Those are facts. No skid marks, a truck gearing down, a turn indicator on. Those are facts. How would a reasonable person explain all those facts?''

"I don't know," said Jenner. "As far as I can tell, there aren't any reasonable people listening." That comment earned him a frown and he shut up.

"A reasonable person would say that maybe there aren't any skid marks because Amy Steele couldn't stop—and that trucker knew it and was trying to get his rig off I-40 and out of her way."

Jenner wiped his shirt sleeve across his forehead. Schroder was right. He could feel it. That was why he was sweating and shivering at the same time. He could almost feel himself in the cab of that truck, fighting the gears and knowing he wasn't going to make it to that exit. "Why? What was wrong with Amy Steele?"

Schroder ground out his cigarette under the heel of one scuffed, unpolished shoe and peered at Jenner from underneath bristly eyebrows. "I don't know."

"What do you mean, you don't know? You're the detective. You're supposed to know. You can explain everything else."

"We collect a lot of facts, reconstruct the crime scene up to a point, and . . ." He hesitated, looking at the burned Continental. "A murder investigation is a lot like a river, Sergeant. We know what's on this side, and we can see the other side, but the bridge is in pieces. So we start constructing the bridge: a support here, a railing there, check the stress, sink the piling deep in the riverbed. But sometimes we're missing a piece and the bridge won't hold a man's weight and we can't get to the other side. That's when a murderer goes free. Because that bridge has to be one solid piece. The jury's gonna stand on that bridge, jump up and down on it, and if it drops their asses in the river, they're gonna let that man walk. The wreck's on this side of the river and we know something's not right about it. Jim Steele's on the other side and we know he had a motive, a good motive, for causing that wreck. But we're missing a piece of the bridge and if we don't find it in the car, then we're gonna have to leave that man to God.''

Jenner felt the hairs on his arms spring erect. Schroder sounded like an old-time revival evangelist. But he was preaching to an empty tent. ''There's no missing piece, Schroder. That car's been scoured six ways to Sunday.''

''That's right,'' he agreed. ''Everybody looked at the outside, underneath, under the hood. But nobody took the *inside* of that car apart. That's where the missing piece is gonna be—inside the car. Amy Steele was all right when she left Canadian and all right for almost two hours afterwards. So whatever she ate or drank or breathed that made her ram that truck, she brought with her inside that car. You been certified as a police photographer?''

''I took some courses, but I don't know how good I am.'' He paused in the act of picking up the camera as his intuition suddenly awoke. ''Schroder, how come it's just me and you? How come the whole Special Crimes Unit isn't here?''

Schroder took a crowbar out of the leather satchel. ''Special Crimes isn't involved.''

''What do you mean not involved? Oh, God, Schroder, your lieutenant doesn't know anything about this, does he? You're acting on your own, aren't you? And you dragged me along. We could get suspended. Goddamn, I can't afford to be suspended; I've got a wife and three kids. I've got six more payments to the orthodontist on Melissa's braces.''

Schroder pried open the door on the driver's side. ''Take a photograph and stop worrying. If we find something, I'll tell the lieutenant. If we don't, there's no point in ruining everybody's weekend.''

''I don't know why the hell not. You're ruining mine.''

Schroder gave him a look that plainly expressed displeasure and Jenner quickly took a photograph. A displeased Schroder could be as bad as suspension. Maybe worse.

At the end of an hour, the driver's side of the car was gutted. The bucket seat, or rather its charred remains, sat in the middle of the floor. Jenner derived no pleasure in looking at it. The outline of Amy Steele's body could still be seen as more lightly burned patches of vinyl. And he was fairly certain that those threads adhering to the headrest weren't threads at all but a few pitiful hairs from her head.

Schroder wiped his face with a grimy handkerchief and managed to spread the soot over the few remaining clean patches. He resembled the end man at a minstrel show. But nobody would look at him and laugh, thought Jenner. Not with that determined expression on his face. Schroder looked like one mean papa bear.

He followed Schroder around the car to the passenger side and obediently snapped a picture of the door being pried open, then several pictures of the interior. "All yours," he said, stepping back to watch. He hated to admit it, but watching Schroder was an education. First he looked over the interior, then with a flashlight he went over every inch of the floorboard and the passenger seat. Next he bent over and peered under the seat, although how someone with Schroder's square body could bend at the waist was one of life's unsolved mysteries, thought Jenner. Schroder didn't have a waist. He was one solid block from shoulders to thighs.

He shifted the camera from hand to hand and waited for the detective to move on to the next step: prying up the seat. He wiped his face and grimaced as he saw the soot on his hand. That's all they were going to find: soot and Amy Steele's singed head hairs. This car couldn't tell them anything. It was as mute as the grave. As mute as Amy Steele.

Schroder backed out and squatted by the side of the car. "Hand me the crowbar," he grunted, his blue eyes hard and still.

"This is the end, isn't it?" asked Jenner, giving him

the crowbar. "If there's nothing in the front seat, we're not going to find anything in the back either."

"It's the end of something," he agreed, gently prying up the outer edge of the seat. "Take a picture of the missing piece of the bridge, Sergeant Jenner."

CHAPTER
FIVE

"JOHN LLOYD! I'M SO GLAD . . . OH, GOD!" THE YOUNG woman's voice broke in a gasp.

Lydia glanced over her shoulder. No one there but John Lloyd, and even in the dim light he couldn't be mistaken for God.

"Christy Steele, may I present my legal clerk, Miss Lydia Fairchild."

"You're a woman!"

"Since birth," agreed Lydia. "But don't tell John Lloyd. He thinks I'm a female impersonator," she whispered, staring into Christy Steele's shocked eyes.

"Miss Fairchild has no small reputation for audacity. And wit of a certain sort." John Lloyd's voice held its customary drawl, but his grip on Lydia's arm was more in the nature of a vise. "Miss Fairchild, our hostess for the evening, Mrs. James Steele."

Next to Christy Steele, Lydia felt like an overgrown ox. Petite women always had that effect on her. They reminded her of being in the seventh grade again and already standing five feet eight in her bare feet. Christy

43

Steele was a pocket-sized Venus with honey-colored hair, big honey-colored eyes, and a figure that would raise the dead, if the dead in question were male. If Christy Steele had a flat tire, a thousand men would offer to change it. Those same men would merely loan Lydia a tire tool.

Lydia shuffled her size-nine feet and fumbled for something to say. After her previous comment, she'd better keep it simple. "Hi," she said and limply shook hands. Limply because John Lloyd still had a death grip on her arm and her fingers were going numb.

Christy Steele was equally brief: a quick smile that appeared oddly relieved, a soft "Come in," a graceful welcoming motion of a dainty hand, and John Lloyd was steering Lydia into the house.

"Let go of my arm, sir," Lydia whispered. "You're cutting off the circulation."

"Perhaps I should be holding your tongue instead. A loss of circulation to that organ might improve your conversational topics immensely."

"All right, I'll admit it. I made a stupid comment. I shocked our hostess."

"That's not what shocked her," he said softly as they followed the second Mrs. Steele into a large square room with a twelve-foot ceiling, white plaster walls, and a stone fireplace ample enough to roast a steer in. And antiques everywhere: marble-topped tables, solid oak bookcases with glass doors, an enormous sideboard, two high-backed velvet couches in front of the fireplace. There was an ancient upright piano and a round game table with six chairs—all appropriate for a frontier town saloon. Nothing in the room looked to have been purchased more recently than the Crimean War. Except a very modern computer, and it was sitting on a rolltop desk only slightly smaller than John Lloyd's, and certainly no newer. Jim Steele wrote western historical fiction, so maybe the combination of the computer and the aged desk was appropriate: contemporary man using modern technology to write of the Old West.

"Miss Fairchild." John Lloyd squeezed her arm to gain her attention. "May I introduce the matriarch of the Steele clan: Mrs. Alice Steele."

The gray-haired woman in the wheelchair gave Lydia a single startled look, then glanced at John Lloyd with a reproachful look in her eyes. "Don't pay any attention to him," she said to Lydia. "A matriarch wears high-necked dresses, smells like a lilac bush, and is an interfering, bossy old woman. I should know: my mother-in-law was one. I'm old, but I hate lilac water and don't interfere. Even when I should," she added. "Let go of her, John Lloyd. She's not going to run away. Stand still, young woman, and let me look at you. I don't see many new faces, and I like to get to know the ones I do see."

Lines fanned out from the corners of Alice Steele's eyes and mouth, and her skin was sallow and weathered from too many years out-of-doors in the hot sun and dusty wind. But there was nothing old or dim about the turquoise blue eyes that examined Lydia with a thoroughness that made her feel like a rare virus under a microscope.

Alice sighed and her measuring look shifted into one of relief. "It's the height," she said to John Lloyd. "And that hair, of course. I don't know what you have in mind and I don't want to know. But sometimes you scare me, young man, and this is one time I think you'd better be scared yourself."

John Lloyd's eyes were black expressionless caverns. "I do what is necessary."

"You're a hard man, Lawyer Branson," said Alice.

Lydia glanced from Alice to John Lloyd, trying to decipher the conversation. They were speaking English, but she wasn't sure what the words meant. She started when Alice spoke abruptly to her.

"You're a natural blonde, aren't you? Very unusual, that color of silver-blonde. Most women get theirs from a bottle. Maybe they can fool a man, but then most men are ready to be fooled. Harder to fool another woman.''

There was an oath and the sound of shattering glass from the far end of the room. Christy Steele's voice was high and quivering. "Jim! I knew you were going to break a glass using that mantel as a table. The stones are uneven and a glass tips over before you can catch it. Would you please get some paper towels and another glass from the kitchen while I pour Miss Fairchild and John Lloyd a drink?"

A tall, black-haired man with turquoise eyes identical to Alice's stood in front of the fireplace, a broken glass clutched in one fist. Eyes closed, he was rubbing his forehead with his free hand. He opened his eyes and smiled at his wife. "I'm okay. You needn't send me out of the room. Miss Fairchild, I'm Jim Steele, your clumsy host," he said, shifting his eyes to Lydia. "Get our guests some drinks, Christy."

Christy Steele whirled around and walked toward the sideboard that served as a bar. "Would you like some wine, Miss Fairchild? John Lloyd, your usual?"

Lydia hated wine. Why was it always assumed women prefer soured grape juice over something more alcoholic? "A bourbon, please, Mrs. Steele. No water," she added with a defiant look at John Lloyd. It was wasted. John Lloyd was watching Jim Steele rake broken glass off the mantel into a wastebasket. In fact, everyone seemed to be watching Jim Steele. Alice Steele leaned forward, her hands gripping the arms of her wheelchair. Her eyes were like chips of turquoise hard and bright and expressionless, and focused totally on her son. Christy was more subtle. Her back was to the room as she mixed the drinks, but her eyes were trained on her husband's reflection in a mirror over the bar.

Lydia frowned and marched across the room to sit on one of the velvet couches. If she was being rude by sitting without being asked, that was too damn bad. She'd driven eight hours today, her feet hurt, and she'd been stared at by the Steeles as if she were a Saturday night call girl who'd stayed over for Sunday dinner. If anyone was rude, it was Jim Steele. His glass hadn't tipped over; he'd slammed it down on the stone mantel. She had terrific peripheral vision and she'd observed him while everyone else thought she was looking at Alice. What had his mother been saying at that particular moment? Something about her blonde hair and fooling men. Oh, hell, what difference did it make? She still felt like an actress in a play in which everyone knew their lines but her, and she'd never even seen the script.

Abruptly the actors moved, the scene changed, the dramatic tension lessened. Jim Steele set the wastebasket on the hearth; John Lloyd joined her on the couch; Alice folded her hands and rested them on her lap; Christy briefly closed her eyes and leaned against the bar. Lydia sat up straighter in anticipation. Next act and our intrepid girl lawyer is ready, she thought. All I need is my cue.

Jim Steele leaned against the fireplace, one arm resting on the mantel. "When John Lloyd told us he was hiring a legal clerk, we assumed it would be some serious young man breaking in his first three-piece suit."

"I believe Miss Fairchild's three-piece suit has a skirt instead of trousers," said John Lloyd dryly. "But she promises to be very serious."

"As if I had any choice," retorted Lydia, thinking of the dean's threat of expulsion. "I mean, John Lloyd is sooo dedicated he just inspires me," she added dramatically, looking up at Jim Steele and batting her lashes in fine Southern style. He, however, was looking at John Lloyd.

"You're right, Miss Fairchild. He is dedicated. More than that, he's committed with every fiber of his loyal, steadfast soul. He's a damn Boy Scout." Jim stepped closer to the couch, his voice urgent. "Give it up, John Lloyd. It's over. Bury the past . . ."

"The past must first be dead to be buried. That is not

the case." John Lloyd's voice cut off Jim's sentence like a rapier slicing through paper.

"It is dead! It's time to quit trying to commit suttee . . ."

"I believe suttee is the Indian custom in which a wife throws herself on the funeral pyre of her husband. You certainly have more experience with that custom than I. Metaphorically, of course."

Jim Steele's face lost all color. "If you're speaking of . . ."

"Miss Fairchild! Here's your drink. Straight, just like you asked." Christy pushed a glass into Lydia's hands. "I poured you some of what Jim calls his sipping whiskey. I hope you like it. John Lloyd, your brandy. Shall we make a toast to Miss Fairchild's success as Canadian's first lady lawyer?"

Christy Steele's voice was high and fast, almost frantic, and Lydia again experienced the sensation of stumbling on stage without a script. It was obviously her line but she didn't want to pick up her cue. Every time she'd opened her mouth tonight, she'd precipitated a violent reaction. "Thank you, Mrs. Steele," she said cautiously.

The other woman seized on Lydia's response as a lifeline. "Please call me Christy. I've only been married two months. I'm not really used to being Mrs. Steele."

"I always thought brides liked being called by their married names," said Lydia, taking a big swallow of her whiskey. If she drank enough, maybe this whole evening would make sense.

Christy chewed her thumbnail, realized what she was doing, and immediately folded her hands together like a child caught raiding a cookie jar. "I—I do. But it's confusing with Jim's mother . . ." Her voice trailed off.

"It's a case of too many Mrs. Steeles, so maybe you better call me Alice," said Jim's mother. Her voice wasn't as frantic, Lydia noticed, but the old woman was clutching the arms of her wheelchair again. "Everyone

does and always has. My mother-in-law was Mrs. Steele
in capital letters. She only let me use it on sufferance.
To this day I always look over my shoulder whenever
someone says Mrs. Steele. My mother-in-law's been dead
for thirty years and I'm still not sure it took." She handed
her glass to Christy. "Fill it up, Christy. Talking about
Jim's grandmother always makes me want another
drink."

Christy took the glass. "I didn't think you liked the
taste of liquor."

Alice Steele chuckled. "I don't, but my mother-in-law
was president of the Women's Christian Temperance
Union. Don't you think that a sufficient reason for a second drink, Lydia?"

"I can't imagine a better one," replied Lydia. "In
fact I'll join you." The WCTU! The deceased Mrs.
Steele sounded about as much fun as a case of the
hives.

"She was president for years. Canadian's dry, has been
since 1903. Mostly my mother-in-law's doing. Prohibi-
tion gave her an itch for reforming and she was always
scratching it. I remember the time she tried to reform the
cowboys out of their chewing tobacco. They all quit during spring roundup. It was the only time I ever saw Jim's
grandfather lose his temper. He told her to keep her cru-
sades out of the bunkhouse. Then he pulled a cigar out
of his pocket, lit it, saddled his horse, and rode into Canadian to hire more cowboys. She went to the house with
her tail between her legs."

Christy brought the fresh drinks and Alice took a sip
and grimaced. "You're probably thinking I'm a silly old
woman, drinking something I don't enjoy just because
someone told me I couldn't. And you'd be right. I am
being silly. Furthermore, I'm being unfair. In many ways
my mother-in-law was an admirable woman. According
to her own lights, that is."

"My grandmother was a stiff-necked old bitch," interrupted Jim Steele. "John Lloyd, you remember when
she caught us smoking those cigarettes we stole from one

of the cowboys? What were we? Eight, nine? God, I'll never forget the whipping we got.''

"John Lloyd *stole* something! I'm shocked.'' Lydia heard Alice sigh and knew another crisis had been avoided. This dinner party had more crises than the Middle East.

"I've never claimed to be a saint, Miss Fairchild,'' he said, lighting a thin brown cigar.

"You don't have to. You assume it's self-evident,'' retorted Lydia, then flinched when she realized what she'd said.

"John Lloyd a saint? Let me tell you about the first time we went to Amarillo by ourselves. John Lloyd had just gotten his driver's license and we had some fake I.D. we'd bought from some college kids . . .''

John interrupted. "I'm sure Miss Fairchild is not interested in my youthful peccadillos.''

"Oh, but I am,'' said Lydia, trying to imagine John Lloyd Branson at sixteen. He hadn't been born wearing three-piece suits and a Phi Beta Kappa key. He had to have been young once. And he still was, or relatively so. Jim Steele and John Lloyd were the same age, somewhere in their middle to late thirties. But there the resemblance ended. Jim Steele was tall, broad-shouldered, sexy. He was everything he should be and a little extra. But if it meant saving her still intact virtue, she couldn't figure out why John Lloyd appealed to her more. Must be all that bourbon on an empty stomach. Canadian might be dry, but she wasn't.

"Do I have a wart on my nose or something caught between my teeth, Miss Fairchild?''

"What? No.''

"I'm relieved to hear it.'' John Lloyd took a sip of his drink. "You were staring at me so intently, you were beginning to make me nervous.''

Lydia giggled, noticed John Lloyd's disapproving look, and giggled again. Nerves were what others caught from John Lloyd. He didn't suffer from the disease himself. But Jim and Christy Steele evidently did.

The bride chewed her fingernails and the groom end-lessly tapped his fingers on the mantel. She expected both of them to erupt in hysterical fits any second, and she might as well have another drink while she waited. Jim Steele's sipping whiskey was the best thing about this evening.

She rose unsteadily, took a few steps, noticed the floor seemed to have developed a slight tilt, and grabbed the back of the couch. That's when she heard the sound. It was not quite a scream, but definitely more than a gasp. She looked up toward the old-fashioned sliding doors that opened onto the hall. "My God!" she breathed and sobered up immediately.

"Cammie!" whispered Christy and started toward the figure cowering in the doorway.

"Hello, Cammie," said Jim, catching his wife's arm and holding her back. "Come in and meet John Lloyd's new legal clerk. Her name is Lydia Fairchild." He spoke in a conversational tone of voice, but more slowly, as one would to a child. "Lydia, may I introduce Camilla Armstrong, Cammie to the family. She's Mother's com-panion and my friend."

Lydia started forward, her hand held out, her stomach churning with so much pity, she felt it rising in her throat like bile. Please, God, she thought; don't let this poor woman see what I'm feeling. "Hi, Cammie. I was about to have another drink before dinner. In memory of Alice's mother-in-law. Can I fix you one, too?"

The fear and hatred faded slowly from the woman's eyes and she straightened her shoulders from their defen-sive slump. "No, thank you, Miss Fairchild." She turned her head toward Jim's mother. "Dinner's ready, Alice."

"Cammie," said John Lloyd softly, his black eyes like soft warm velvet.

He's vulnerable, Lydia realized suddenly. He's not guarding himself against Cammie. He can be hurt just like anyone else. She drew a deep breath and held it.

Cammie slowly turned and stared at John Lloyd. Her

light brown hair was twisted into a knot at the back of her neck and did nothing to distract from her ruined face. She raised her hand in an attempt to cover the vivid pink scar that seared down the left side of her face and neck and disappeared under the collar of her dress. Still more red, puckered scars marred her hand and wrist. The unblemished half of her face turned a mottled red. Humiliation, thought Lydia. She's humiliated by John Lloyd's seeing her. He's destroying what's left of her self-esteem and he doesn't even realize it.

"Cammie," said John Lloyd again, stretching out his hand toward her.

Cammie's mouth twisted grotesquely for a moment, then stilled. She glanced at Lydia with some unreadable expression in her eyes, turned her back on John Lloyd and fled down the hall.

Lydia walked over to the bar. Not because she wanted another drink, but because she needed to lean against something and to be offstage. This was the third act in a Eugene O'Neill tragedy and she didn't want to deliver any lines.

"I'm sorry I didn't interfere, John Lloyd," said Alice. "You were wrong to try to change anything."

"You're a manipulating bastard, Lawyer Branson. You knew what would happen when you brought *her*." Jim Steele pointed an accusing finger at Lydia.

Lydia opened her mouth to protest, but Alice Steele frowned and shook her head.

The black eyes blinked slowly in the thin, austere face. "Let us rather say that I suspected. I had hoped I was wrong. I was not. I cannot afford to indulge myself in such wishful thinking again."

"God save us from your wishful thinking and your Machiavellian mind. All you've done is bring it all back to her . . ."

"It has never left her!" said John Lloyd sharply. "Because you denied her justice."

Jim sucked in his breath. "There are never any mitigating circumstances for you, are there? No human weaknesses, no faulty judgments allowed? Just blind commitment to an idol called justice? Well, it's your commitment and your idol, not mine. I didn't let you hound her then, and I won't let you disgrace her memory now in the name of some abstract justice. Leave it alone, John Lloyd.''

"I had hoped to spare you, but I see I cannot," murmured John Lloyd.

"Please." The voice was loud and firm, much too loud and firm to have issued from the petite body of Christy Steele. "Please. I don't think I can stand spending another evening with Amy's ghost." She turned to her husband. "Although if you insist, Jim, we can set another place at dinner. Isn't that another mourning custom, John Lloyd, dining with the dead?"

Jim Steele slammed his fist into the palm of his hand. "For God's sake, Christy! You knew I was a widower before you married me. Stop acting like a jealous shrew. Amy is dead!"

"Not to Cammie!"

"It was an accident!"

"How was Cammie scarred?" The question burst out almost before Lydia was aware she was going to ask. Like it or not, she was a member of this cast if only because the Steeles and John Lloyd didn't have the decency not to air their secrets before strangers. For some unknown reason she was a pivotal character in this play and be damned if she intended to continue blundering around without a script. "How was Cammie scarred?" she repeated.

Alice and Christy Steele stared at her, but oddly enough their eyes held no censure. It was as though she had broached a subject they knew needed to be discussed, but had been afraid of. Jim's face was a shuttered window whose chinks of light gave no hint of what occurred within. She glanced at John Lloyd and nearly lost her breath. His obsidian black eyes were narrowed in concentration as he switched his attention from Jim Steele to herself and back again. Like a director. Or a damn master puppeteer moving real people on some cosmic stage and doing it so skillfully that the actors didn't even feel the strings.

She looked at him and felt goose bumps form on her arms. Jim Steele was right! John Lloyd Branson was a manipulative bastard and as soon as she got out of this ranch house she was going to tell him so. But not now—because she could feel the strings tugging, feel the force of his will, and knew she'd play this act out to the end. "How was Cammie scarred?" she asked for the third time.

"She was in a car wreck," Jim finally said.

John Lloyd leaned heavily on his cane and looked at him. Lydia didn't have to see his eyes to know the insistent power they were exerting. Jim brushed his hand over his face. "Amy was driving," he began reluctantly. "Apparently the car skidded on the gravel, hit a rock, and Cammie was thrown against the windshield and knocked unconscious. She was burned when the car caught fire."

"And Amy was killed?"

Jim jerked his head to look at Lydia as if he'd forgotten to whom he'd been talking. "No. She went for help. Not everybody can be a goddamned hero." He turned and gripped the stone mantel of the fireplace with both hands and rubbed his face on his sleeve. Suddenly he pushed himself back and whirled around. "But she's dead now. Killed in another car wreck. Burned, charred, incinerated like trash no one wanted. An eye for an eye, a mutilation for a mutilation. Isn't that enough for you, John Lloyd?"

John Lloyd lifted his head and Lydia was reminded of a bird dog who had scented a pheasant. But that was wrong. Bird dogs were nice, spotted, floppy-eared pets. No one would ever scratch John Lloyd behind the ears. John Lloyd was a dangerous predator. "You are still her champion?" he asked in a drawl.

"She was my wife!"

"Perhaps you should devote an hour's interpretive

thought to theology; to wit, the biblical reference to turning a sow's ear into a silk purse, or the admonition against casting pearls before swine." The last word louder, sharper, lingered unpleasantly in the air like a stench of uncertain origin.

"Shut up, damn you!"

John Lloyd hesitated. His shoulders seemed to sag, then straighten, as though he had accepted some burden. He tilted his head to one side almost as though he were listening, then crossed his hands over the silver head of his cane. "So be it. You cannot face up to Amy dead because you could not face up to your feelings for Amy alive. You are blind because you *choose* blindness." His drawl was so pronounced it was like molasses dribbling slowly between outstretched fingers. "So be it," he said again.

Lydia felt the tiny hairs on her arms stand erect. She wished John Lloyd did not remind her so much of a biblical prophet pronouncing doom. She could almost hear it approaching on stiletto heels, tapping against the hardwood floors of the hall. Except doom wouldn't be wearing stiletto heels. But someone was. The tapping came closer, changed direction, entered the room, and stopped.

All she had to do was turn around to see whoever or whatever her host and hostesses were staring at, but she didn't want to. The evening was rapidly becoming more Edgar Allan Poe and less Eugene O'Neill, and Poe had always given her nightmares. The faces in front of her appeared to be living through a nightmare. Shock, horror, and fear took turns painting the features of Alice and Christy. Disbelief bleached Jim's face until the only color left was the turquoise of his eyes.

"Jim, darling, have I changed so much?" The voice was low, honey-smooth, and intimate.

The air was so saturated with tension Lydia was surprised there was sufficient oxygen to breathe. She felt twelve years old again, sitting in a darkened movie theatre during a horror movie and peeking at the monster

CHAPTER
SIX

SERGEANT LARRY JENNER TOLD HIMSELF HE WAS NOT A violent man. He had never been a violent man. He didn't abuse his children or beat his wife. In fact, some of the other cops thought he was a soft touch. He always bought cookies from the Girl Scouts, popcorn from the Boy Scouts, candy from the PTA, lemonade from a kid's neighborhood stand. He was always the first to reach in his pocket when the hat was passed for some cop who was a new father, or was in the hospital, or got a promotion, or had a birthday. He was a generous guy, a good guy who wore a white hat. He didn't lie, or at least not about anything serious. He didn't cheat on his wife or on his tax return, at least not much. He always tried to live right, to be kind to small children and elderly ladies. So why in the hell had this happened to him?

He slammed out of the police station, ignoring the greetings from the other officers who were spit and polished in their medium blue uniforms. He wasn't in the mood to exchange gossip about last night's drug raid or the latest move the Chief was planning against the pros-

titutes on Amarillo Boulevard. He was planning a few
moves of his own.

He crossed Pierce against the light, a dangerous proposition at eight o'clock in the morning, but he was in a
dangerous mood. Maybe even a violent mood, he
thought, ignoring the angry looks and squealing brakes
as he dodged the traffic. He leaped on the curb a split
second before a passing car would have made a medium
blue grease spot out of his six-foot body. He then realized he was definitely in a violent mood and walking the
block and a half to the beige brick storefront at Sixth and
Taylor that housed the Potter County Annex was not
going to be far enough to dissipate it. Halfway to the
Canadian River wouldn't be far enough.

Hesitating a few seconds in front of the outer glass
door, he consciously unclenched his teeth. No sense in
scaring the receptionist half to death. She hadn't done
anything wrong. Carefully he entered the first door, took
a deep breath and opened the second. He supposed climate control was the reason for the little cubicle between
the doors. Not a bad idea, given that the building faced
north and winter winds in the Panhandle came straight
off the North Pole with an intermediate stop in Nebraska.
But it was June and his temper and the weather were both
hot as hell.

The receptionist's eyes were round as an owl's behind
her blue-tinted glasses. "Sergeant, are you all right?"

Jenner smiled, realized he was grinding his teeth again,
and relaxed his jaw before he spoke. "I'm fine, just fine.
Or will be in a few minutes." He would, too, when he
had his hands around Schroder's neck.

"I wasn't sure. Your face is red. Must be the heat."

"Blood pressure," Jenner corrected, heading down the
hall.

"Gracious," said the receptionist. "Have you seen
your doctor?"

"Don't need to," he called over his shoulder. "It's a
temporary condition." Caused by a scruffy, overweight,

obnoxious, irritating, low-down investigator, he added silently.

He jerked open the second door on his right. "Schroder, you son of a bitch! I'm going to kill you!" he yelled, and broke into a fit of coughing.

Schroder was sitting behind a desk as battered as he, a newspaper in one large hand, the telephone in the other, and a grin on his face. His square, heavy-set bulk dominated the room, but then it was a small room, just wide enough for a desk, filing cabinet, and two chairs. It was also filled with cigarette smoke. He covered the telephone receiver and motioned toward the room's one unoccupied chair. "Sit down."

"Goddamn it, how the hell can you breath in here?" Jenner gasped between coughs. "And I'm not sitting down. I didn't come over here for a visit."

Schroder ignored him and continued both his phone conversation and his grinning. "Federal Express brought it yesterday?" He lit another cigarette and Jenner gagged. "Yeah, I was in a hurry. Didn't want to wait over the weekend until the post office opened. It figures in a real interesting murder case we got down here. Got any results yet?"

"Schroder, I want to talk to you."

Schroder listened, but to the voice on the other end of the line, a frown replacing the grin. "You've had it twenty-four hours."

"Schroder, read my lips. I won't do it!" Jenner said emphatically, then sat down on the chair and clenched his teeth again. No point in wasting his breath as long as his adversary was on the phone.

Schroder was listening again, rolling his cigarette between his lips. Ashes showered unnoticed onto the desk to join the gray layers already there. "Just because the evidence is eight months old is no reason for you experts to take another eight months running those toxicology tests. Didn't you read the lab letter I sent with the package? The one requesting the tests and giving you the facts of the case? This is murder and the murderer's already had eight months of freedom he didn't deserve. Now what have you folks got so far?" He inhaled deeply and smoke trickled out of his nose. He reminded Jenner of a moose breathing on a cold morning. "Send your report by express mail. I don't want to have to wait. I got a murderer to catch."

He hung up the phone and loosened his tie, which Jenner noticed was the narrow variety popular ten years ago. "Have to prod those FBI types sometimes. Claim they're overworked. Every cop's overworked too; no excuse for being slow. You upset about something?" he asked as he ground out his cigarette in an ashtray filled with a pyramid-shaped mound of butts.

"Upset?" Jenner got up and paced the width of the office, a matter of ten feet or so. "Am I upset, the man asks. No, I'm not upset. I'm goddamned livid!" He leaned over and put both hands on the desk. "I go to work this morning expecting a day like all days: driving my patrol car, handing out a few tickets, tying down the scene on a few fender benders, rousting out winos that might be sleeping in the reading room down at the library, maybe even helping an old lady across the street. What happens instead? The Chief calls me in and tells me I've been temporarily reassigned. So I think maybe it's the Metro Squad, something nice and clean and straightforward. No, says the Chief; it's Special Crimes! You did this to me, Schroder, and you can just undo it. I don't want to be in the Special Crimes Unit. You people deal with the real filth. Next to a murderer, a prostitute's a Sunday school teacher."

He straightened, leaving two handprints in the grit on the desk. "God!" he blurted, jerking a clean handkerchief out of his pocket and scrubbing his hands. "Don't you ever clean this pigpen?"

"No one touches my desk."

"I can understand that. Who'd risk choking to death on the dust?"

"You've got Scotch Guard on your uniform. A little dirt'll brush off."

"The Scotch Guard is so *blood* won't stain my uniform. The *dust* in this office would eat through solid lead!" He dropped onto the chair, looked at his handkerchief, grimaced, and dropped it in the wastebasket. "Oh, hell," he groaned, wiping his hands over his face. "Why am I talking about dust?"

"No idea." Schroder's voice was low and somnolent, like insects around a pond in midsummer. It also sounded self-satisfied, maybe even a little smug.

"I won't do it." Jenner's was also low, but it sounded more like someone in the throes of an asthma attack. He used an aerosol antihistamine to ease his swollen sinuses. "I won't work for you. I won't be involved with Special Crimes. And I *won't* sit here breathing this polluted air."

"You won't have to," replied Schroder, pulling a thick red book out of his bottom drawer.

Jenner slumped back in his chair. It was easier than he thought. Too easy, in fact. He leaned forward and glared at the stocky man behind the desk. "I don't have to what?"

"Dizziness, drowsiness, light-headedness, ataxia, confusion, hallucinations, euphoria, paradoxical excitement, plus difficulty focusing or blurred vision. Also heartburn, upset stomach, dry mouth, bitter taste . . ."

"I've got heartburn and a dry mouth, and it's difficult focusing with all this smoke in the air. What are you talking about, Schroder?" he shouted.

The investigator looked up. He was smiling again. Just like a shit-eating possum, thought Jenner. "Adverse reactions to an overdose of Quindat, one of the few, one of the very few, water-soluble sedatives. Prescribed dose is fifteen to thirty mg. The coffee contained at least seventy-five milligrams."

"What coffee? What the hell are you talking about, Schroder?"

"The burned thermos we found in the car. It contained coffee laced with Quindat and sugar. The sugar must have masked the taste of the drug. Think about it, Jenner. She drank a cup of coffee; her body absorbed the Quindat almost immediately. She felt euphoric, restless, maybe a little dizzy. She couldn't focus so she didn't know how close she was to that truck. Ataxia means her coordination was disturbed. She realized at the last minute she was going to hit the truck, but she couldn't move her foot from the gas pedal to the brake. Same reason she didn't swerve: no coordination, impaired reactions, confusion.''

"She drove all the way from Canadian in that state?''

"No. Didn't you hear me say the body absorbed the drug almost immediately? She drank that coffee ten to fifteen minutes before the wreck. Maybe she was feeling a little sleepy—it was one o'clock in the morning—and had some coffee to wake up. If she hadn't drunk the coffee at that particular time; if she hadn't been behind that particular truck; if she'd been driving through open, flat country, and passed out, gone off the road, she might still be alive.'' He tapped a page in the open book he'd been reading aloud. "Or maybe not. The *Physicians' Desk Reference* doesn't specify a lethal dosage. She could have gone into a coma and died.''

"You know what's wrong with your reconstruction, Schroder? It's a damn iffy way to commit murder. What if she hadn't swallowed the coffee? What if it was bitter and she spat it out?'' Schroder looked at him with approval and Jenner was irritated at himself for saying anything at all. He had a feeling Schroder's approval meant more trouble than Schroder's displeasure.

"You're a good cop, Jenner. A good cop always looks at the crime scene from all angles and asks questions. So what's the answer?''

"Hell, I don't know! That's what I've been trying to tell you. I'm not a homicide investigator. I don't want to work with Special Crimes because homicide and suspicious death are all you deal with. It's not the dead bodies, Schroder—I see dead bodies too damn often working traffic—it's the way they got dead that bothers me. If somebody dies in a traffic accident, I can handle it. They died because of mechanical failure, or poor judgment, or a damn drunk driver, and it's a stupid, useless way to die, but there's nothing"—he searched for a word —"evil about it. But murder, that's something else.

"I've caught homicide squeals. I've preserved the scene until Special Crimes could get there to take over. I remember one in particular, and I wish to hell I could forget it. It was October. Why is it always October? I've been a cop ten years, and every October there's some kind of brutal damn murder." He noticed his hands were shaking and clenched them together. "It was cold and wet and miserable that day, but there was a gas heater in that garage apartment and it was hot. I stood in the doorway with my back to the living room preserving the scene and waiting for Special Crimes. That was the longest wait of my life. Just me and two dead bodies in that dirty little apartment. And blood, Schroder. There was blood everywhere I looked: splashed on the wall, soaked into the carpet, pooled underneath the man's body, smeared on that young girl until it looked like body paint. When I was relieved, I called in sick and went home. I took a shower. Used all the hot water and most of a bar of soap. I sprayed my wife's perfume all over the bathroom and still couldn't quit smelling blood."

"How did you feel?" asked Schroder.

"Sick. And angry. Someone walked into that apartment, held a gun against that girl's face and . . ." He stopped and swallowed. "If I'd had the murderer in front of me, I'd have shot him."

"I don't think so," said Schroder. "You don't have it in you to kill someone. If you did, I wouldn't let you in this pigpen." He grinned and Jenner reluctantly smiled back. "But you won't have to stay here and breathe the polluted air . . ."

"Thanks, Schroder, I appreciate that. Listen, I didn't mean to come on so strong, talking about the blood and all, but I didn't want you to think it was anything against you . . ."

". . . because we're going to Canadian. There's a few

people up there who aren't expecting us and I want to visit with them.''

"What! Goddamn it, Schroder! Didn't you listen to me? I'm no good to you. I'm not objective.''

Schroder heaved himself out of his chair. "If I wanted objective, I'd use a computer. Objective's no good in a case like this.''

"Why not? Oh, hell, it doesn't matter. This case is going nowhere. We"—he saw Schroder grin at the word *we*—and corrected himself—"*you* don't have a case. The D.A. would throw you out of his office if you asked for an arrest warrant because some woman mixed her sleeping pills with coffee. You can't even open a murder investigation with nothing but that. Besides, Canadian's in Hemphill County and Special Crimes doesn't have jurisdiction unless you're invited. You can question Jim Steele, and he'll tell you his wife regularly took her pills in coffee. Then where will you be? Nowhere. Jim Steele's gonna walk on this one, Schroder, and there's not a damn thing we can do about it. I don't want the bellyache getting mad about it would cause, so count me out.''

"You read the paper this morning?''

"No. I didn't have time. And quit changing the subject.''

Schroder tightened his tie and made ineffectual tucking motions where his shirt had bunched around his waist. "What if there is evidence of a death occurring under suspicious circumstances in Potter County? What if an investigation is opened? What if we had Hemphill County's blessings, or at least cooperation to question citizens in their jurisdiction? Suppose we could show Jim Steele had opportunity as well as motive to dope his wife's coffee?'' His voice dropped to a husky whisper. "What if we had a witness who could prove Amy Steele didn't dissolve her sleeping pills in coffee, and in fact, almost never took sleeping pills? How would you feel then? Would you still back off?''

Schroder was offering him an out. There was no way the bastard could prove all that. Hell, he couldn't even get his lieutenant to authorize an investigation. Why was it, then, that he felt he was being pushed into a corner?

"Well, Jenner? This is your chance to have a murderer standing in front of you. Not to shoot him, but to cancel his freedom like he canceled that young woman's life."

"All right! All right, Schroder. If there's an investigation, I'll help." He got up, feeling light-headed with relief. "Until then, I'm going back on patrol. I'd like to stay and bullshit with you, but we're undermanned on this shift. Maybe we can have lunch some time." But not if I see you first, he thought silently.

"We'll grab a sandwich in Canadian," said Schroder, fishing a key ring from his pocket.

"Canadian! What are you talking about now, Schroder?"

On his way out the door, the stocky investigator gave Jenner a newspaper. "Why don't you read the front page while I bring the car around?"

Jenner took the paper and noticed his hands were shaking. He was sweating again, too. He'd been had. He knew it, but he couldn't figure out how. Thirty seconds later he had his answer. He couldn't miss the article; it decorated most of the front page "Schroder, you son of a bitch!" he swore at the absent detective. "You tricked me!"

CHAPTER
SEVEN

"MRS. AMY STEELE, FIRST WIFE OF PANHANDLE rancher and novelist James Steele, came back from the dead last Friday evening to confront her husband and his second wife. 'I didn't know Jim believed I was dead,' declared the first Mrs. Steele, wiping tears from her eyes. 'I thought he didn't want to see me again and that's why he never tried to find me. To come home and find he married again just breaks my heart.' "

Lydia broke off her recitation and, clutching the newspaper to her chest, rolled her eyes toward the ceiling. "Doesn't that just break your heart?" she asked Mrs. Dinwittie in a falsetto voice. "That woman is an absolute barracuda. If she ever saw a heart, she'd eat it."

Mrs. Dinwittie put her hands over her scarlet mouth and laughed. "Miss Fairchild, you're just a breath of fresh air in this musty old office. You're always so cheerful and funny. I told Mr. Branson you were a ray of sunshine sent to brighten our lives."

Lydia smiled. John Lloyd's secretary was a sweet lady, but her conversation included every cliché known to the English-speaking world and some known only to Mrs.

Dinwittie. "That's me: little Mary Sunshine." God, she thought, I never knew clichés were contagious.

"What else does the paper say, Miss Fairchild?"

Lydia scanned the rest of the article. "More of the same, I'm afraid. Quotes from poor pitiful Amy on how Jim done her wrong. Ah, here's one from our own Mr. Branson delivered in his indubitable style. 'Mr. James Steele declines to answer Amy Steele's aspersions, as his breeding forbids his making accusations of falsehood against a member of the opposite sex.' "

Mrs. Dinwittie had the face of an aging Kewpie doll with dyed black hair, a round spot of rouge in the middle of each cheek, and pink-tinted bifocals in frames vaguely the shape of cats' eyes. She looked like a *puzzled* Kewpie doll as Lydia finished reading the quotation. "It must be wonderful to know as many words as Mr. Branson does, but sometimes I don't understand him. What did he say, Miss Fairchild?"

"He called Amy Steele a damn liar. But politely, of course."

"Mr. Branson is always a polite gentleman." Mrs. Dinwittie's face bore the adoring expression she customarily wore when speaking of John Lloyd. Lydia wanted to gag. "What else does it say, Miss Fairchild?"

"That's all. A quote from John Lloyd is enough to intimidate any reporter into laying down his pencil." She slapped the paper down on Mrs. Dinwittie's desk. "It's all garbage anyway. The article makes it sound as if poor Amy Steele had been persecuted and browbeaten, thrown off the ranch by Jim like a discarded tissue. It wasn't that way at all. She walked into that room as if she owned the ranch and everybody else was there on her sufferance. What's worse, she's right. She's Jim Steele's legal wife, and according to the Texas community property laws, she owns part of that ranch. But that didn't give her the right to walk up to Jim and twine around him like a snake. I doubt etiquette books cover proper behavior when confronting a bigamous husband, but shouldn't you be satisfied with a handshake until you know whose bed you're going to be sleeping in? Or maybe I should say whose bed *he's* going to be sleeping in.''

"She kissed him?'' asked Mrs. Dinwittie.

"It wasn't a peck on the cheek.''

"What happened next?''

"I don't know,'' answered Lydia, thinking this was the most exciting event Mrs. Dinwittie had ever been involved in. At least since she took an ax and gave her husband forty whacks. "John Lloyd sent the 'ladies' out of the room with some comment about the inappropriateness of the gentler sex witnessing any further exchanges. So we cooled our heels in the dining room with all the cheerfulness of three people sitting around waiting for a root canal.''

Lydia shifted on the hard dining room chair and glanced at her watch again. Twenty minutes! She and Alice and Christy had been sitting in absolute silence for twenty minutes while whatever was happening in the other room was . . . happening. People have been born and died in twenty minutes, battles won and lost, kingdoms overthrown, revolutions launched, the Gettysburg Address written. Nothing of that magnitude was occurring now. Just the death of a marriage, she thought, looking at Christy's white face. Maybe two marriages were ending simultaneously, which made for a sick kind of logic since both were running concurrently.

"Alice, shall I serve dinner?'' Cammie held open the swinging door into the kitchen. Her eyes flickered. "What's wrong? Where's Jim and''—she hesitated—"John Lloyd?''

Christy laughed, and the sound gave Lydia cold chills. "Our ghost is alive.''

Cammie nodded toward Lydia. "Her, you mean?''

"No. Amy's back. She's alive.''

Cammie touched her scar. "That's impossible. She burned to death in a car wreck. I saw her buried.''

"We should've driven a stake through her heart,'' said Alice grimly. "Provided she has one.''

"My God!" exclaimed Lydia, then wished she'd kept quiet as three pairs of accusing eyes focused on her. "I'm sorry. I shouldn't have said anything." She swallowed. "Sometimes I talk too much."

"It's a common failing tonight, Miss Fairchild," said John Lloyd. Lydia jerked around in her chair. How anyone in boots and with a bad limp could walk as soundlessly as John Lloyd Branson was one of the mysteries of the universe. "She's gone, Alice, but not exorcised."

A red-faced Jim Steele followed him into the room. Christy rose to her feet and held out her hand. "Jim," she said.

He ignored her. "For God's sake, John Lloyd, do you want me to throw her out like some piece of garbage?"

"The idea has merit; however, being aware of your blindness in respect to your former wife, I shall do it for you."

"What?"

"My God!" interjected Lydia.

John Lloyd's eyes were glittering like a crusader's facing the infidel. "I shall conduct the ritualistic, legalistic bloodletting we call divorce in such a manner that as little of your blood will be spilled as possible."

"I'm warning you, John Lloyd. None of your tricks. I'm trying to be honorable about this whole thing. I owe her some consideration."

"You owe her nothing!" John Lloyd's voice snapped like a bullwhip. "When she *deserted* you, she cleaned out your bank accounts in both Canadian and Amarillo. Two hundred and fifty thousand dollars is more consideration than she deserves."

Jim's voice had a strained quality, as though he were desperately tired and forcing himself to continue. "She was my wife. I made a commitment that I'm breaking— again. I promised her the divorce would be handled as quietly as possible so she wouldn't have to face any unpleasantness."

"My God!" exclaimed Lydia again as she heard

Christy gasp, and wondered if Jim Steele was deliberately cruel or merely stupid.

"Unpleasantness!" screamed Christy, her face so white it looked bloodless. Jim looked at her with surprised shock.

He's stupid, decided Lydia.

"What about the unpleasantness I'm facing?" demanded Christy. "All of a sudden I'm your mistress instead of your wife. I'm a scarlet woman."

"Don't exaggerate, Christy. I know you're angry and upset, but it'll all be over soon. I'll bunk in with the cowboys until we can be married again. Nobody can call you names if I'm sleeping in the bunkhouse. Trust me, honey."

"You may sleep in the bunkhouse, the barn, or in the cellar with the rats for all I care. I'm going home. When I marry again, it won't be you. It'll be a man who isn't in the habit of wearing sackcloth and ashes for his former wife." She walked toward the door.

Jim clutched her arm. "God, don't leave me, Christy. You're still my wife—except for a legal technicality." She stared at him until he released her arm, then continued through the door. "Christy . . ."

"My God!" interrupted Lydia. "That technicality must stand five feet ten inches in its stocking feet."

"Miss Fairchild, your calling upon the Deity with every breath is beginning to sound as monotonous as a Gregorian chant. If you could refrain from addressing Him quite so frequently, or at least quite so loudly, I shall endeavor to enlighten the family as to just what that legal technicality means to their future financial planning."

Alice maneuvered her wheelchair away from the dining table and toward John Lloyd with a series of jerky movements that threatened to short circuit its electric motor. "You mean we may not have a pot to piss in or a window to throw it out of when that bloodsucking vampire gets through with us?"

"My G—," Lydia started to say until she saw the expression in John Lloyd's eyes.

"If you wish to use the vernacular, Alice, then I may be able to save the pot. However, I have serious reservations about how much of the window I can salvage."

". . . So if anyone was driven off the ranch, it was Christy." Lydia tapped the paper. "But there's not a word about what she's suffering." She frowned. "Wait. There is another article about the whole mess. That's strange. It seems to be an interview with a Sergeant Ed Schroder of the Special Crimes Unit. He's opening an investigation into the death of whoever was driving Amy's car." Lydia looked at Mrs. Dinwittie. "Why should they do that? Wasn't it a simple traffic accident?"

"There's the little matter of whose body is buried under Amy Steele's headstone, Miss Fairchild." John Lloyd stood in the open doorway, his cane in one hand, a bulging briefcase in the other. "Unfortunately, it is not the body of Amy Steele. The Almighty saw fit to inflict us with her corporeal presence yet again. Mrs. Dinwittie, if you would be so kind as to serve Miss Fairchild and myself some coffee, I should be forever grateful. We shall be in my office."

"That was a callous statement," said Lydia as she followed John Lloyd into his office and sat down behind the oak library table she was using as a desk.

John Lloyd hung his Stetson on the wooden hat rack behind his desk, hooked his cane over the arm of his chair, and sat down. "I thought I asked for coffee quite nicely. In these days of women's liberation, one does have to be careful. Of course I did have the foresight to include making and serving coffee in Mrs. Dinwittie's job description; therefore, technically speaking, I could phrase the request in the form of an order. There is the matter of good manners, however."

Lydia turned her chair around to face him. "I was referring to your statement about Amy Steele."

John Lloyd's eyes glittered as if diamond chips were

embedded in coal. "Amy Steele negates good manners," he snapped. His lids half closed over his black eyes and he leaned back, folding his hands over his trim belly. "Is this the summer thaw, Miss Fairchild?" he asked in his usual drawl.

"I don't know what you're talking about."

"I am referring to the sheath of ice covering every word, few though they were, that you addressed to me yesterday. The atmosphere in this office was distinctly chilly."

"You shouldn't complain. Think of the money you'll save on air-conditioning," she said, her tone at least fifty degrees cooler than room temperature.

"I find your remark unusually flippant, your attitude stereotypically feminine . . ."

Lydia gripped the arms of her chair. "How do you expect me to act? Like a man?"

". . . your behavior inappropriately juvenile . . ."

She leaned forward, her voice beyond lukewarm, but not quite hot. "It is not!"

". . . and marginally unacceptable."

She stood up, now at the boiling point. "Marginally! Only marginally? If you're going to talk like a male chauvinist horse's ass, don't stop halfway, John Lloyd."

"I use that adjective because I wish to give you the benefit of a doubt. I am assuming your behavior is uncharacteristic, and is therefore a calculated response to some emotional stimuli. Used judiciously, under the proper circumstances, and against the right man, sulking can be a valuable psychological weapon. I, however, am not the right man."

"I was not sulking!" yelled Lydia. "I was just too damn mad to talk to you."

John Lloyd touched palms and fingers together in a prayful attitude, and Lydia felt like a blasphemer in an ecclesiastical court. "You were subjecting me to the . . . I believe the term is silent treatment?"

"That's a better description than sulking."

"Surely a matter of semantics, Miss Fairchild. The end result is the same: a lack of communication."

His eyes were watchful, but there was another expression in their black depths. If he were anyone else, Lydia would diagnose loneliness. But John Lloyd was too self-sufficient to be lonely, so the tautness she could feel somewhere in the vicinity of her stomach must be hunger instead of sympathy. Imagine being sorry for John Lloyd Branson. "Don't talk to me about communication. Getting information out of you is like trying to predict the future by examining the entrails of a chicken."

He tilted his head. "You seem fond of animal imagery, Miss Fairchild."

"There you go again. You're always talking, but you never say anything."

He placed his hand over his heart. "I've always prided myself on being an articulate man. I'm devastated by your comment."

"You are a pompous ass, John Lloyd Branson," she announced.

There was a gasp from the general direction of the doorway. "I brought your coffee," said Mrs. Dinwittie, giving Lydia a disapproving look.

Lydia felt her face heat up like a blast furnace. So did her temper when she heard John Lloyd's soft drawl in her ear as he stood in deference to his secretary. "Is that in addition to, or in place of, being a horse's ass?"

There was another gasp from Mrs. Dinwittie, and Lydia wished she'd never heard of Mrs. Dinwittie, Canadian, Texas, or John Lloyd Branson. She cleared her throat and clasped her hands at waist level in her best Queen Victoria manner. "Mr. Branson and I were attempting to have a meaningful dialogue."

Mrs. Dinwittie set the tray on Lydia's desk. She examined John Lloyd, then Lydia, her eyes suddenly shrewd behind their pink lenses. "Mr. Dinwittie and I had our little spats, too."

"That will be all, Mrs. Dinwittie," said John Lloyd quickly.

"Yes, sir," the secretary said as she left, lavishing on each of them a last penetrating gaze.

Lydia sat down. "Well! I never knew a Kewpie doll could look enigmatic. It must come from working for you."

John Lloyd poured her a cup of coffee. "You find me an enigma?" he asked, raising one eyebrow.

"I find you irritating, egotistical, and manipulative, Mr. Branson. If you aren't careful, I'll follow Mrs. Dinwittie's example and take after you with an ax."

He sat down and contemplated her over the rim of his cup. "I would choose that over your previous behavior. I always prefer forthrightness."

Lydia slammed her cup down on the desk and got up. "Ha!"

"Please sit down, Miss Fairchild. You keep jumping up like a jack-in-the-box."

"Certainly." She slipped between the two desks, pulled one of the upholstered client chairs into the middle of the office, and sat down. "Just let me sit far enough away so my dress won't be singed."

"I fail to grasp your meaning," said John Lloyd with a frown.

"When the lightning bolt strikes you dead for lying." She jumped and paced. "Forthrightness! My God, John Lloyd. You wouldn't know forthrightness if you stumbled over it. Or is that a trait that's only desirable in other people? So you'll always know what the other person is thinking, and he, or in this case, she, will blunder around making a complete fool of herself. Why didn't you tell me that I looked like Amy Steele?"

John Lloyd waved away the accusation. "A superficial resemblance. Amy Steele"—he formed the words with distaste—"is merely an imitation produced for a less discriminating public."

Lydia stopped to stare at him. "What?"

"No person of judgment will mistake a rhinestone for a diamond."

Lydia blinked in disbelief. He was complimenting her!

Undoubtedly for some devious reason—such as changing the subject. "Then the Steeles don't have any judgment, because they certainly thought I was Amy. When I think of poor, sick, crippled Alice Steele . . . She might've had a heart attack."

"Alice Steele is as healthy as you are, Miss Fairchild. The loss of the use of her limbs hardly justifies your sympathy."

"What about Cammie?" demanded Lydia.

John Lloyd stiffened. "Tread softly, Miss Fairchild."

"I've treaded softly since Friday night, anticipating some kind of explanation. Even a few words would do, something in the nature of 'I'm sorry I didn't prepare you for the possible effect your appearance would have on the Steeles.' But no! An explanation, or, God forbid, an apology, is too forthright for your convoluted mind. Or do you have a guilty conscience? You accuse me of unacceptable behavior in order to cover up your own."

"If memory serves, my primary accusation was that of sulking, Miss Fairchild, and the thrust of your heated remarks leads me to believe I was correct in so charging you. My only doubt concerns your motivation. Are you displeased because I failed to inform you of my strategy, or are you displeased because you disapprove of my tactics?" He leaned forward in his chair, his obsidian eyes as hypnotic as the drugging effect of his drawl.

Lydia gasped and whirled around, walking to the window to look down at the town below. Canadian, Texas, was a mélange of red brick buildings, mellowed with age, and old Victorian homes built on gentle hills. And everywhere giant cottonwood trees, their trunks massive gray columns, lent a peaceful serenity. But there was no serenity for her. Not with John Lloyd Branson staring holes in her back. And not with a guilty conscience.

She turned around and walked back to the middle of the room. "All right, John Lloyd. I was mad because you didn't confide in me."

His eyelids half-closed, giving him a harmless sleepy look. Like a lion before it pounces on the gazelle, thought

Lydia. "At least you are not accusing me of manipulating you."

She laughed, then wondered why. Except if she didn't laugh, she'd cry. "No, you didn't manipulate me. I could've stopped playing in your little scenario, apologized to the Steeles, and thumbed a ride home from a passing cowboy. But I didn't. I was having fun. And I wanted to know what happened next. I don't like myself very much, John Lloyd, and I don't like you at all for making me your tactical weapon."

John Lloyd held out a white linen handkerchief. "Wipe your eyes, Miss Fairchild. I trust your mascara isn't indelible. And I apologize."

"I'm not crying and I don't wear mascara, but I'll pour some India ink on it just to make you feel better." She took the handkerchief and blotted her eyes. "Damn you, John Lloyd. I haven't cried in years."

"I haven't apologized in years, Miss Fairchild," he observed. "You seem to be a disturbing influence in my life."

"I'm disturbing all right. Just ask the Steeles. I don't think they enjoyed my influence any more than you did. And Cammie. My God, did you see her eyes? She was terrified of me at first. Aren't you even ashamed of frightening that pathetic woman? Where's your common decency, John Lloyd? Isn't it enough that she has to live with those scars the rest of her life? Do you have to play games with her peace of mind?"

John Lloyd came off his chair, his eyes as deadly as a coiled rattler's. "She has no peace of mind, Miss Fairchild. None of them do. It's a house of damned souls."

She laughed nervously. "Lighten up, John Lloyd. I didn't smell any sulphur last night."

"This isn't a matter for flippancy, Miss Fairchild," he said, stalking toward her, his voice as cold as his eyes.

Lydia took a step backward. It wasn't that she was afraid of John Lloyd, but she didn't want to tempt fate either. And John Lloyd was fate with a capital *F*, an impersonal, inevitable force controlling destinies and predetermining events. She rubbed her forehead. If she didn't get her imagination under control, she'd be assigning some obscure metaphysical meaning to the ham sandwich and stuffed celery she'd brought for lunch. Besides, she thought while gazing at John Lloyd, in Greek mythology Fate was a goddess. Three goddesses to be precise.

"I didn't meant to be flippant, but I've never liked tragedies. All that talk of doom, of gods interfering with men. Did anybody ask Helen if she wanted to go to Troy? Did Menelaus stop to wonder if one shopworn wife was worth it? Did anybody tell Achilles to buy a pair of high-top work boots? Then there was poor Oedipus. How was he supposed to know he'd married his own mother? Let's not forget Hamlet. Why didn't he just sue his uncle for wrongful death? But he couldn't do something simple like that, could he? His father's ghost was skulking around the ramparts keeping the heat on."

Lydia stopped abruptly. "Like I was doing last night," she said slowly. "I was playing Amy's ghost. I wasn't only keeping the heat on, I was turning it up until the pot boiled over. How did you like the climax to the tragedy you were directing, John Lloyd? Did you enjoy seeing Cammie run from the room because she couldn't face her memories? Did you get your kicks watching Jim and Christy Steele rend each other to bits? And how about Jim Steele's defense of his dead wife? Great theatre, wasn't it? How do you think it'll play on Broadway?"

"I think your dramatic criticism may be somewhat superficial, Miss Fairchild. And your knowledge of structure is sadly lacking. You seem to have missed the real climax."

"You mean the appearance of the real Amy Steele? I'm not including that scene in your play. It's good drama, I'll admit, but rather coincidental." She walked closer and poked his chest. "Even you aren't capable of arranging outside events, although your last line was prophetic. 'So be it,' you said, with your head tilted to one side as if you were listening for her entrance."

If she hadn't been touching his chest, she would have missed his almost imperceptible stiffening. If she hadn't been watching his eyes, she would have missed the slight dilation of his pupils. But she was, and she didn't.

Jerking her hand away from his chest, she doubled it into a fist and sank it as far into his belly as anger and a strong right arm could manage. "You son of a bitch! You knew Amy was alive!"

CHAPTER
EIGHT

IT WAS A CHOICE BETWEEN THE HEAT AND SCHRODER'S cigarette smoke. Leave the car windows up and be cool while choking; roll the window down and sweat while breathing. Jenner opted for breathing.

"You're letting the air-conditioning out," protested Schroder.

"No, I'm not. I'm letting oxygen in. Goddamn it, can't you drive five miles without firing up one of those things? The smoke is playing hell with my sinuses."

The burly investigator sighed and rolled down his window. Jenner loosened his collar and hoped his deodorant would last the day. He looked out on still another wheat field, or what he supposed was a wheat field. He was more familiar with that grain in the form of cereal or a loaf of bread. For all he knew, those rows of green plants could be weeds—except he didn't think farmers would spend the money irrigating weeds.

"Ever been to Canadian?" asked Schroder, flicking his steel lighter open and shut with his right hand.

"No," said Jenner, grinding his teeth together with every click of the lighter. Then he noticed the older man's left hand. One finger was resting on the bottom of the steering wheel. That was all. One finger steering a vehicle traveling at—he squinted at the speedometer—seventy-five miles an hour!

"Holy shit! Would you keep your hands on the wheel?"

Schroder cocked one bushy red eyebrow. "Anybody ever tell you to stop worrying so much? You're as nervous as a forty-year-old virgin in a roomful of gigolos."

"I'm a traffic cop. I can't help being nervous when someone else is driving. Hell, sometimes I'm nervous when *I'm* driving. So humor me and put at least one hand on the wheel."

Schroder sighed, lit another cigarette, and grabbed the wheel firmly with both hands. "You need to learn to relax, son. Way you're going now, you're a candidate for high blood pressure."

Jenner silently counted to ten, took a deep breath, and continued on to twenty. "So what do we do first when we get to Canadian?"

"See the sheriff, tell him we'll be doing a little investigating in Hemphill County. Standard procedure when Special Crimes is out of Potter, Randall, and Armstrong counties. Don't stomp around on somebody else's turf without telling them first. It's procedure, and it's polite."

Jenner sensed Schroder was more concerned about being polite than he was about proper procedure. "Ever had anybody tell you to get stuffed, to get out of their territory?" He saw the expression in the investigator's eyes, and pulled at his collar. "Guess not, huh?" Schroder grunted and Jenner decided the man who could tell Ed Schroder to get stuffed hadn't been born yet.

"So we see the sheriff first, then Jim Steele?"

"No. We talk to Amy Steele just in case she doped her own coffee. Sheriff Taylor's probably going to tag along with us, and we'll let him."

"Procedure, again?"

"Politics," grunted Schroder. "Canadian's a real

small town, and everybody in it likes Jim Steele. How far do you think we'll get poking into the affairs of the community's most popular boy without the local sheriff along to kind of smooth the way?''

Schroder might be a slob, but you couldn't fault his psychology, Jenner thought as he and the investigator sat across the desk from Sheriff William G. "Buster" Taylor of Hemphill County, Texas. "So you want to interview Amy Steele," he said as he squinted at Schroder's identification. "The whole town turned out for her funeral, or what we thought was her funeral. It wasn't out of respect, either. We just wanted to be sure she was dead and buried so maybe the Steeles could draw an easy breath. We were a little too fast off the mark, I guess, but how were we to know we were barin' our heads over the wrong body? Hell, Amy Steele wasn't accommodatin' when she was alive. Can't expect her to be any different when she's dead.''

He got up, a tall, middle-aged man whose thinning brown hair was mixed with gray. He reached for his Stetson. "You can just follow me down to the Cottonwood Inn Motel where Amy Steele's stayin'. Her mouthpiece got here Sunday. Fellow by the name of H. Curtis Rutherford. I don't know what the H. stands for, but I probably wouldn't like him any better if I knew. He's got one of them tanning parlor tans, clear polish on his fingernails, and acts like he don't put his pants on one leg at a time like everybody else. Folks all agree that he's going to be just as as well liked as Amy, and you know how fond we are of her. I don't suppose you're here to arrest her for murder, are you?'' he asked hopefully.

Schroder's eyes were bland. "Just need to ask a few questions about who was driving her car, and maybe clear up some other details. We'll meet you at the motel, Sheriff.''

The whole of Hemphill County might have fewer people than the Wolflin Village area of Amarillo, and Sheriff Taylor might seem like a good old country boy, but Jenner noticed he had a cop's eyes: shrewd, cynical, weary, and resigned. The odds of a cop with eyes like that buying Schroder's story were as good as a snowball's chances in hell. Maybe even less, Jenner thought as the sheriff hesitated in his office doorway.

"You wouldn't like to tell me something about those other details, now would you, Sergeant Schroder? I like to stay on top of what's happening in my county. Folks expect it."

Schroder shifted his holster to a more comfortable position and tucked a loose shirttail back inside his pants. "That's a little hard to do, Sheriff, because some of those details depend on what Mrs. Steele tells me."

The sheriff clapped his hat on his head. "You want to be careful, Sergeant Schroder, 'cause that woman's the best damn liar I ever met. She believes everything she says, too, so it's real hard to figure out when she fibbin' and when she's not."

Amy Steele might be a liar, thought Jenner a little later as he watched her pose on the couch in her motel suite, but she was one of the most beautiful liars he'd ever seen—if you liked ice sculpture, that is. His male hormones, not to mention his experience as a cop, told him this lady was frozen from the neck down. She knew all the right moves—stretching, leaning over, touching herself, crossing her legs, licking her lips—designed to show off the goods. He'd seen whores on Amarillo Boulevard do the same thing. But whores were more honest: cash on the dresser for services rendered. He wasn't sure what medium of exchange Amy Steele used, but he'd bet it wasn't one as straightforward as money.

"I'm not sure I understand why you're here, Sergeant Schroder," said Amy, her long black lashes closing over oddly light blue eyes, then fluttering open again. "I know nothing about the car wreck; I wasn't there. But if Sheriff Taylor thinks I should talk to you"—she leaned over and patted Taylor's knee—"then I'll do so."

The sheriff cleared his throat and moved his chair back

out of range. Jenner took the opportunity to check out
the view afforded by Amy's gaping blouse and made a
notation in his notebook: knockers—8. He considered,
crossed through the eight and substituted seven. He preferred a lighter pink.

"Just a minute, Amy. Sergeant Schroder, my client
has just stated that she was not at the scene of the accident and has no information to give you. Any further
questions of my client in her distraught condition might
be construed as harassment." H. Curtis Rutherford's
voice was well-bred, well-trained, bland, and utterly de-
void of character.

"You wait just a minute yourself. Nobody's ever accused me of harassment, and you're not about to now.
These officers have a job to do and they're tryin' to do it
as polite as they know how, so you just shut your mouth
about harassment and let them proceed."

Sheriff Taylor pulled his hat down lower over his eyes
and glared at the attorney. Jenner wondered if Amy or
Rutherford realized that the sheriff's failure to remove his
hat was a mark of disrespect just short of spitting in their
faces.

Amy frowned at her attorney. "Sit down, Curtis. I'm
willing to let the sergeant do his worst." She managed a
flash of thigh as she crossed her legs. Schroder either
didn't notice or was immune. He moved his chair closer
to the lamp table at the end of the couch, laid out his
cigarettes and lighter, positioned an ashtray, chose a pen
from the several in his shirt pocket, opened his tiny spiral
notebook, and smiled pleasantly at Amy. Schroder's idea
of a pleasant smile gave Jenner the shudders.

"Mrs. Steele, whose body was found in your burned
car?"

Amy's face went blank. Whatever question she expected, it obviously wasn't that one. "I don't know,"
she finally said.

"You don't know who was driving your car?"

"It was some girl wearing scruffy jeans and carrying
a backpack. I met her at the airport in Amarillo while I

was waiting for a plane to Dallas. I merely made her a business proposition. I offered her a thousand dollars to drive my car to California. She was just a drifter with no particular destination in mind, so she accepted the offer. I gave her an address in Los Angeles, and told her to leave the car there."

"Why?" asked Schroder.

"Why what?"

"Why did you want her to drive the car to Los Angeles?"

Amy's smile was ugly. "I didn't. I didn't care if she drove it to Los Angeles, or stole it, or pushed it off a cliff, just as long as that car was found a long way from Texas."

"Why?" asked Jenner, ignoring Schroder's frown.

"I advise you not to answer," interjected Rutherford.

She blinked and Jenner noticed her eyes were just marginally too close together. "Because I wanted Jim Steele to suffer! I wanted him to wonder what had happened to me! I wanted him . . ."

"Amy!" cried Rutherford, and grabbed her arm.

Sheriff Taylor's face turned red. "Someone's daughter died in your place and is buried under a tombstone with your name on it. Doesn't that bother you?"

Amy shrugged her shoulders. "I can't bring her back from the dead and ask her what her name is, can I?"

"That's enough, Sheriff! You're being abusive to my client. She didn't plan on a car wreck killing that girl. In fact, she didn't even know the girl was dead until she read that magazine article."

"She could at least feel sorry for the poor little girl."

"Mr. Rutherford is within his rights, Sheriff Taylor. You are being abusive. We're not here to accuse Mrs. Steele." Schroder leaned over and grasped Amy's hand between his own ham-sized ones. "It's all right, little lady. No need to get agitated. We know you're just an innocent victim of circumstances. Let's see if we can't clear up those circumstances."

"What the hell!" exclaimed Taylor.

Only ten years as a cop involved in interrogations kept Jenner's mouth from falling open. What kind of game was Schroder playing? If anyone was a victim of circumstances, it was the Jane Doe rotting in Amy Steele's casket.

Amy fluttered her lashes at Schroder and he stared at her with a lustful expression. Jenner's mouth did fall open. Schroder thinking of sex! Everybody in the department knew his only notice of sex consisted of circling the *M* instead of the *F* on a credit card application.

"Sergeant Schroder, if you could only relieve my mind about that wreck," cooed Amy, scooting closer and putting her other hand on his thick knee. Schroder wiggled appreciatively and Jenner heard Sheriff Taylor mutter a four-letter word.

"I'll try my best, little lady. I know you're upset right now, and I'll bet you were upset the night you left. Sometimes when a person's upset, it helps to talk about it. So if you'll just tell me what happened, it'll help me understand the circumstances behind your giving your car to that girl. Start at the beginning and kind of relive the evening, and just maybe you'll remember something else about the girl that'll help us identify her. And you'll feel better by getting it off your chest."

"Oh, Sergeant, you're so understanding." She blinked her eyes and sniffed. Schroder gallantly pulled a rumpled handkerchief out of his coat pocket and presented it to her while keeping a secure hold of one of her hands. Jenner gave her ten points for bravery for even touching the piece of cloth, much less actually dabbing at her eyes with it. He made another notation in his notebook: eyes— 5. He never did like women who wore false eyelashes.

"I hardly know where to start, Sergeant. I've lived in misery for so long."

"Just start with that day, Mrs. Steele," said Schroder.

"Amy, I feel it's my ethical duty to caution you against saying anything."

"Shut up, Curtis. I hired you to handle my divorce. I'll manage everything else." She turned back to Schroder. "I ran errands most of the day, had supper with a friend, so it was close to nine when I got back to the ranch. The minute I saw Dr. Bailey's car, I got a headache."

"Who is Dr. Bailey?" asked Schroder. "I don't believe he was mentioned in Sergeant Jenner's incident report." His quick look at the younger man promised retribution, but Jenner shrugged his shoulders. The Steeles hadn't mentioned any Dr. Bailey when he'd questioned them after the wreck. How was he supposed to know he was dealing with a homicide and they were covering up information? After all, he'd told Schroder he wasn't a trained murder investigator.

"He's a physician. *And* my godfather. He's known me forever; he even introduced me to Jim. But that doesn't make him my friend. He didn't want me to marry Jim, and he's spent the last five years telling him what a mistake he made."

"That's terrible!" exclaimed Schroder. "Why should he do that?"

"Money," said Amy, nodding her head at the investigator's surprised look. "Money. Christy Steele is his niece. With her married to Jim, the Steele money was his for the asking for his grandiose schemes. Restoring old buildings in Canadian to preserve her past as the cultural center of the Panhandle. Did you ever hear of anything so ridiculous? As if this area had any culture. There's hardly a decent store in the entire Panhandle."

"Now just a damn minute!" interjected Sheriff Taylor. "Don't you go slanderin' Canadian. We even had a opera house, the only one between Dallas and Kansas City. We had culture when Amarillo was just a wide place in the road."

"Now there you go again, Sheriff Taylor, abusing this poor little lady," said Schroder. His voice was mild, but the stare he directed at the sheriff was nothing short of ferocious. He turned back to Amy. "You go on with your story. You saw Dr. Bailey's car . . ."

"I went in the house. I could hear voices in the living

room, loud voices. I heard Jim say my name in an angry voice. I didn't go in; I couldn't stand another argument. I went to the kitchen for a drink. There, sitting at the table with Cammie and looking as mealy-mouthed as ever, was my husband's whore, Christy Deveraux Steele.''

The look Schroder flashed at Jenner had degenerated from promising retribution, to specifying the method of retribution as dismemberment. ''It's hard to believe a man could be so cruel to his wife,'' he murmured in his hoarse voice.

Amy dabbed at her eyes again, an unnecessary action in Jenner's opinion. He hadn't noticed any tears to begin with. ''You just don't know, Sergeant Schroder. I ordered her out of the house, and I went up to my room to pack. Jim came in to ask what I was doing. I told him I was leaving, that he'd finally driven me away, but that he'd better not even think of a divorce or I'd take half of everything and tell the upstanding citizens of Canadian just what kind of a man he was.'' She was panting and there were little beads of sweat above her upper lip.

It was silent in the motel room and Jenner shifted on his chair. That was it: a large cast of suspects, motive out the kazoo, opportunity. Amy had put Jim Steele's neck in a noose. Except for one thing: she hadn't mentioned anything about a thermos of coffee, and he and Schroder had no proof the Steeles had ever heard of Quindat, much less possessed any. If Schroder went to the Potter County D.A. with what he had gathered and asked for an arrest warrant, he'd get his ass kicked out of the Courts Building and back across the street to Special Crimes. Hot damn, he thought. That would mean he could go back to working traffic and forget Schroder.

''Was this girl driving your car on drugs?'' asked Schroder, rubbing Amy's wrist.

''I don't think so. Of course, I don't know much about drugs—I never take them myself, not even an aspirin— but she wasn't staggering, and her speech wasn't slurred.''

Schroder gazed vacuously into Amy's eyes. "I knew you weren't the type to take stimulants."

"I do drink coffee and occasionally some white wine at dinner. I'm not perfect, Sergeant," she said in a tone that implied the opposite.

Even Schroder didn't pick up that cue. "Coffee," he said in an abstracted tone of voice. "Didn't we find a thermos of coffee in Mrs. Steele's car, Sergeant Jenner?"

"Uh, yeah, we did," he said.

"I always take a thermos of coffee with me when I drive. Jim used to make fun of me, but it's boring driving in the Panhandle. There's no scenery except all that empty land, so I drink coffee to keep from falling asleep at the wheel."

"Did you drink any that night?" asked Schroder, continuing to stroke her wrist.

Amy abruptly pulled her hand out of Schroder's grip and wound a lock of blonde hair around one finger. "No, I didn't. I was too angry to fall asleep, so I didn't need coffee."

"And you left the thermos in the car?"

"I left it on the kitchen cabinet. My faithless husband practically threw it at me as I was leaving. My witch of a mother-in-law said she hoped I choked on it. You should have seen their faces when I walked into that living room last Friday night. They were afraid, both of them. And that cheap slut Jim married looked like she'd seen a ghost." A flash of some expression, like a primeval beast surfacing in a dank swamp, appeared in her eyes only to vanish before Jenner could decipher it. "Why are you asking questions about the coffee? Did that stupid girl try to pour some while she was driving? Did she lose control of the car? Is that how the wreck happened?"

"We're not absolutely sure," lied Schroder. "But in an investigation we have to know if an object was an inherent part of the scene, or if it was added to the scene later. In other words, was the thermos already in the car, or did the girl bring it with her? A lot of police work is asking boring, trivial questions that don't seem very important.''

"Sergeant Schroder, your harassing Mrs. Steele about a thermos of coffee won't help you identify your deceased driver. I really must advise my client against answering any more of your boring, unimportant questions." Rutherford smoothed his expensively cut hair with one well-manicured hand and looked pleased with himself.

The investigator gave a dramatic sigh. "There's always a material witness attachment, Mr. Rutherford.''

"Because you're investigating a traffic accident?" asked Rutherford with contempt. "You're not talking to some illiterate hooligan, Sergeant. I'm an attorney. Don't try to frighten me with your threats. No judge will sign an attachment order on a case like this."

Schroder bared his nicotine-stained teeth in a smile that reminded Jenner of his last visit to a zoo: the orangutan had grinned just like that right before he pissed on the zookeeper. "Mr. Rutherford, I never said I was investigating a traffic accident—that's Sergeant Jenner's responsibility. Mine is investigating suspicious deaths."

Rutherford seemed to have trouble finding his voice. "You're persecuting my client because of her divorce action against James Steele. I've heard how you people in the Panhandle close ranks against outsiders, and thanks to her dislike of this backward region, Mrs. Steele is considered an outsider. As long as it was Amy Steele dead in that wreck, you were willing to call it an accident. But let Amy Steele be alive, and all of a sudden it's homicide."

"That's right," agreed Schroder.

"What! You admit it?"

"Circumstances have changed. Instead of an identified body, we have a Jane Doe. That's enough to reopen the investigation, and in Potter County, a dead Jane Doe is automatically a case for the Special Crimes Unit. Acting upon information received, certain procedures were be-

gun and in the course of my investigation, new evidence
has turned up.''

"What new evidence?" demanded Rutherford.

"Your client's statement."

"Was that thermos of coffee one of the *details* you
were talking about a while ago, Sergeant?" demanded
Sheriff Taylor as he stood almost nose to nose with
Schroder in the motel parking lot a few minutes later.

"Yes," Schroder replied, pulling a cigarette out of his
pocket.

"What in hell is so important about it?" Taylor asked,
stepping back to avoid have his nose singed by Schroder's lighter.

"It's full of enough sedative to make anyone drinking
it comatose."

The sheriff's stunned expression gradually changed to
one of a man who's eaten something that disagreed with
him. "Shit! I told you Amy Steele wasn't accommodating.
She couldn't even drink that coffee like she would've any
other time. If it weren't for that poor dead girl, killin'
Amy Steele would've been a public service."

CHAPTER
NINE

"WHY DID YOU DO IT, JOHN LLOYD?" DEMANDED LYDIA.

"Please keep the ice bag securely on your hand, Miss Fairchild," drawled John Lloyd. "The doctor was quite insistent."

"Tighten your tape. And answer my question."

"My ribs are not taped. The doctor assures me that procedure has been found to be unnecessary for a simple fracture with no displacement of the bone. An occasional rib belt is sometimes prescribed, but my injury is not severe."

"If you weren't such a snob, neither one of us would've been injured," said Lydia, adjusting the ice pack more comfortably on her throbbing knuckles.

"Once again I fail to grasp your meaning, Miss Fairchild," said John Lloyd, his drawl slightly less pronounced.

"Your Phi Beta Kappa Key. If you weren't a snob, you wouldn't be wearing it, and if you hadn't been wearing it, I wouldn't have hit it, and neither one of us would've been injured," explained Lydia.

John Lloyd peered through the windshield at the narrow concrete strip of highway running between the desolate pastures. "Miss Fairchild, your mental processes can only be compared to those of a career politician explaining to his angry constituents that his voting to raise their taxes while lowering their deductions is for their own benefit. You are truly formidable. I am not a snob. However, in the interest of both our skeletal structures, I shall discontinue wearing baubles of any kind on my watch chain."

"Oh! You arrogant bast—! Oh, God, I think I'm dying!" A second later she was sure of it as John Lloyd slammed on the brakes. As she was already leaning over clutching her swollen hand, the sudden stop threw her forward into the dashboard. She saw stars and heard someone scream her name at the same time.

"Lydia!"

She stayed where she was, her forehead resting against the padded dash, and wondered who was cursing and why the car had stopped. There was a logical explanation and she'd think of it in a minute. She felt two hands tugging at her waist and wondered whose hands they were. A second later she had something else to think about. Her seat belt and harness were whipped away and she was lifted until she lay prone across John Lloyd's lap, her head resting firmly against his left shoulder.

He looked down at her, his long-fingered hand gently touching her forehead. "Lie still, Miss Fairchild, and let me examine you."

"The last man who tried that line on me got kneed in the groin. Ouch!"

"A slight lump just above the hairline. I doubt it's serious, but an X-ray might be the proper procedure. I shall take you back to town."

She caught his hand in her uninjured one. "John Lloyd, I'm all right. I've gotten worse bumps walking into low-hanging light fixtures."

His eyes were deep and black and worried. "Miss Fairchild, spare me your witty attempts at stoicism. You screamed out in a very creditable expression of pain immediately prior to my stopping. Indeed, your cry of pain was the motive for my stopping.''

Lydia realized three things at once. The first was that John Lloyd was not thin as she'd first thought, but lean and very muscular. Amazing how those funeral parlor suits he wore disguised what felt from her perspective, at least, a very spectacular male body. The second was that she was very, very comfortable and had no desire to move. At five feet ten and one-half inches, she so seldom found a man tall and strong enough to make her feel delicate. Actually she'd never found one. Until now. She curled her fingers around the hand that still rested against her face, and snuggled back against his shoulder. She estimated she had approximately forty-five seconds to en-joy John Lloyd the hunk before he turned back into John Lloyd the stuffed shirt, arrogant, unethical slimeball of an employer. Because the third thing she realized was that he was going to be madder than hell when she told him why she screamed.

''Miss Fairchild, your eyes are glazed. Are you able to comprehend what I'm saying?''

She felt her romantic bubble burst. ''I clenched my fists.''

He was silent and she tilted her head back to find him looking down at her with an odd expression in his eyes. ''Well?'' she demanded.

''You clenched your fist.''

''Yes!''

''No doubt with another physical assault upon my per-son in mind.''

''It was an irresistible impulse,'' she said, glaring at him. ''You're not angry? *Why* aren't you angry?'' she asked in confusion.

His lips twitched. ''Your propensity for violent phys-ical responses to stimuli notwithstanding, Miss Fairchild, I find you quite an acceptable companion.''

''Thanks a lot,'' said Lydia, scrambling out of his lap and back to her side of the car. ''You make us sound like the Lone Ranger and Tonto.''

He chuckled. God, she thought, even his laughter has a drawl. "I had in mind Don Quixote and Sancho."

"Do you tilt at windmills, John Lloyd?"

He eased back in the driver's seat and put the car in gear. "Perhaps," he said finally. "At least in regard to Jim Steele."

"Speaking of the Steeles, are you going to tell me why? And don't you dare raise that eyebrow and ask why *what*," she added as she saw one dark blond brow began to arch.

His sigh contained a sharpness that told her she was stepping in forbidden territory. Too bad, but she was going to get an answer if she had to sock him in the ribs again. Maybe not the ribs, she thought as she saw him grimace as he whipped the car in a sharp right turn over a cattle guard and onto the gravel road that led to the Bar-S headquarters.

"Well," she said sharply.

John Lloyd shot her an exasperated look. "You are overly fond of that exclamatory word."

Lydia folded her arms and glared at him. "I'm waiting."

"Has anyone ever told you that being so completely single-minded is not always wise?" He glanced at her stubborn face and sighed again. "You were correct in accusing me of knowing Amy Steele was alive. Her lawyer, an urban android with a particularly unctuous manner, called me Friday with the unwelcome news. Rather than immediately inform Jim Steele, I instead filed divorce papers. Waiting until almost five o'clock, of course, to avoid having the information passed along to the Steeles before I had the opportunity to prepare them."

"You prepared them. You marched me out there like a carbon copy to give them all fainting spells. It was unethical, John Lloyd."

"It was necessary! All of them are suffering from a severe case of disassociative neurosis. Particularly Jim."

"Could you convey that in words of one syllable? Please," she added.

"Simply put, Miss Fairchild, they refuse to face the realities of their feelings toward Amy, and Jim Steele is the source of that refusal. My strategy, impetuously planned after I saw you, was to divide and conquer. If Alice and Christy could be persuaded out of their compliance with Jim's wishes not to discuss Amy . . ."

"You didn't persuade; you bludgeoned."

" . . . then the combined force of our demands would conquer his reluctance to examine his guilt."

"What does he have to feel guilty about? Did he beat Amy? Did he have affairs? And what business is it of yours?"

"He did not beat her, and to my knowledge he did not have affairs. And before you interrupt again, let me assure you that in a town the size of Canadian, I would know if either event occurred. Secrets are a community effort, not an individual one. Except in the case of Jim Steele. I don't know why he feels guilty. And I must know."

"And I repeat: what business is it of yours?"

"The divorce, Miss Fairchild. And the hearing on temporary alimony. The Steeles must present a strong united front. They must be prepared to fight. Our position vis-à-vis Amy Steele on the property settlement is most precarious. The judge is allowed a certain amount of discretion in awarding a property settlement. Amy Steele could end up owning half the Bar-S Land and Cattle Company. She could sell, lease, or build a condominium on half the ranch and give the Steeles hell for the rest of their lives."

John Lloyd's eyes were glittering pools of blackness in a harsh, austere face and Lydia hesitated to point out the weakness in his argument. But someone had to, and it was obvious John Lloyd was suffering from his own case of disassociative neurosis. Taking a deep breath, she crossed the fingers of her one unswollen hand, and plunged in. "But as Jim's wife she's entitled to half of all the community property."

"She is entitled to nothing! And as God is my witness, nothing, or as close to it as I can manage, is exactly what she will receive. But I must know Jim's guilty secret. I can not go into the arena armed with a shield and sword only to discover that my challenger has an automatic weapon."

"You make it sound like a game, John Lloyd," Lydia protested.

His hands tightened on the steering wheel and she suddenly noticed how strong his hands looked. He could wield a sword or a lance. And be totally merciless. "What are games but life reduced to symbolic rituals? Trials are a symbolic reenactment of the ancient practice of settling disputes by armed combat. Attorneys are champions chosen by each side to represent them on the field. We use statutes and case law rather than crude weapons, but we must use them just as skillfully. But my skill is useless if I cannot counter the thrust of my opponent's sword because my limbs are bound and I lack freedom of movement."

He tapped the steering wheel with the fingers of one hand, the first overt nervous gesture Lydia had ever seen him make. "She has chosen to engage in combat on my home ground, Miss Fairchild, a most illogical strategic move. Why should she do so? Jim Steele is well known and well liked in Canadian. She is known but uniformly despised. We shall almost certainly have a sympathetic jury. She could have quietly filed for divorce in Dallas. Instead her attorney called to alert me of her continued existence and further informed me of her intention of speaking to Jim about a reconciliation, thus allowing me time to file our own petition for divorce. Upon reflection, I conclude that I have been manipulated. Why? Why is she so confident that she will fare better with a jury of Jim's friends than with one of objective strangers? What is her secret weapon? What knowledge does she have that can harm Jim if she shares it with the community?"

His voice rose in a crescendo of sharply pronounced syllables and Lydia held her breath. "Goddamn it!" he shouted suddenly, pounding on the dashboard. "I have to know what he's hiding!"

"John Lloyd!" cried Lydia, then debated climbing out the passenger window. An angry, sarcastic John Lloyd she could handle. A John Lloyd so out of control he'd actually curse and abandon his usual polysyllabic style was another matter entirely.

He looked at his fist as if he'd never seen one before. Lydia had the feeling his own actions horrified him. "My apologies, Miss Fairchild. My language was inexcusable." His voice was even more stiff than his body.

"Forget it, John Lloyd. I've heard worse. As a matter of fact, I've used worse. I'm just glad to know you're human."

"It is a condition I try to rise above, Miss Fairchild. Jack the Ripper was human; so was Attila the Hun."

"And so was Albert Schweitzer."

"Unfortunately, history's miscreants far outnumber the saints, a fact that lends credibility to the doctrine of original sin."

"Oh, for God's sake, John Lloyd. No wonder you dress like the chief mourner at a Victorian funeral. You always expect the worst."

"And I am seldom disappointed. The present instance supports my philosophy." He parked next to the most disreputable-looking vehicle Lydia had ever seen. "Wherever you find that mechanical monstrosity, you may rest assured the worst has already happened and prepare yourself accordingly."

Lydia got out of the car and waited for John Lloyd to join her. "Why are we out here and what does that loser in a demolition derby have to do with anything?"

"It bears a harbinger of doom, Miss Fairchild, one whom you are about to meet." He took her elbow and escorted her to the porch where Jim Steele waited with a group of three men.

"What took you so long, John Lloyd?" demanded the rancher, glaring at him from bloodshot eyes.

"Miss Fairchild had a mishap that required medical treatment. As I told you over the phone, I cannot prevent a search of your premises as long as the warrant is properly drawn up and signed by a magistrate."

Sheriff Taylor pushed his Stetson to the back of his head. "It is, John Lloyd. I'm sorrier than hell and so is the county judge, but the sergeant here's got good probable cause. I'd be lying if I said otherwise. I hope they don't find anything and you can send them back to Amarillo with their tails between their legs. I've done all I can by gettin' them to wait for you. They didn't have to, you know. The sergeant explained he's done it as a kind of professional courtesy." The sheriff leaned closer to John Lloyd. "He also said he didn't want any bullshit about an invalid search when this case got to court." He tipped his hat to Lydia. "Pardon my French, ma'am."

"Spare yourself any feelings of embarrassment, Sheriff Taylor. Miss Fairchild informs me she speaks the language quite well." He grasped Lydia's elbow again before she could say anything. "Shall we speak with the second most dangerous man in the Panhandle?"

Lydia looked at him. "So who's the first most dangerous?"

John Lloyd's voice had a matter-of-fact flatness to it. "I am, Miss Fairchild." She believed him absolutely.

He nodded to a thick-bodied, middle-aged man with the stub of a cigarette emerging from one side of his mouth. "Sergeant Schroder, I haven't seen you since that distressing business last fall."

"The body in the mesquite tree, I believe it was, Mr. Branson," said Schroder, his lips widening in what Lydia assumed was a smile.

"And the matter of the single sumac leaf." John Lloyd returned Schroder's smile with one equally false. "An object lesson in the danger of misinterpreting trace evidence."

"Maybe," grunted Schroder. "But no danger of that

in this case. None of your fancy talking is going to explain away this evidence, or reinterpret it, either. No sumac leaf on this mesquite tree, Mr. Branson. Just plain cut-and-dried facts with no room for reasonable doubt about what was done or how.''

''You seem to have left out the *who* in the case, Sergeant. Does that mean there's room for reasonable doubt about that particular fact?'' asked John Lloyd softly.

''You ain't going to like trying that kind of defense. Sheriff Taylor tells me all these folks are friends of yours. You raise any reasonable doubt about the guilt of one, you're pointing the finger at the others. Hell of a position for a man to be in.''

CHAPTER TEN

"WILL YOU LOOK AT THAT!" EXCLAIMED JENNER. "That's the damnedest thing I ever saw. And in a bedroom, too."

The mahogany bar, its wood polished to a high gloss, its brass footrail gleaming, ran the full length of the room. A painting of a reclining woman, nude except for a few wisps of gold cloth hiding her vital statistics, hung above it. It was opulent, unexpected, and decadent as hell, at least in Jenner's mind.

"Beautiful," he said to the tall blonde gently rubbing her hand over the polished wood of the bar. What was her name? Fairchild? Perfect name for her, at least part of it was. She was fair, but she damn sure was no child. He'd thought for a minute—no, not even a minute; a second—that she looked like Amy Steele. Must have been the heat from waiting out on that porch with the Panhandle sun baking his brains because this one wasn't anything like the other one. Except the hair, and he'd bet his next paycheck Miss Fairchild's hair was the real thing. Everything about her was real. No false eyelashes, no thin lips, and her eyes were widely spaced and the deep blue of—he hesitated—of the water in a swimming pool. How did that scarecrow of a lawyer get anything done with someone like her in his office? She beat the hell out of looking at law books.

"The bar or the painting?" asked Lydia with a smile.

"Uh?" he asked, staring at her teeth. God, what perfect teeth! His gaze dropped below her chin and he gulped.

A hand clamped on his shoulder. "I also would find the answer to that question most interesting, Miss Fairchild."

Jenner felt his face turn brick red. He was over thirty, happily married, had never indulged in adultery, never even been tempted, and be damned if this country lawyer didn't make him feel like he'd just been caught with his pants down playing doctor with the little girl next door. "I was talking about the bar," he said, jerking away from John Lloyd. "Beautiful lines, and the wood feels as smooth as a woman's, uh, skin." He froze at the expression in the lawyer's eyes. He'd never seen eyes that black.

"I concur with both observations, Sergeant, but from a strictly aesthetic point of view. Keeping in mind its intrinsic value and its unsullied nature, a certain amount of reverence is proper, don't you agree?"

"Yeah, sure," agreed Jenner. He sank limply against the bar as John Lloyd took Lydia's arm and led her toward the door. After reaching for his handkerchief, he remembered he had thrown it in Schroder's wastebasket. His only recourse was to blot his forehead on his uniform sleeve. He looked up to see Schroder watching him with disapproval. "Don't you get on my ass. I was just looking."

"You're a married man."

"That's doesn't mean I'm blind! Don't you ever just look, Schroder? No, I guess not," he added as Schroder's expression went from mild to severe disapproval. "Damn it, is everybody around here a eunuch?"

"Not yet, son," said Sheriff Taylor with a grin. "But you will be if you mess around with John Lloyd."

"That lanky guy with the cane? You're kidding!"

The sheriff's grin faded. "Nobody around Canadian ever kids about John Lloyd. He'll have your balls and you won't even know it until you start talking like a choir girl. And we don't mention his cane, either."

"What happened to his leg?"

"That's something else we don't mention."

"Does anybody ever mention anything around this town?"

"Not if it's about John Lloyd Branson, we don't. He's kind of an institution, or a landmark."

"He dresses like a historical landmark. And the way he talks. Unsullied! I don't think I've ever heard anybody say that word out loud. Does he always talk like that?" he asked the sheriff. "I never knew it took so many words to tell a man to keep his eyes to himself. *If* that's what he's was talking about."

"It is precisely what I was saying, young man. Miss Fairchild has a healthy unawareness of her potential for wreaking havoc on the male sex in this community. I would prefer she remain in ignorance for the duration of her employment. I have neither the time nor temperament to deal sympathetically with a multitude of smitten swains disturbing the tranquillity of my legal establishment."

John Lloyd stood in the bedroom doorway leaning on his cane and looking, at least to Jenner's eyes, capable of breaking any man's balls. Since the balls in danger were his, he decided an explanation might be the best defense. He cleared his throat, looked at the expression in the lawyer's black eyes, and decided on an abject apology instead. Groveling beat the hell out of conversing in a soprano voice.

"I didn't mean to stare, Mr. Branson, but"—he searched for words—"damn, she's a fox." God, he thought; that was some apology. He should have kept his stupid, adolescent mouth shut.

"True, if not eloquent," said John Lloyd as he limped

toward the bar. "Sergeant Schroder, it has been a stimulating, if exhausting morning, and I am confident that you will provide an equally exhausting afternoon. In the interest of our being able to retire at a decent hour this evening, I would appreciate it if you could execute your search warrant without any further delay."

Schroder's brows drew together in a gargantuan frown. "You planning on tagging along?"

"Strictly as an observer."

"Don't step on my toes, Branson. You interfere with this search in any way and I'll haul you before a judge so fast, you won't know what hit you."

"Are you accusing me of suborning justice?"

Schroder looked over the lawyer's shoulder toward the door. "No, but I wouldn't put it past you to distract it a little."

Jenner switched his attention back to John Lloyd. He'd never heard a cop threaten a lawyer before. Most cops wanted to at some time or another—they even talked about it in the squad room—but they all knew better than to try it. Threatening a lawyer would get your ass in a crack and the department in court. Judging from the expression on the lawyer's face, Schroder's ass was already in a bear trap.

"Miss Fairchild!" John Lloyd's voice boomed out as he turned toward the door.

Jenner blotted his face on his other sleeve. That sneaky bastard had posted his assistant to eavesdrop. Schroder was in trouble up to his fat neck, and guess who was in it with him: Sergeant Larry Jenner, innocent victim.

Lydia stepped into the room. "John Lloyd, Alice doesn't need me to hold her hand. I couldn't anyway. She's busy holding a glass of Jim's sipping whiskey. So I came to watch the search . . ."

"Jenner, you keep your eyes on your business," Schroder muttered out of the side of his mouth.

". . . but since you and Sergeant Schroder are not

making me feel very welcome, I'll go with Sergeant Jenner. At least he's not frowning at me."

"Shit!" said Amarillo's finest under his breath.

Jenner hooked his boot heels on the rung of the chair and tilted it back. "I don't think anybody goes to sleep naturally in this house. We found those sleeping pills in Jim Steele's bathroom, Alice Steele's bathroom, and Cammie Armstrong's bedroom. The bottles all say Quindat, but I suppose you're going to have them analyzed?"

"Yeah," grunted Schroder. He lit a cigarette and looked at the sheriff through a cloud of smoke. "We'll need to subpoena those pharmacy records. I want to know when those prescriptions were filled and if anybody suddenly needed a refill just after Amy Steele's accident."

The sheriff scratched his chin. "That's going to be a waste of time. Nobody with any sense would get a refill of something they just used to murder someone. Besides, they could've saved up pills one at a time for weeks."

Schroder shook his head. "You're wrong. My gut tells me this death wasn't planned. It was an impulse kill. Somebody got a bellyful of Amy Steele and saw an opportunity to do something about it. He used the nearest handy weapon, the Quindat, and put it in her coffee. He didn't stop to think that it was a stupid way to commit murder. She might not drink the coffee; she might feel sleepy and park by the side of the road; she might taste something in the coffee and pour it out; anything could happen. And it did. When her supposed death was treated as an accident, he thought he was home free and could've refilled that prescription without worrying."

"You keep saying *he*. Are you that damn sure it was Jim Steele?"

"When a wife is murdered, the first person you suspect is the husband and most of the time you're right. Jim Steele had the motive, the means, and according to Amy

Steele, the opportunity. He went to the kitchen and got the thermos. Thirty seconds, a minute at the most, to grab the nearest bottle of Quindat, dump half the pills in the coffee, screw the lid back on the thermos, and give his wife a parting gift. But I'll keep an open mind. There were four other people in this house, three of them women. Poison is traditionally used more by women than men.''

Sheriff Taylor looked horrified. ''But Alice Steele is in a wheelchair.''

''There's nothing wrong with her hands, Sheriff. She could open a bottle of pills and unscrew the lid of a thermos just as quickly as her son. In fact, she may be a better suspect. She was downstairs the entire time Amy was in the house. She had plenty of time. And then there's Cammie Armstrong. She was actually in the kitchen with the coffee. We can't forget Dr. Bailey. He was downstairs. He knew there was Quindat in the house because his name was on all the bottles as the prescribing physician. All he had to do was look in Alice Steele's medicine cabinet and palm several pills. He's also a candidate because, out of all those people, he would know that Quindat is water soluble. Most sedatives aren't. Last is Christy Steele. She has a strong motive, but I have strong reasonable doubt about her. How would she know there was Quindat in the house unless she just happened to run across it while looking for an aspirin?''

The sheriff pounded his fist into the palm of his other hand. ''Goddamn it! I just don't believe any of them did it. I've known them all my life. My oldest daughter was in the same grade as Christy Steele. There's got to be another answer.''

Schroder lined up the three bottles of Quindat on the table. ''What is it, Sheriff? A passing motorist who stopped to ask directions? The highway is seven miles from this house. A vagrant who was taking a shortcut across the ranch? A neighbor who wanted to borrow a cup of sugar?'' He shook his head, his eyes sympathetic.

"It was someone who lived here, or at least knew the house and the habits of everyone in it. It was someone who knew Amy Steele always took a thermos of coffee whenever she drove her car. Face it, Sheriff. Our murderer is someone who *knew* Amy Steele. It was someone here, in this house, on that night."

Sheriff Taylor wiped his face, then the sweatband of his hat, with a handkerchief. He tucked the handkerchief back in his pocket and put his hat on. He got up and hooked his thumbs in his belt. "I'm going back to town, Schroder. I don't think I can sit in Jim Steele's living room with my feet under the table his granddaddy bought from his favorite saloon when the county went dry, and hear him accused of murder. And I damn sure don't want to hear him, or his mama, or anybody they love confess to trying to kill that brass-plated bitch. It ain't my case, so I don't have to listen. I'm sorry it's not Amy Steele who's dead, and I'm sorry it's that poor little girl instead, but most of all, I'm sorry you ever came to Hemphill County, Schroder."

He was almost to the door before he slowed. Turning, he gazed back at the room. "This was the original headquarters, this one room. Jim's great-granddaddy built it with just his wife and a bunch of kids to help. He cut down a couple of giant cottonwood trees and cut them into planks and laid this floor. Cottonwood ain't supposed to make good floors but this one's lasted over a hundred years. He carried those stones up from the river to build the fireplace. He lost his wife in childbirth, and all his kids except one boy and a daughter to typhoid. His daughter ran off to marry a gambler who owned a saloon in Canadian. He disinherited her and they never spoke another word to each other. He never compromised, the old man didn't, and that's a hard way to live. He maintained his own code and everything and everybody was measured against it. Once he gave his word he kept it, even when his best interests weren't being served. His great-grandsons are a lot like him. That's why I think you're wrong, Schroder. Jim Steele wouldn't kill his wife. He gave his word to take care of her when he married her. He'd never go back on his word."

"And if he did, are you going to stand back and watch him walk away?"

The sheriff looked at the three bottles of Quindat. His face aged before their very eyes. "I'll call from town about the prescriptions." He disappeared through the door, a tall unhappy man who had just admitted that before he was a friend, he was a cop.

Jenner rubbed his arms where the hair was standing on end. He looked down at the floor and thought about how long it took one man with nothing but hand tools to saw and plane and sand each board to build something that would last a hundred years. It only took his great-grandson a bottle of pills and a few seconds to destroy what it stood for. And Amy Steele. All this mess started with her.

"Damn it, Schroder, Amy Steele isn't worth this floor."

Schroder brushed some ash off his coat. "Not worth the powder it'd take to blow her to hell."

"I want out of this investigation. I want to go back to Amarillo. This is a dirty business and I'm no good at it. I told you that before."

"What did the girl in the car look like?"

Jenner stared at him. "How the hell do I know? When I saw her, I couldn't even tell she was female. She looked like a burned side of beef."

"Do you suppose her great-granddaddy ever built a house?"

"I don't know! I don't even know who she is." He corrected himself. "Was."

"You think maybe her mama is old and crippled?"

"For God's sake, what are you getting at?"

"She doesn't have anybody to tell pretty stories about her family. We don't even know if she has a family. She's just a girl that got in the way and is giving Jim Steele a lot of trouble. Oh, everybody's sorry she's dead, but that's as far as it goes. Nobody really cares. Nobody but an overweight investigator that smokes too much, and a young traffic cop that thinks murder is a dirty business. We're all she's got, Jenner, and I'm going to make someone very sorry she's dead. Now go get Jim Steele.''

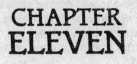

CHAPTER
ELEVEN

LYDIA WAS BEGINNING TO HATE THE DINING ROOM. NOT
that there was anything wrong with it structurally. It was
long and narrow with five windows on one end and wide
double doors leading to the hall on the other. A door set
in one thick wall led to Cammie's room, while a louvered
swinging door in the opposite wall led to the kitchen.
The furniture was all right, too, if you liked massive
sideboards and an antique dining table and chairs. She
squirmed uncomfortably. In her opinion a modern chair
with a thick foam padded seat beat an antique any day.
No wonder the pioneers had a reputation for being tough.
They had to be—considering nothing they had to sit on
or lie on was comfortable.

But discomfort had nothing to do with why she hated
the room. It was the role she played every time she entered it. Or rather the lack of a role. Was she supposed
to play warden or chaplain? Neither part appealed to her.
She'd make an awful warden, and any self-respecting de-
nomination would defrock her in an instant for her pro-
fessed views that God was more likely to worry about
skid row winos than the Ladies' Aid Society.

In any event, none of her wards were acting exactly like condemned prisoners. Except Jim, and according to John Lloyd, he had a wardrobe of hair shirts. Cammie and Alice were merely sitting at the table as if they were waiting to peruse the menu. Maybe she should offer some comfort, talk about justice. The problem was she wasn't sure what justice was in this case, and at any rate she suspected the spirits in Alice's glass provided more comfort than she could.

She glanced at John Lloyd sitting at the head of the table. What was she feeling guilty about? She was the second chair, the assistant, the flunky in this case. John Lloyd ought to be saying something instead of watching everyone in the room like a hawk waiting to pounce on a rabbit. His hooded glance switched from Jim to Alice to Cammie. Only when he looked at Cammie did his expression soften.

"It was that magazine article, Jim," said Alice suddenly. Lydia felt relieved that at least someone still had vocal cords. "Amy saw that article and knew she had you over a barrel and could pick your pockets clean. I knew talking to that reporter was a mistake. Your grandmother always said that decent folks never had their names in the paper except when they were born, got married, and got buried. For once, I'll have to agree with the old bat."

"She would've come back sometime, Mother," said Jim, sitting and staring at his clasped hands.

"When she felt you'd been punished enough for whatever she thought you'd done to her this time," said Cammie, looking across the table at Jim. "She likes punishing people."

"And animals," said Alice. "I had to shoot my favorite mare because Amy punished it for throwing her."

Jim looked up, white lines bracketing his mouth. "Damn it, she was terrified and angry. Haven't you ever done anything in anger that you were sorry for later?"

Alice slammed her glass of whiskey down on the table.

"Yes! But I never waited three days to do it! And I never *killed* anything. When she picked up a board and broke that mare's legs, she killed it just as surely as if she'd shot it instead of me. She knew a horse with a broken leg had to be put down."

"It was an accident!" Jim's voice held a pleading note.

"I don't have any use for somebody who'd hurt an animal or a child, and I don't care who they are."

Lydia decided John Lloyd wasn't exaggerating when he described the Steeles as damned. Jim Steele was a man with an intimate acquaintance with hell. His hollow voice sounded as if he were an empty shell. "She was sorry. She apologized."

Alice gripped the arms of her wheelchair until her knuckles were bloodless. "Not to me she didn't."

"I was in the kitchen when she came back from that ride," said Cammie, rubbing her cheek as Lydia noticed she always did when speaking of Amy. "She didn't look like someone who'd been thrown. She wasn't even dusty. She hurt that mare because you loved it, Alice. She was like that. She'd hurt whatever a person loved. If you crossed her, she paid you back."

"Stop it, both of you!" Jim rubbed a trembling hand over his face. "She's back, and I don't want to hear any more accusations against her."

Alice Steele slumped back in her wheelchair and took a sip of whiskey. "Amy is just like a bad penny: she's going to keep turning up until someone melts her down."

"I think someone tried to," Lydia blurted.

The silence that followed definitely qualified as a pregnant pause, fecund with a thousand possible emotional responses, most of them disapproving and practically all of them directed at her. She wished she were back in her Dallas apartment listening to her bathroom faucet drip.

Cammie turned her ruined face toward her. "You're a stranger. You don't know anything about it."

Alice set her glass down with a thud. "Lydia, I was beginning to like you, but that wasn't a nice thing to say."

Jim came out of his chair and leaned over the table. "It was a damn lousy thing to say."

"But true," interjected John Lloyd.

"I think you better explain yourself," Jim said. "Lawyer Branson," he added, his eyes as hard as the turquoise that matched their color.

Lydia felt more than saw John Lloyd stiffen at Jim's derogatory address. "Miss Fairchild may have many faults, but stupidity is not one of them. She is quite capable of drawing reasonable conclusions from observable facts."

"What facts?" demanded Jim.

"You are not feebleminded, although I suspect that in these circumstances you have acted as though you were. I am endlessly disappointed to discover that clients I had supposed to be quite intelligent have failed to read a legal instrument." He pulled a document out of his pocket. "The search warrant was quite clear. 'The thermos found in the vehicle contained coffee, which upon chemical analysis, was determined to have been adulterated with a sizable quantity of Quindat, a prescription sedative. The quantity of Quindat present in the coffee was such that a reasonable doubt exists that its introduction was accidental.' In a word of one syllable: murder."

"That was two syllables," muttered Lydia. "You've never used a one-syllable word in your life if you could avoid it."

John Lloyd ignored her. "Did you think the police were searching your house because they had nothing better to do? Obviously Sergeant Schroder suspects that someone in this house attempted to hasten Amy's departure from this vale of tears by introducing Quindat into her coffee."

"Dead or alive, that woman's been nothing but trouble to this family," said Alice, picking up her glass and draining it.

"Before Sergeant Schroder proceeds with his interrogation, I wish to know which of you is guilty of attempted homicide."

Even Lydia gasped at John Lloyd's question. Jim's reaction was more physical. He kicked back his chair and rounded the table, his hands clenched into fists. "You son of a bitch, you think we're guilty."

John Lloyd didn't move. "Sit down!" he commanded. "We haven't the time for you to indulge in the understandable desire for fisticuffs. Answer my question."

"None of us are guilty!"

"Of course, you are," said John Lloyd softly. "But of what? Murder? Or something else?"

Jim seemed to shrink as if he'd finally lost a long-fought battle. "Guilty. Innocent. What difference does it make?"

"About ninety-nine years," said Lydia. "Unless the state can prove the murder was committed during the commission of another felony, in which case the maximum penalty is death by lethal injection."

"Miss Fairchild, you are not answering questions in a criminal law class. Mr. Steele was speaking rhetorically. He does not require a dissertation on the difference between murder and capital murder as defined by the state of Texas. You must learn self-restraint in your choice of conversational topics."

Lydia experienced a feeling of déjà vu. John Lloyd was hatching another plot. Otherwise, why would he accuse Jim Steele of murder in one breath, and chastise her for mentioning the subject in the next? Whatever underhanded stategy he constructed this time wasn't going to work. At least, not if he was planning to use her as a tactical weapon again.

"But you just asked who had attempted homicide?" protested Lydia.

"I am not infallible. There is a remote possibility that I have misjudged the situation. It is not likely, but a good attorney examines every likelihood. Now, perhaps you would be good enough to procure a notebook from that oversized handbag of yours and be prepared to take notes during the interrogations. I am particularly interested in an accurate record of Sergeant Schroder's questions."

Lydia wanted to wallop him over the head, preferably with her oversized handbag. In his usual convoluted style he had eloquently explained nothing. "Aren't you worried about the answers?" she asked, showing her teeth in an insincere smile.

He raised one eyebrow. "Miss Fairchild, why should I be? I can always direct my client not to answer. Sergeant Schroder, on the other hand, must ask questions. Thus I shall gain more information than he, because questions are often more revealing than answers."

He unhooked his cane from the arm of his chair. "I believe I hear the approaching footsteps of the messenger from our guardian of the public peace. Remember that you may give your name, age, and residence," he said to the Steeles and Cammie. "Beyond that, look to me for instructions." Bracing himself on his cane he rose to his feet. "Ah, Sergeant Jenner, you are our escort to the smoke-filled room in which lurks the inestimable Ed Schroder."

"Sergeant Schroder wanted to see Mr. Steele. He didn't say anything about you," said Jenner, being very careful not to look at Lydia.

John Lloyd casually raised his hand. "Where my client goes, so go I. Miss Fairchild, if you will please accompany me. We shall beard the beast in his den."

"I hope you're not allergic to cigarette smoke," muttered Jenner, standing back to allow Jim Steele to precede him down the hall.

"I shall endeavor to persevere," said John Lloyd. "Miss Fairchild, if you would be so good as to offer me the use of your youth and strength. My leg seems stiffer than usual."

"Let me help you." Jenner quickly grasped John Lloyd's shoulder. "Sir," he added when the lawyer looked at him.

John Lloyd quickly stepped back and clutched Lydia's arm. "That won't be necessary, Sergeant. In addition to being more attractive, Miss Fairchild is quite practiced at aiding me without endangering my masculine pride. I'm sure you understand.''

Jenner grinned. "Yeah, I see your point."

''I rather thought you would,'' replied John Lloyd dryly. He leaned against the wall and closed his eyes.

Lydia put her arm around his waist. "Are you all right, John Lloyd? It's your ribs, isn't it? I knew the doctor should've taped them.''

He slung one arm over her shoulders and leaned against her. "Keep your voice down, Miss Fairchild," he whispered, watching until Jenner disappeared into the living room behind Jim Steele. "While comforting a maiden in the confines of a car did cause me some discomfort, I am not incapacitated. I merely needed a word with you in private.''

Lydia attempted to pull free and found herself held firmly against John Lloyd's side. "You are devious," she said through gritted teeth.

''Perhaps,'' he agreed. "But trust me in spite of my unattractive character traits. This is a complex case, almost diabolical in some respects, and requires deviousness to solve it.''

''It seems straightforward to me,'' she said. "It's just a matter of discovering who slipped Amy a Mickey Finn.''

She heard a strangled sound and looked back toward the dining room. Cammie stood in the doorway, torment clouding her gray eyes. Lydia felt John Lloyd's fingers dig into her shoulder and looked up at him to see an equally tormented expression. "You're in love with her," she said.

He turned his back on Cammie and all emotion disappeared from his face. "Nothing is straightforward, Miss Fairchild. Particularly not in this house." He urged her toward the living room.

''But what about Cammie? She must have misunderstood what she saw. I don't want her thinking . . .''

CHAPTER
TWELVE

"IN THIS ROOM, PLEASE, MR. STEELE," SAID JENNER, motioning the rancher through the door, and taking a quick look back down the hall at Branson and his gorgeous clerk. She was giving him hell about something while the scarred woman watched. Jenner had never seen such a sad look on a woman's face.

Jim Steele straightened his shoulders and strolled through the door. "Thank you very much, Sergeant, for inviting me into my own living room."

Schroder heaved his bulk out of the chair to the accompaniment of creaking wood. "We appreciate the use of the room, sir, and regret the inconvenience to you and your family." Jenner controlled the profane remark welling inside as he took a seat next to the investigator. Schroder didn't give a damn whether he inconvenienced God himself if it meant catching a killer.

Jim Steele sat down. "You can skip the apologies."

Schroder also sat down and squirmed around until his weight was evenly distributed on the chair seat. "Where's Branson? He doesn't let his clients go to the men's room by themselves, much less answer questions."

Jenner flipped open his notebook. "He's coming. His leg's giving him problems and Miss, er, Fairchild is lending him a shoulder to lean on."

Schroder looked at him and made a sound that resembled a bull snorting. "John Lloyd Branson would crawl on his belly before accepting that kind of help. He had another reason, like getting me riled."

"Sergeant Schroder, I apologize for my delay." John Lloyd leaned more heavily on Lydia as they entered the living room. "Ah! Gathered around the saloon table, I see. Appropriate, although I doubt that in all the poker games played around this table, the stakes were as high as they are today."

Allowing Lydia to pull out a chair, he released her shoulder and sank onto it, smothering an Academy Award-winning groan at the same time. "Miss Fairchild, were you aware that in the early West, trials were quite often held in the saloons, those establishments in many cases predating a courthouse?"

Schroder added another circle of smoke to the haze over the table and Jenner hastily used his nose spray. "This isn't a trial, Mr. Branson. It's a friendly talk with your client about certain incidents that occurred on the night of October fifteenth of last year."

"Said the spider to the fly," Jenner murmured to himself. Question is: who's the spider and who's the fly?

"Perhaps you'd like to be more specific," John Lloyd said, his voice resuming its usual deep drawl.

"Your wife came in late that night, Mr. Steele?" Schroder asked. "About nine o'clock?"

John Lloyd held up his hand. "Is the time of Amy Steele's arrival one of the incidents you were referring to, Sergeant?"

Schroder shifted his bulk in the chair. "Just getting a little background."

"I think you will have to manage without the background. I fail to see the relevance of that question."

Jim raked his fingers through his hair. "For God's sake, John Lloyd, what difference does it make?"

John Lloyd's eyes appeared to project a light from behind
the pupils. It was the first time Jenner could honestly say
someone had fire in their eyes. "You will not answer that
question. I have no intention of allowing the sergeant to engage in a fishing expedition. Next question, please."

Schroder ground out his cigarette so vigorously that
Jenner suspected he was imagining it was John Lloyd
Branson. However, when he spoke his voice sounded as
flat and hoarse as before. "Mr. Steele, when did you first
see your wife that night?"

"Get to something germane to the incidents raised by
the search warrant, Sergeant." John Lloyd sounded bored.
He even looked bored, sitting slumped over the table,
bracing himself with his elbows.

"Where were you when Amy Steele entered the
house?"

Jenner glanced at John Lloyd, waiting for him to interrupt. He folded his hands as if in prayer and gazed at
the opposite wall while listening to Jim's answer. "I was
in this room with my mother and Dr. Bailey.

"Why were you and Dr. Bailey arguing?" asked
Schroder.

John Lloyd cleared his throat. "I do not believe I shall
allow my client to answer that question. It's immaterial
to the issue of Amy Steele."

Schroder lit another cigarette and took several puffs.
He polished his lighter on his coat sleeve, a futile exercise in Jenner's opinion since any finish had worn off
about the time Columbus set sail for the New World. He
leaned back in his chair and hiked his right leg over his
left, staring daggers at John Lloyd Branson.

It wasn't going to work, thought Jenner as he caught
himself doodling on his notepad and heard the tapping of
Jim Steele's fingers on the arm of his chair. Lydia Fairchild kept tucking the same strand of hair behind her ear.
Schroder could mess around lighting cigarettes and saying nothing until the rest of us started squirming like we
had ants in our pants and that cold fish lawyer still
wouldn't show any sign of nerves.

Rolling his cigarette into one corner of his mouth, Schroder finally spoke. "You got a short memory, Branson. I already said this wasn't a trial, so you might as well quit using words like *immaterial* and *irrelevant* because when I'm investigating a murder everything is material unless *I* say it isn't. Any fact at all that might indicate state of mind is relevant."

John Lloyd leaned back in his chair and reached in his coat pocket. Jenner tensed. Branson looked enough like a nineteenth-century gambler to be carrying a derringer. He wasn't. He pulled out a long, thin cigar and Jenner shuddered. If cigarettes weren't bad enough, now he had to suffer cigars.

The lawyer clipped the end of the cigar, rolled it between his fingers a moment, then lit it with a silver lighter inset with turquoise. Pushing his chair back, he stretched out his long legs and crossed them at the ankles. He draped his arm over the back of Lydia's chair and blew a puff of cigar smoke into the remaining breathable air. The angle of the late afternoon sun and the blue haze of smoke combined to shadow John Lloyd's face.

Jenner blinked his watery eyes. There was something about the dim room with its high ceilings, old wooden floor, the round gaming table with one of those old-fashioned lamps hanging over it, something that made the hair on the back of his neck stand up.

He looked from Schroder to Branson and back again. The fat man and the thin man: the lawman and . . . the gambler! This wasn't an interrogation; it was a goddamn poker party. Schroder had raised his bet by challenging the lawyer and now John Lloyd had to throw in his hand or see the bet and call.

He called. "Perhaps my semantics are out of place, but I have also made my position clear. I will not allow my client to answer questions which might elicit self-incriminatory responses. Now shall we continue?"

Jenner made a small mark in his notebook under a column labeled BRANSON. The lawyer took that hand, but the pot was small. Schroder really hadn't lost much. It wasn't all that important to know when Amy Steele arrived at the house. And he had won the admission from Jim Steele as to where he was and who he was with at the time of her arrival. But he'd lost on the issue of the argument. The argument was important, very important.

New deal: Schroder opened. "Mr. Steele, according to a witness, you were heard to say your wife's name in an angry voice. Why?"

Jim glanced at John Lloyd, received no signal to stand pat, and answered. "I was defending her."

"Against whom?"

"Uh, Dr. Bailey. He had made some remarks that I didn't like, and I told him to leave Amy alone."

"What kind of remarks?"

"I'm not going to repeat them."

Schroder nodded, and raised the bet again. "Who told you that your wife was home?"

Again Jim glanced at John Lloyd and again received no signal. He rubbed his hands together. "I think it was Cammie."

"You only think. You don't know?"

Jim wet his lips. "It was Cammie."

"What did she tell you?"

"That Amy had returned, that she was upset, that she was leaving."

Schroder leaned forward, his eyes intent, and raised the bet again. "And did Cammie say why Amy was upset?"

Jim clenched his fists. Tiny beads of sweat reflected the light from the Tiffany lamp overhead. John Lloyd called and laid down his cards. "Do not answer that question."

Schroder allowed himself a smile. "He doesn't have to, Mr. Branson. I already know; she was upset because she came home to find Christy Deveraux sitting in her kitchen as if she belonged there. Her husband's paramour was in her house."

John Lloyd sat up a little straighter and Jenner was prepared to swear that the lawyer hadn't known that

Christy Deveraux had been in the house that night. Very interesting, he thought, exchanging a look with Schroder; the Steeles didn't even tell their lawyer the whole story.

Jim kicked his chair back. "She was not my lover, and you keep your filthy mouth shut!"

"Sit down!" John Lloyd's voice echoed from the room's high ceiling. "We shall not discuss Christy Steele in any terms, particularly not obscene ones."

Jenner made a mark in the column under Schroder's name. Branson had lost that hand. He drew brackets around the lawyer's name. The question was why. Why in hell did Branson allow Jim Steele to say anything at all?

Schroder dealt the cards and bet. "What did you do after Mrs. Armstrong told you your wife was back?"

"I went up to Amy's bedroom. She was throwing clothes and things into a suitcase."

"You and your wife didn't sleep together?" Schroder's eyes were half closed, like a cardsharp with a straight flush.

John Lloyd raised the bet. "Questions of such a personal nature are not only in bad taste; they are immaterial to the issues."

Schroder leaned forward and his cigarette ash fell on the table. "Any questions about the relationship between Steele and his wife are material, Branson."

John Lloyd took another puff of his cigar. "Which wife is the subject of your question, Sergeant?" He smiled at Lydia and stroked her shoulder as if she were a saloon girl bringing him luck. Jenner gave the lawyer ten points for continuing his sentence without a break after his clerk kicked him. "My client has recently had difficulty in keeping up with his wives. I have suggested buying a software package to aid him."

"Goddamn it, Branson! You know which wife I mean. The one who nearly got herself murdered!"

John Lloyd doubled his bet. "Are you accusing my client of murdering his wife?"

Schroder took time out to light a cigarette and think, or so Jenner devoutly hoped. The burly investigator had blown it. If he said yes, he suspected Steele of murder; then Branson would not allow his client to say another word. If he said no, Branson would claim his client had no pertinent information. Either way it was Branson's pot.

Schroder saw the bet and raised again. "I'm investigating the death of a Jane Doe. Information received indicates that Mrs. *Amy* Steele was the intended victim and that Mr. Steele is a material witness."

John Lloyd bet again, and Jenner hitched his chair a little closer to the table. "A matter of semantics on your part, Sergeant Schroder. Material witness indeed! My client will answer no more questions."

Schroder smiled, and Jenner noticed Lydia shiver. Smart girl. She recognized a crocodile when she saw one. "Mr. Branson. I'll serve an attachment order, haul your client's butt off to Amarillo, and he can answer the grand jury's questions. And you know how grand juries are; they get real mad when a witness takes the Fifth. They figure the witness has got something to hide."

John Lloyd carefully laid his cigar in the ashtray and Jenner knew he was about to bet all his chips. "Sergeant Schroder," the lawyer began, "what can Jim Steele possibly be trying to conceal? He has answered your questions concerning his whereabouts that evening. He has even informed you that he defended his wife against slurs made by Dr. Bailey. He has refused to speak of his marital relations with his wife, but that is the natural reluctance of a gentleman to discuss matters that might embarrass his spouse."

Schroder slapped the tabletop with one large hand. "Save that kind of comment for the reporters, Branson. Steele doesn't want to talk about marital relations because he and Amy Steele didn't have any. They didn't sleep together and hadn't slept together for months. During those same months he was seen in the company of Miss Christy Deveraux. That'll look just great to a grand jury, Branson. Especially when that same Christy Deveraux becomes the second Mrs. Steele upon the supposed death of the first Mrs. Steele, and when the miraculously alive Amy Steele testifies that she would take half of everything if Jim Steele attempted to divorce her. But what's really going to put the frosting on the cake, Mr. Branson, is when the grand jury hears that Jim Steele gave that thermos of coffee to Amy Steele just before she left. A thermos of coffee that contained enough Quindat to put a horse out for the count, much less that innocent young woman who drank it.''

John Lloyd's voice was so soft that Jenner could hardly hear it. ''You are talking about motive, Schroder.''

Schroder recklessly bet the rest of his chips and the deed to his house. ''Yes! The state doesn't have to prove motive, but every good cop knows that once you discover the motive, you backtrack right to the murderer.''

John Lloyd picked up his cigar and Jenner had a premonition that the hand wasn't over yet. ''I wish you the best of luck with finding a motive, Sergeant. With a woman of Amy Steele's sterling character, it shouldn't be difficult. A survey of any ten members of the general population should identify at least eight with a motive for murdering Amy Steele. However, James Steele is not one of the eight. James Steele would have rid himself of Amy Steele within sixty days without committing a rather clumsy murder, and without it costing him more than a nominal legal fee of one dollar, one Continental automobile, and approximately twenty-five thousand dollars.''

''What!''

John Lloyd arched one eyebrow. ''You needn't shout, Sergeant Schroder. I am not deaf. I said that James Steele would have rid . . .''

''I heard what you said. What in the hell do you mean?''

The lawyer contemplated the end of his cigar. ''Texas is a community property state, a fact with which I am sure you are familiar. At the time of the divorce, property, in whatever form, accumulated during the marriage, is theoretically divided in half. Property held by each party prior to marriage is not considered to be community property if a divorce occurs. However, it is not quite that simple. If monies are commingled, or assets used for the mutual benefit, then it becomes more difficult to determine what is separate and what is community property. It is not common knowledge, but James Steele did not own the Bar-S or any part of the oil and gas within its environs until approximately six weeks ago. His father, distrusting Amy Steele after a very brief acquaintance, very wisely changed his will just prior to his untimely death to leave his entire estate to his wife, Alice, who is also very wise. With my assistance, Alice Steele and I scrutinized every dime spent on the Bar-S to ensure that none of Jim's somewhat irregular income would be used on the property. No commingling of assets was allowed. Therefore, James and Amy Steele had no community property except their cars, bank accounts, and the clothes on their backs. The divorce would have been very simple and uninvolved.''

Jenner shook his head in admiration and drew a star under Branson's column in his notebook. The son of a bitch had been holding a royal flush all along.

CHAPTER
THIRTEEN

"Sergeant Schroder." Cammie stood in the doorway, carefully avoiding looking at anyone but the investigator. "You have a phone call."

"Take it in my bedroom," said Jim, pushing back his chair and rising. "I'm sure you remember where it is. I'm going to the barn. I've got a mare with a new foal that I need to check. If you need me, that's where I'll be. It's the big red building behind the house, the one that smells like horse shit." He shoved his chair under the table and followed Cammie out the door.

Schroder's chair creaked as he got up and Lydia wondered if it would survive any more interviews. "It's not over yet, Branson," he vowed. "There's a lot of different motives for murder. Money's just one. We'll talk to the mother when I get back. Wouldn't be the first time a mother killed for a child."

Lydia rubbed her arms as she watched him lumber out of the room. He reminded her of a bear, and she'd read somewhere that it was dangerous to bait a bear. Glancing at John Lloyd, she wondered if he was ever frightened of anything or anyone. If he hadn't been so concerned about her this afternoon, she'd think he had no emotions at all except irritation at the foibles of lesser beings like herself. But he felt something for Cammie, whether it was romantic love or concern or something else. Cammie felt something for him, too, and if John Lloyd Branson wasn't going to illumine that scene outside the dining room, then she, Lydia Ann Fairchild, reader of romances, would.

"I'm going to get a cup of coffee," she announced casually.

John Lloyd grabbed her wrist. "You are going to get into trouble, Miss Fairchild. I warned you about meddling."

Lydia reached down and pried his fingers loose. She blinked her eyes in her best Southern-belle style. "Why, whatever do you mean, Mr. Branson, suh?"

"Do you have something in your eye?"

"No!"

"Then please refrain from batting your lashes. It's most disconcerting to the observer. One feels the urge to offer you eyedrops."

Lydia stifled her retort when she remembered Sergeant Jenner. She smiled at him, thinking what a truly handsome man he was, and wondering why he always seemed so nervous around her. "Excuse us, Sergeant. John Lloyd takes his responsibility toward me very seriously. Almost like a father," she added. A tiny flame of some kind seemed to glow behind John Lloyd's black eyes, and she wondered if baiting him might be dangerous, too.

She dismissed the thought as she pushed open the kitchen door. John Lloyd might drive her into screaming hysterics, but he'd never hurt her. She hoped.

"Cammie, may I speak to you?" she asked.

Cammie turned from the stove, her face tilted slightly to the left so her scar was only hinted at. Her profile was cameo pure. Before her accident she must have been a beautiful woman. Her figure was slim, and if she'd only stand straight and proud, she'd still be an attractive woman in spite of her scar.

Almost as if Cammie realized what Lydia was thinking, she deliberately turned full face toward her. "Are you here to coach me?"

"Coach you?" asked Lydia, realizing how wrong she'd been. Cammie Armstrong would never be attractive again. Her face looked as if one side had been melted and someone had tried unsuccessfully to remold it.

"For my third degree," said Cammie.

"Oh, no. This is John Lloyd's game. I'm just here to take notes and learn. He'd skin me alive if I interfered. In his legal business," she added hastily. She wondered how her hide would look on his office wall, because he'd certainly skin her for interfering in his personal affairs.

Cammie's eyes were wary. "Then what do you want?"

"I'm sorry you saw that scene in the hall. It didn't mean anything; John Lloyd was trying to fool the sergeant, and he needed to talk to me . . ." Her voice trailed off. She felt like a fool.

"And you thought I was hurt?"

Lydia nodded. "Yes."

Cammie rubbed the back of her hand, tracing the edges of the scars as if she could erase them. "I was hurt," she admitted. "But John Lloyd needs to get on with his own life and I can't be a part of it."

"Why? Because you have a scar? John Lloyd's no horny teenager who can't see past the surface. Do you think a scar would bother him?"

Cammie flushed a mottled shade that turned her scar into a livid red brand. "You stand there with your perfect face and perfect body and talk about me as if I'd burned my hand frying chicken. Do you think my scars stop with my face and arm?" She ripped open the first few buttons of her dress and pulled it down over her left shoulder to expose glistening red scar tissue. "My whole left side to the waist, my hips, the backs of my thighs, all look like that, Miss Fairchild. I do have one unscarred breast and half my face left," she said as she fastened her dress. "One old biddy from town told me I should be thankful for that. Should I offer those to John Lloyd and ask him to imagine the rest?''

Lydia swiped at the tears rolling down her cheeks. ''If he loves you . . .'' she began.

''Oh, he does. From a long time ago. But I married someone else and we were very happy together. My husband died about the time John Lloyd came back to Canadian and we drifted together again. But there was never any passion between us, not when we were young, and not now. The earth never moved when he kissed me. I don't think it moved for him either. Don't think I'd give him up, though, if I weren't scarred. I'd marry him like we'd planned, and I'd make him send you back to Dallas so fast your head would swim.''

''But you're acting jealous and I've been trying to tell you there's no reason. John Lloyd is just my employer.''

Cammie laughed, showing even white teeth. ''You get under his skin like a burr under a saddle. I've never seen that happen before, not in all the years I've known him. Did you know we grew up together, John Lloyd, Jim, and I?''

''No, I didn't. John Lloyd doesn't volunteer much information about his personal life.''

''Those were the rainbow days.'' She smiled. ''That's my word for happy times. And they were happy for all of us, even baby Christy. Bailey would come to dinner sometimes and bring her. He raised her, you know. We all loved her, but Jim absolutely doted on her.''

''Then why did he marry the Wicked Witch of the West? Why didn't he marry Christy to start with?''

Cammie looked surprised. ''He was fourteen years older. He was past thirty before she was grown enough for him to notice she wasn't a baby he could hold on his lap. Then he didn't know what to do. If a thirty-two-year-old man takes a sixteen-year-old girl out on a date, folks in Canadian would think the worst. Most of the time they'd be right. So he waited around pawing the ground like a bull that can't get through the fence to the prize heifer. Then Amy came to visit and six weeks later

Jim married her and the rainbows disappeared. He's not the same person he was, and I'm not either. I'm ugly underneath all these scars, but not quite so ugly that I'll try to hold John Lloyd to his word. I've got enough human decency left not to do that. At least, I do today. Tomorrow, I don't know.''

She opened a cabinet and took out a canister. Taking off the lid, she took out two cellophane-wrapped pieces of dried meat. ''Beef jerky,'' she said handing one to Lydia. ''Everyone laughs at me, but I love the stuff.'' She unwrapped hers and began folding the cellophane into a tiny square. ''Can you imagine John Lloyd eating jerky?''

Lydia unwrapped hers, wondering how she was going to fake eating it. Pity and embarrassment and regret for meddling had nauseated her. ''He doesn't seem the type,'' she said. ''Sirloin is more his style.''

''You're right, and sirloin and beef jerky don't go together any more than John Lloyd and I do. But we would've managed if it hadn't been for Amy.''

She walked over to the sink and looked out the window. Her voice came high and rapid. ''Amy and I were coming back from town, and she was driving too fast. She always drove too fast. I told her to slow down, that the gravel road was dangerous, but she laughed.'' Cammie turned around to face Lydia. ''Have you noticed that big boulder about halfway between the highway and the house?''

Lydia nodded. ''The huge one with the black streaks on it?''

Cammie closed her eyes for a moment. ''The black streaks are smoke. She skidded out of control and crashed into that boulder. I was trapped in the car because the crash broke both my arms.'' She looked beyond Lydia, her eyes unfocused. ''I couldn't open the door. And she just stood there, not even trying to help me, like she was fascinated by what was happening. I sat there and watched that rock turn black from the smoke and knew I was going to die.''

"But Jim said you were knocked unconscious, and that Amy went for help," protested Lydia, not sure she believed what Cammie was saying, but very, very sure that Cammie did.

Cammie's laugh held no humor. "That's what Amy told him. But I wasn't unconscious. At least, not all the time. Pain has a way of waking you up. And where could she go for help? Three miles back to the highway? Four miles to the house? I would've been dead before she walked a mile either way." Her voice dropped to a whisper. "But she didn't want me dead, because she started walking back to the car, wrapping her coat around her hands and arms. Then I saw her stop, then turn and run up the road toward the ranch. One of the cowboys had seen the smoke and rode up and pulled me out. Or so I was told. I was unconscious by then."

"I don't understand what you're saying," said Lydia. Actually she didn't want to understand. It was too horrible.

Cammie took out another piece of jerky and began to unwrap it. "I'm not surprised. You're a stranger. You don't know us. Even knowing Amy as well as I did, I didn't believe it for a long time. I spent the months in the hospital thinking about what Amy did—I was still trying to be charitable, you see—and I finally came to the only logical conclusion. Amy decided I'd been punished enough and she was going to pull me out. Think of what a heroine she'd have been. Articles in the newspaper, maybe even parades. All the attention she could want. But the cowboy rode up, and he might have wondered why she waited so long. So she ran. I don't hate her for the accident. I hate her because she was going to let me live."

Lydia rushed to the sink and leaned over it, breathing deeply and hoping she wouldn't lose everything she'd eaten for the last three days. She turned on the water and bathed her face. She felt Cammie's arm around her shoulders, smelled the sunshine trapped in the dish towel that the older woman used to wipe her face. "Oh, God," she mumbled as Cammie helped her over to a kitchen chair. "Oh, God, I can't believe it."

Cammie tilted her head to one side and contemplated Lydia. "You're nothing like the other one. You don't even really look like her. And you're decent and brave, like I used to be. Otherwise you wouldn't be in here talking to me. John Lloyd's not going to like it, but I think you knew that beforehand."

"I just wanted you to know you misinterpreted what you saw. Between John Lloyd and me."

Cammie dismissed the comment with a wave of her hand. "Like I misinterpreted what Amy did?"

Lydia threw the dish towel on the kitchen table. "You must have," she insisted. "Otherwise Jim wouldn't keep defending her like a mealy-mouthed weakling."

"You're defending her, and you aren't married to her. Besides, I never told him. John Lloyd did. That's why Jim was going to divorce her."

"Then he did believe it!"

"Maybe deep down, but that wasn't why he finally agreed to divorce her. John Lloyd threatened to file suit against her. John Lloyd believed me, but then she never fooled him," she said with an odd inflection in her voice.

Lydia's stomach lurched again. There was something else. My God, she thought. How many something elses could there be. "I can't imagine anyone fooling John Lloyd. Those black eyes could see through six inches of steel, not to mention a lie."

Cammie shook her head. "That isn't what I mean."

Lydia stared at her, a wild idea flitting through her mind. "Not John Lloyd! She didn't go after John Lloyd!"

Cammie smiled. "Mrs. Dinwittie is a friend of mine. But even if she weren't, I would've heard about it. The town's too small to keep secrets. He threw her out of his office. Picked her up and dropped her in the middle of the hall. She was lucky he didn't throw her down the stairs and out into the street. It was the next day that the wreck happened. John Lloyd crossed her, and she punished both of us."

Lydia got up, proud that her legs weren't shaking and that she didn't feel weak anymore. Amazing what anger would do for a person. ''I believe you, and do you know why? Because anyone so self-centered and arrogant as to think John Lloyd Branson would betray a friend is capable of anything.'' She opened the back door and looked toward the barn. ''I'm going to go tell Jim Steele exactly what I think of him.''

Cammie started toward her. ''No! Leave him alone!''

''Too many people have been doing that, and I'll be damned if I'll be one of them.'' Lydia slammed the door behind her and started running toward the barn.

CHAPTER
FOURTEEN

"ONE MOMENT, SERGEANT SCHRODER. WHERE IS MISS Fairchild?"

"She's in the kitchen with Cammie," said Alice, wheeling herself over to the massive sideboard that served as a bar. "Would anyone else like a drink? No? Well, I would. Talking about Amy is hard to take stone sober."

"Damn that exasperating woman!" said John Lloyd, thumping his cane on the floor.

"I wouldn't call Amy exasperating exactly," said Alice, pouring herself four fingers of whiskey. "That's kind of a mild term for her."

"I was speaking of Miss Fairchild," said John Lloyd. Jenner thought the lawyer sounded a little exasperated himself.

Alice came back to the table. "I don't think I've ever heard you talk about a woman like that before. A cuss word even. I'm glad to hear it. It shows your blood's starting to circulate again. You were turning brittle as an old stick, but you've got sap left."

"Madam, you may leave my state of health out of this

conversation, and please stop mixing your metaphors.''

Jenner grinned. The old boy's face was even turning red.

"I don't know what a metaphor is," replied Alice, taking a generous swallow of her whiskey and smacking her lips. "But I'll mix them all day to see you acting like a stallion instead of a gelding."

John Lloyd closed his eyes and Jenner had the feeling he was counting to ten. Probably in Latin. Black eyes blinked open and focused on Schroder. "You may begin your questions, Sergeant."

Schroder was grinning, at least that's how Jenner interpreted the facial grimace. "Sure you wouldn't like to go find your little blonde? You and your friend, Mr. Steele, can't seem to keep up with your women."

John Lloyd's eyes were deadly, like a rattler getting ready to strike. "Shall we continue with the interrogation without any further unnecessary remarks? From either of you," he added, giving Alice Steele a look that should have boiled the whiskey out of her glass. Jenner wanted to chuckle, but lost the urge when John Lloyd focused on him.

Schroder evidently felt the same way because he cleared his throat and shifted his chair around to face Alice. "Mrs. Steele, where were you when Amy Steele returned home?"

"You may answer that question, Alice," said John Lloyd, writing a note in Lydia's notebook.

"I intended to anyway," she snapped. "It's getting late. I want my dinner, and these two still have to talk to Cammie. I'll get right to the point. I didn't try to kill that woman. Not that I didn't want to, or think about it from time to time. But I wouldn't use a method like that. Doping her coffee! That's as bad as shooting someone in the back, and it's not my style. If I'd tried to kill her, I would have shot her, and there wouldn't have been any trying to it. I'd have killed her, period."

"Alice! That's enough!" John Lloyd's voice was missing its drawl, Jenner noticed.

"I'll agree with you, John Lloyd," she said, taking another drink and lowering the level of liquid in her glass by at least an inch. "They want to know who doped her coffee, and I told them I didn't. And that's that."

"Not quite, Mrs. Steele," said Schroder. "You didn't answer my question. Where were you when Amy Steele came home?"

Alice expelled a deep breath. "In the living room with Dr. Bailey and my son."

"And they were arguing?"

She started to answer, but glanced at John Lloyd, who was slowly shaking his head. "They were having a disagreement," she admitted.

"What was the subject of the disagreement?" asked Schroder.

Alice exchanged a look with John Lloyd. "That's personal."

"Nothing's personal in a murder investigation."

"My client has said all I intend for her to say on that subject," interjected John Lloyd, writing another note.

Now it was Schroder's turn to look exasperated. "Branson, if you want your clients clear, you'd better tell them to start cooperating. So far, everyone's still under suspicion, including Jim Steele. You might think you proved he didn't have a motive, but he gave that thermos to his wife."

"Now you listen to me, you nosy smokestack," said Alice. "My son didn't dope that coffee. He only went into the kitchen to get it after she told him to. He didn't remember anything about it. There were three people watching him pick up that thermos and he didn't make any detours with it. He came out of the kitchen, straight down the hall, and out the front door. I know. I was watching."

Jenner interrupted. "She *told* him to get her coffee?"

Alice nodded, a pleased expression on her face. "That's right, and if she told you anything different, she's lying."

"I believe that clears Jim Steele," said John Lloyd, his drawl back. "Thank you, Alice."

"Just a minute!" said Schroder, half rising from his chair. "I'm not through. How do you know there were three people in the kitchen?"

"Don't answer that question," said John Lloyd quickly.

Schroder sat back down, brushed some ash off the table in front of him and stamped out his cigarette. "She doesn't have to. The only way she could know how many people were in the kitchen is if she'd been in there. Were you handling the thermos, Mrs. Steele? Maybe complaining about your daughter-in-law to distract everyone else while you dumped a handful of Quindats in the thermos and poured coffee over them?"

"I didn't pour—"

"Quiet, Alice!" snapped John Lloyd, grabbing her arm.

"Who did pour the coffee?" asked Schroder, his hoarse voice sounding like a cougar purring after eating a rancher's calf.

"I didn't see anyone pour it," she answered quickly. "I heard Amy and Jim come downstairs, so I went out to meet them by the front door."

"Let's go back to the events in the living room," said Schroder, changing tacks. "Cammie Armstrong comes in to tell Jim Steele that his wife is back and he goes upstairs. Who leaves the living room next?"

"Dr. Bailey."

"Where does he go?"

"To find Christy. She's a little upset. Amy called her a"—she hesitated—"an ugly name."

Schroder lit another cigarette. "Called her a whore, didn't she?"

"That's hearsay," said John Lloyd. "Mrs. Steele was not present."

Schroder exhaled a cloud of smoke. "I told you this isn't a trial; it's a preliminary investigation. Hearsay is fine."

John Lloyd picked up his discarded cigar and twirled it around with his thumb and forefinger. "There's no judge and no jury, but this is a trial, Sergeant. If I can persuade you that your reasoning is faulty, your evidence weak, and the motives not what you think, then you'll start looking in another direction."

Schroder hitched his chair forward, loosened his tie, which Jenner noticed had a freshly burned hole, and pulled the ashtray a little closer. "I'm agreeable. Let's try another direction. The one Christy Deveraux took when she left the kitchen. Where did she go, Mrs. Steele?"

Alice didn't even look at John Lloyd for instructions. She closed her mouth tightly and stared back at Schroder.

The investigator put his lighter on the table next to his nearly empty pack of cigarettes. He pulled a paperback western out of his pocket and placed it opposite the cigarettes. A half-used book of matches joined the other objects. "Now let's see if we can't figure out where Miss Deveraux went. This lighter," he said, touching its battered surface, "is Cammie Armstrong's room, which is opposite the kitchen. Did she go in there, Mrs. Steele?" He observed Alice's passive face. "She didn't, did she? She wouldn't be safe there because I don't think Amy Steele would think twice about following her in there."

His blunt finger tapped the paperback western. "This is the living room, but she didn't go in there, either, did she? You or your son would have mentioned it because it's a safe room. No Quindat and no coffee in the living room. Now that leaves us with two rooms. This one"—he touched the book of matches lying next to the western—"is Jim Steele's room. She definitely wouldn't go in there. She'd just been called a whore by Jim Steele's wife so the last place she'd go would be his room with that great big oil painting of her hanging on the wall."

He smiled at John Lloyd's startled movement. "I've done my homework, Counselor, I talked to the drapery hanger, who happened to be from Amarillo and didn't give a damn about keeping his mouth shut concerning Jim Steele like the folks in Canadian do. That painting was hanging over the bar from the time that room was built, which was a year or more before Amy Steele took off with a thermos of doped coffee in the seat beside her.''

His hand hovered over the pack of cigarettes. "So what room does that leave? What room might Amy Steele be reluctant to enter?'' His hand covered the cigarettes. "Your room, Mrs. Steele, with your Quindat sitting in the medicine cabinet in your private bathroom. And who follows her, but her uncle, the family doctor, who not only knows that Alice Steele has Quindat, but that it's water soluble. He knows Amy Steele is leaving because he heard Cammie tell Jim Steele. And he would also know about Amy Steele's addiction to coffee and fast driving. *Because he knew Amy Steele as well as any of you.*'' His voice dropped back to a low growl. "He was her godfather and a doctor. Giving a sedative would be *his* style more than yours, wouldn't it, Mrs. Steele?''

Jenner touched Schroder's arm.''Hey, take it easy. Mrs. Steele doesn't look too good. Can I get you a glass of water, ma'am?'' he asked. She needed something, he decided. Her skin was gray and she had deep grooves on either side of her mouth. Schroder must have guessed right, or she wouldn't look so sick.

"The Jane Doe in that grave doesn't look so good either, Sergeant Jenner,'' said Schroder. "Why did the doctor and Christy Deveraux go into the kitchen? Because they *were* in the kitchen, weren't they? They and Cammie Armstrong. Those were the three people watching Jim Steele pick up a thermos of coffee and leave the kitchen. But the door into the kitchen is a swinging door. Once he walked through it into the dining room, they couldn't see him. And neither could you, Mrs. Steele; not until he walked through the double doors and into the hall.''

John Lloyd slapped his hand on the table. "I believe we dispensed with any suspicion that might attach itself to James Steele earlier this afternoon. He had no motive for disposing of his wife in such a careless fashion. He was divorcing her."

Schroder turned his head toward John Lloyd. "But he didn't announce it, did he? He was still defending her to Dr. Bailey after he allegedly decided to divorce her."

"The papers were filed that day, Sergeant Schroder," said John Lloyd. "It was a matter of public record."

"Was it a matter of private record, too? Did Dr. Bailey know? Had the small-town grapevine gotten the word to him yet? I don't think so, or was he stupid enough to bring his niece out to her lover's house on the day he files for divorce? I think even Canadian, as much as the folks here dislike Amy Steele, might find it hard to stomach their having a victory dinner together."

He stopped and lit another cigarette, his faded blue eyes never breaking contact with John Lloyd's black ones. "I'm looking in another direction, Branson. Do you like what I'm seeing? What about it, Mrs. Steele? I've got your boy with the opportunity and the means. I don't have to prove motive. Would you like to tell me more about the Quindat in your bathroom, or do you want to see your son in prison in Huntsville? He's a good-looking man; he wouldn't have an easy time of it. Would you like to know what might happen to him?"

"Goddamn it, Schroder!" cried Jenner.

"That is enough, Sergeant!" John Lloyd stood up, his tall figure a dark silhouette against the gloom outside the pool of light from the Tiffany lamp.

"What do you want me to say? No, John Lloyd, I won't be quiet. Dr. Bailey and Christy went to the kitchen to be with Cammie. She'd only been out of the hospital a week and Amy upset her. But they knew about the divorce; we all did. We knew we were finally getting rid of the bitch."

''But she'd just called Christy Deveraux a whore. What was she going to call her in court, Mrs. Steele? That divorce wasn't going to be as uncomplicated as John Lloyd wants me to believe. Amy Steele was planning to throw as much mud at Christy Deveraux as possible. She and Jim Steele were gong to provide this town with something to talk about for a long time. Jim Steele could look forward to walking into his favorite store and have everybody look at him and snicker. And the doctor's practice might fall off because of the scandal.''

He looked at her for a minute, his face impassive. ''Why did you fill your prescription for Quindat the day after Amy left? You'd had it filled the week before. How did you use a month's supply of sleeping pills in less than a week?''

John Lloyd leaned over and grasped her shoulder. ''Don't answer that question, Alice.''

She shook his hand off. ''I dropped the bottle,'' she said. ''My hands shake sometimes. It fell in the toilet. You can believe that or not, Sergeant Schroder, but it's the truth.''

''I don't believe it, Mrs. Steele, and I don't think a jury will either.''

Alice clutched John Lloyd's arm. ''Get me out of here, please.''

John Lloyd turned her wheelchair. ''You, sir,'' he said to Schroder, ''are an unmitigated bastard.''

Schroder nodded. ''That makes two of us, doesn't it, Branson?''

John Lloyd pushed Alice's chair toward the door. He stopped suddenly and turned around. ''Ask yourself who has the character, and the most to gain from this.''

''I have, and I keep coming up with the same answer: the Steeles.''

John Lloyd made an impatient sound. ''They had nothing to gain from her death six months ago. You are confusing the present situation with the past.''

CHAPTER
FIFTEEN

LYDIA SHIELDED HER EYES AGAINST THE SUN. IT WAS just above the horizon, its light already beginning to turn red and orange from the haze of dust in the air. Lydia had heard that the Panhandle produced some of the most beautiful sunsets in the world, but she could do without witnessing one. Right now she was more concerned with watching where she stepped. None of the heroines in the western romances she read had to worry about stepping in horse manure. It was unfair that fiction didn't mirror reality a little more closely.

"Damn it!" she exclaimed when she felt her heel sink into something soft. She pulled her shoe out and practically doubled over to watch the path. She felt as if she'd won the Boston Marathon when she finally stumbled through the barn door.

She stood still, letting her eyes adjust to the gloomy interior. She squinted down the center of the barn with its rows of stalls on each side. The air was full of dust motes dancing on the tiny ribbons of sun that slipped through the cracks in the sides of the old building. She quickly pressed her upper lip to prevent a sneeze. An-

other strike against romantic novels. Real barns stank of
horse manure, leather, old hay. The dirt floor had sus-
piciously damp spots that she didn't think were puddles
from a spring shower. She sneezed. There was a dull
thud from a nearby stall and a loud whinny. Lydia jerked
violently and sneezed again.

"Miss Fairchild." Jim Steele pushed open a stall door
and stood looking at her. "What are you doing out here?"

She sneezed again. "I came out here to tell you what
a weak-kneed, wishy-washy nerd you are." She took
another deep breath, sneezed several times, stepped
backward, and felt an unidentified liquid ooze into her
open-toed sandals. "Shit!" she exclaimed.

Jim's lips twitched and he rubbed his hand across them.
"That's not what you stepped in."

She wiped her eyes on the hem of her skirt. "What
was it?"

Jim came toward her. "You're better off not knowing." He took her arm. "Come here. I want to show you
something."

"What?" she demanded, pulling back.

Jim frowned. "Not my etchings. And I'm not going
to try to murder you, so relax."

"I didn't think of murder."

"You don't have to worry about seduction either. After
the last four days, I'm thinking of taking a vow of
celibacy. Watch where you put your feet," he cau-
tioned.

She did a quick sidestep and kept her eyes on her feet
as she followed him. "It's your own fault."

"You can look up now, Miss Fairchild," he said
as he released her arm and stepped inside the horse
stall.

"Oh, how beautiful! It's a baby horse!"

Jim chuckled. "I guess you could call it that. Technically it's a foal. That's a baby horse under a year
old. After a year, we'll call this fellow a colt. You can
pet him. You smell enough like a horse after your trip
out here that I don't think his dam will bother you.

If she lays her ears back, get the hell out of the stall fast.''

Lydia jerked her hand back and looked at the mare. The mare's nostrils quivered once, then she snorted and dipped her head for another mouthful of hay. There was something disconcerting about being told you stink by a horse, she thought, then forgot it as she gently touched the white star on the foal's forehead. "He's so beautiful," she whispered. "All skinny legs and big eyes."

Jim hooked the toe of his boot between two slats in the stall gate and rested his forearm on his thigh. "You don't like me very much, do you?"

She looked at him over her shoulder. He was different out here, taller, stronger, more sure of himself. He appeared—looser, relaxed, at home in his scuffed boots and faded Levi's. He looked like the western historical writer he was. In fact, he looked like a romantic hero from one of his own books, and she wished she could like him. But he wasn't and she didn't. "No, I don't," she admitted. "I'm sorry."

He pushed his hat back on his head. "At least you're honest."

She stroked the foal's neck, enjoying the softness of its coat. "I try to be."

"What happened to your hand?"

She looked down at her swollen knuckles. "I hit something."

"With your fist?"

She turned around to face him. "That's how one usually hits something, isn't it?"

He grinned, a lazy sort of movement that emphasized the squint lines around his eyes. "Not always. Not women anyway. Women usually slap things. Or people, mostly men. I can't see you hitting an object, so I'm going to guess that you hit someone. Since the only someone here you know well enough to hit is John Lloyd, and since I noticed a T-shaped cut on one of your knuckles, I'm going to guess that you hit him right in his Phi Beta Kappa. Care to tell me why?''

"It's complicated."

"It usually is with John Lloyd. He's so damn arrogant sometimes. There's a right way, a wrong way, and John Lloyd's way. The hell of it is, he's usually right."

"He's right about Amy. Why won't you see that? Why don't you believe Cammie? My God, how can you look at Cammie and apologize for that woman?"

She saw him hunch his shoulders defensively. "I knew that was coming when you starting calling me names. It's none of your business, Miss Fairchild, so you can pick your way back to the house and tell John Lloyd to go to hell."

"John Lloyd has nothing to do with this. He doesn't even know I'm talking to you."

"So you decided on your own to stick your nose in my business. You've been in town less than a week, you've met me exactly twice, and suddenly you feel you have the right to ask me personal questions. Your arrogance goes beyond John Lloyd's. Who appointed you my conscience? Who anointed you as James Steele's personal confessor?"

He stood in front of her, both his fists clenched like a fighter waiting to defend himself against the next blow. She drew in a slow breath as she realized what an apt description that was. He didn't strike blows; he defended against them. Friday night and earlier today, when he was repeatedly attacked by John Lloyd, his mother, Christy, he didn't go on the offensive. He defended himself vigorously, but he never retaliated with ugly accusations of his own.

"Who appointed you a martyr?" she asked.

His mouth slackened. "Why do you say that?"

"You didn't deny any of what I said. You just challenged my right to say it. You know Amy is a liar; you know she's cruel; you know she's a monster. What she did to Cammie was inhuman. Yet you continue to defend her. You take her side against your family. You drove Christy away with your damnable stubbornness. You take everything Amy can dish out without fighting back. Just like a martyr, you're marching off to be eaten by the lions without kicking a few people in the groin on the way into the arena. That's all right for you, if that's really what you want. But do you have to take your family with you?''

"My family will be all right."

"Tell that to Cammie. I'm sure she'll find it a comfort the next time she looks in a mirror. You stupid fool, she'll never be all right again. Ever. She won't have any more rainbow days."

She knew she'd made a direct hit by the way the color drained from his face. He turned and gripped the top of the stall door, leaning his forehead against the rough wood. "She was my wife. I promised to cherish her for better or worse. If it was worse, then I was still obligated to take care of her."

Lydia stared at his rigid body, his knuckles slowly turning white from his grip on the stall door, the bunched muscles in his shoulders and arms from his efforts to hold onto his self-control. If ever a man looked ready to self-destruct, it was Jim Steele. "You could've kicked her out, divorced her."

He turned around, his arms outstretched along the top of the door, his hands still gripping the wood. "It's so easy to sit in judgment of someone else. John Lloyd, my mother, Cammie, now you—all saying off with her head. I wish I was so blameless, so goddamn perfect, as all of you are. But I'm not. I wish I could say that I've never done anything to be ashamed of. But I can't say that either. I have to take some of the blame for what Amy is."

Lydia shook her head in bafflement. "Are you telling me that it's your fault that Amy beat a helpless animal until it had to be shot?"

Jim's gaze wavered, and his voice held a note of self-loathing. "Maybe she learned about mistreating helpless things from me. Did you ever think of that, Miss Fairchild? Maybe I taught her how to strike in anger and apologize later. Maybe I taught her everything she knows about seduction.'' His gaze steadied and he looked directly at her. "She deserved more out of this marriage than she ever got.''

Lydia looked at her swollen hand resting between the foal's twitching ears. "I struck John Lloyd when I was angry. Does that mean he's going to kick the next dog he sees? Will he suddenly begin to set fire to cats? Will it be all my fault?''

"No! You're not listening to what I'm saying.''

Lydia took a step toward him. "Yes, I am, and you ought to try listening to yourself for a change. All I'm doing is repeating what you said, but changing the names. If you beat up Amy, you need counseling, not self-flagellation.''

He lowered his arms from the gate, and Lydia relaxed. He didn't look quite so much as if he were waiting to be crucified. "I didn't beat her up.''

"Okay, you slapped her around, mistreated her by locking her in her room.''

"I did not! She wasn't a child. ''

Lydia widened her eyes in mock surprise. "She wasn't? I got the distinct impression from listening to you that Amy was a baby girl clutching her Cabbage Patch doll when she married you. All this talk of teaching her this and teaching her that. I'm surprised you didn't have to teach her to walk.''

She noticed his color had returned. His face was as red as the sunset outside. She hoped he didn't suffer from hypertension, because he certainly looked angry enough to have an apoplectic attack. "I don't even know why I'm talking to you, Miss Fairchild.''

"Because you don't have to apologize to me for anything Amy did. She's hurt everyone around you, and you have to keep making excuses for her. Excuses get in the way of explanations. She never did anything to me, though. And there's another reason, of course.''

''What is it?''

She felt her hands trembling and took a deep breath. She was close to finding out just what power Amy held over him. He was exhausted from the shocks of the past few days. There were cracks in his defenses. The question was: would he crumble into dust or would he tear off his shell and come out fighting?

''I think you're ashamed of whatever you did to Amy, so ashamed you don't want anyone you care about to know. You'd rather have your family and the whole town believe you're a blind idiot than have them know the truth. You think you lose less respect that way. That's why you didn't divorce her years ago. Me, I'm a stranger. I'll be gone by the end of the summer. You don't care so much what I think about you. And you wanted to talk to someone, and I hit John Lloyd.''

''What does that have to do with anything?''

''Maybe you thought I'd understand because I lost my temper and did something I'm ashamed of. Not ashamed enough to borrow one of your hair shirts, but ashamed nevertheless. Now suppose you tell me what you did to Amy.''

There was a hint of admiration in his blue eyes. ''You've got gall, lady.''

''When your feet are as big as mine, there's no point in trying to pussyfoot around an issue. So talk to me, Jim Steele. You've come too far to go back. I know enough now to ask questions of other people, and I don't think you want me doing that.'' Nothing like coaxing someone to confess one minute and threatening them the next, she thought.

He rubbed his hands together as if he were trying to wash them. ''I seduced her and got her pregnant. Then, after we were married, I caused her to miscarry. There were complications, and she ended up sterile as a result. She never forgave me and I've never forgiven myself.''

Lydia swallowed. "Oh, God."

"I doubt God had anything to do with it, Miss Fairchild." John Lloyd pushed open the stall door and stepped on the clean straw. As usual he looked cool and well-groomed, Lydia thought resentfully. She and Jim had sweat running down their faces and dripping off their noses from the heat in the barn.

"What the hell are you doing out here?" demanded Jim. "I thought you said he didn't know you were talking to me," he added, glaring at Lydia.

"Miss Fairchild is innocent of misleading you. She merely underestimated my tenacity in seeking her out. Unsupervised, her impulsiveness may lead her astray. However, in this case it did not."

"You've been eavesdropping!" Jim accused.

One of John Lloyd's eyebrows arched. "You were hardly whispering. And one does occasionally learn something useful by listening at keyholes. Or stall doors, as the case may be."

"That's rude," said Lydia, stomping over to confront him.

"Under ordinary circumstances, yes. However, under ordinary circumstances one is not accused of murder." He shifted his feet and leaned on his cane. "Shall we discuss your confession?"

"I didn't mean to kill my baby," said Jim, looking haunted.

"Spare me the histrionics," said John Lloyd sharply. "Let us begin with the so-called seduction. Based on five years' acquaintance with Amy, I find you innocent of the charge. Your ex-wife would have attempted to seduce her pediatrician before she was out of diapers. I do find you guilty of bedding the viper when your affections were otherwise engaged."

"Christy was too young!"

"At least you aren't claiming you were drunk and didn't know what you were doing," interrupted Lydia.

"I was drunk!" said Jim, shoving his hands into his pockets.

"While your reluctance to bed Christy in consideration of her youth is commendable, your inability to control your libido and your choice of a partner is not. How do you know she was pregnant?"

"I saw the lab report," replied Jim.

"How did you cause her to miscarry?"

"I was trying to finish a book. I had a deadline to meet, and I was behind. Amy had been badgering me all day about taking her somewhere, and I hadn't been able to concentrate. I was tense and angry. When she reached over my shoulder and pulled my disc out of the disc drive and threatened to destroy it, I lost my temper. I took it away from her and she lost her balance and fell. I should've reasoned with her, instead of physically taking back the disc." He wiped his forehead on his sleeve. "She accused me of hating her and wanting her dead. I just stood there. I couldn't even deny it, because at that moment I did want to kill her. She packed a bag and left. She called me a few days later to tell me what had happened. She was hysterical, accused me of murder."

The silence was as intense as the heat and Lydia felt the tears mix with the droplets of sweat on her cheeks. God, no wonder Jim didn't go on the offensive. The last time he had, he'd been responsible for a horrible accident. And no wonder he defended Amy. His own guilt made it impossible for him to do otherwise.

"Where did this alleged miscarriage occur?" asked John Lloyd.

"In New York. And it wasn't alleged!"

John Lloyd rubbed his forehead. "Interesting," he murmured. He looked over at Jim. "You refused to obtain a divorce because of your guilt?"

Jim nodded.

John Lloyd's eyelids lowered, but not before Lydia caught an expression of calculation. "I never would have believed you were a coward."

Jim's head jerked up. "What?"

"To be afraid of having this little episode exposed."

"I'm not a coward!"

"But you are," said John Lloyd, his drawl so pronounced it seemed to extend into infinity. "You allowed those around you to be put in mortal danger because you were too cowardly to face your neighbors' possible censure."

"What do you think would've happened if I had divorced her?" asked Jim angrily. "What kind of mortal danger do you think they'd have been in? As long as I was living with her, I could watch her, maybe keep her from hurting anyone."

"Rather like keeping a pet rattlesnake caged?"

"Yeah, I guess so."

John Lloyd smiled with what Lydia thought was relief. "And you allowed me to blackmail you into divorcing her, not to save her from possible criminal charges, but because she was simply too dangerous to keep."

Jim sagged against the side of the stall. "Yes. I had to take the chance. Thought I could keep everybody safe, get a restraining order maybe, and warn everybody to stay away from her."

"I don't understand," said Lydia. "Why didn't you let John Lloyd press charges in Cammie's name? If Amy was in jail, then she couldn't hurt anyone."

Jim rolled his head against the wall. "She threatened to hurt Christy."

"Kill her?" asked Lydia.

"She didn't kill Cammie, did she?" asked Jim. "Do you think I'd risk anything like that happening to Christy? I couldn't risk it. I thought the divorce would upset her less." He straightened up to look at John Lloyd. "That's why I don't want to fight this temporary alimony. I'll acquiesce to any of her demands if that's what it takes to keep Amy calm. I'll give up the ranch, or my share of it anyway. I'll lie down in the middle of town and let her walk on me if that's what she wants. I haven't any pride left. I'll do anything to keep Christy safe."

"Even murder?" asked John Lloyd softly.

Jim drew a breath. "Even that."

CHAPTER
SIXTEEN

JENNER STUMBLED OUT ON THE PORCH OF THE STEELE ranch house and took several deep breaths. He'd forgotten what it was like to breathe air he couldn't see. God, but it was pretty out here. The land sloped in a series of breaks from the ranch house down to the Canadian River, and he could see the line of trees that shaded its banks. More damn trees than he'd ever seen in one place in the Panhandle, he thought; trees that hadn't been planted by the white settlers, that is. Behind the house, the land was flat, bald prairie, reaching to the horizon with maybe a mesquite tree or a dry streambed to break the monotony.

He'd read somewhere that the Panhandle had freaked out Coronado and his boys. That was back in the days when the grass was still belly high to a horse and there weren't any mesquites at all, just a sea of waving grass with no landmarks. The Spaniards went ape because they couldn't tell where they were going from where they'd been. Once you got away from the river, the land looked the same. He could sympathize with Coronado. He liked a few street signs and stoplights himself. All this open country could make a man feel insignificant.

He heard a tapping sound on the wooden porch and turned around. Now there was someone that he'd bet had never felt insignificant in his life. John Lloyd Branson had stopped to talk to Schroder. The guy looked like the big city in that fancy suit until you noticed the boots and that Stetson. He looked as if he belonged in a Stetson. Not everybody did. You had to have a certain set to your shoulders and a certain expression in your eyes, like you were used to looking beyond that horizon out there. Jenner smiled at himself. Time to get back to Amarillo before he freaked out like Coronado. Next he'd be seeing wagon trains and cavalry, Indians and buffalo.

Schroder brushed past him, a cigarette in his mouth. "Come on, son. Time to go."

"I've got to stop in Canadian to call my wife," said Jenner, following the investigator to the car. "I'm going to be late and she doesn't know where I am."

Schroder grunted as he slid his bulk under the steering wheel. "You can call from this doctor's house. I told Branson we'd meet him there."

"What?" Jenner slammed the car door. "Listen, Schroder, it's after six o'clock. It'll be eight before we get home. Can't we come back tomorrow?"

"Branson'd have the doctor and Christy Steele so rehearsed by morning you'd think they were in the movies."

"He didn't have much time to rehearse that Cammie Armstrong, and we still got zilch from her. Yes, sir, I was in the kitchen. No, sir, I wasn't there alone. No, sir, I didn't notice who poured the coffee into the thermos. Yes, it *could* have been me, but I have no recollection of it. No, sir, I don't remember anyone being in the kitchen by him or herself. No, sir, I didn't like Amy Steele. Yes, sir, she was driving the car when I was injured. Do I blame her for it? I can't answer that question, sir, on the advice of my lawyer. God, talk about someone blind, deaf, and dumb. She swears she didn't notice a damn thing. I'm surprised she admitted being in the house. For someone who crept in the room and huddled in that chair, and seemed more interested in hiding her face than paying attention to us, she turned out to be a tough woman to break.''

Schroder stubbed out his cigarette, dislodging several older butts in the process. "She won't break. Why should she? The worst that can happen to her already has. What's left to be afraid of?''

Jenner eyed the floorboard of the car with distaste. "For God's sake, don't you ever empty your ashtray?''

Schroder ignored him. "We learned more from Alice Steele than either of the other two. In fact, we learned too much. That's not like Branson. He usually keeps a tighter rein on his clients.''

"You've run into him before?''

The investigator nodded. "Lots of times. Murder and Branson go together like wienies and mustard.''

"How come I've never heard much about him?'' asked Jenner, gingerly picking up cigarettes and putting them in a rumpled paper sack he'd found in the glove compartment.

"Because his clients never get charged. Or if they do, the charges are dropped. Sometimes they make it all the way to court. If that happens, you can figure we've caught the client with a smoking gun in his hand with his fingerprints on it, forty eyewitnesses, and video tapes taken by a passing TV cameraman. Not that it does us any good. John Lloyd Branson will either prove the victim was stabbed, not shot, that the eyewitnesses were all legally blind, or that the video tape had been tampered with. If he can't do any of those things, then he'll prove his client acted in self-defense, or under extreme mental duress. I saw one case where the jury not only found Branson's client not guilty, but nominated him as citizen of the year for ridding our streets of the victim, who happened to be a pretty sorry specimen, by the way.''

Jenner managed to extract the ashtray from the dashboard and dump it in the paper sack. "You sound like you admire him.''

Schroder lit another cigarette. "Yeah, I guess I do.

I've seen him defend a man for a dollar fee and then turn down a millionaire.''

"How come?"

"He thought the indigent was being framed, and the millionaire was up on a drug charge. Branson never defends anybody charged with drugs or child abuse.''

"Was the indigent being framed?'' asked Jenner, looking around for a place to dispose of the sack.

"Jury said so.''

Jenner surreptitiously tossed the sack into the backseat. "You two don't act like you think much of each other.''

Schroder turned off the gravel road onto the highway. "Never said I liked him. He's a real bastard. But I've never seen him like he was today. He was acting like he didn't know what was going on, and that he didn't trust his clients to tell him.''

Dr. William Bailey was a dead ringer for Santa Claus, decided Jenner. Except Bailey didn't have a beard. Christy Steele looked like a girl you wanted to stick in your pocket and take home. But not to Momma.

Dr. Bailey's house resembled those you'd see featured in an antiques magazine: a two-story clapboard with a corner turret and an old wooden swing on the front porch. Jenner wished he were sitting on the swing rather than this couch with its high back and curly arms. There were glassed-in bookcases, corner china cabinets, a round table with claw feet, Persian rugs on the hardwood floors, even a fireplace with a marble mantelpiece. He thought the whole damn living room should be dismantled and reassembled in a museum somewhere. He noticed Lydia Fairchild twitching around in an uncomfortable-looking chair upholstered in tapestry of some kind. He wondered what Branson thought about her appearing without her pantyhose or shoes. If she worked for Larry Jenner, the less she appeared in, the better, but he didn't imagine her stiff-necked boss felt that way. Or maybe he did. He sure didn't like her out of his sight.

Schroder began his inquiry. "Dr. Bailey, I have just a few questions for you and Miss Deveraux about the evening of October 15 last year. I wonder which of you would like to talk to me first."

Dr. Bailey was sitting in the only modern piece of furniture in the room: a cozy, thickly upholstered recliner. The physician smiled and Jenner decided he definitely resembled Santa Claus. "We'll both talk to you, Sergeant Schroder. It'll save time, and I'm late making my rounds at the hospital."

Schroder grimaced back at the doctor. "I'm afraid that's a little unorthodox. We usually speak to one person at a time."

Dr. Bailey rubbed the side of his nose. "You'll have to be unorthodox, then, Sergeant, because that's the only way we'll discuss those events. We were together almost all that evening and we can refresh one another's memories."

"That's what I'm afraid of," muttered Schroder.

"What was that?" asked the doctor.

"I could take you down to the sheriff's office and question you there if you prefer."

"Oh, I think not," replied Bailey. "I'm afraid Christy and I wouldn't be able to remember a thing under those circumstances. You know the old saying: a bird in the hand is worth two in the bush."

"I think you had best accept the doctor's conditions, Sergeant," said John Lloyd. "Unless, of course, you prefer to make this whole investigation more formal and thus coercive. I believe such a decision on your part would be most unwise at present. Your position is simply too weak; I should checkmate you at once."

Schroder's brows drew together. "Are you threatening me, Branson?"

The lawyer laid his cane across his knees and stroked the smooth wood for a second. He looked up, his eyes expressing a degree of intelligence that intimidated Jenner. He suspected it would intimidate anyone. Except Schroder. "Sergeant, I do not threaten. It is a wasteful exercise. I am merely stating facts. You have no evidence upon which to support your suspicions of any of my clients except the statement of an unstable woman whose acquaintance with the truth is limited to its spelling. I caution you against interpreting the facts in such a way as to support a favored theory. I remind you again to ask who has the most to gain from putting Quindat in the coffee. Now may we get on with your questions? You still have a long drive home, Miss Fairchild wishes to freshen up before dining, and Dr. Bailey must make his evening rounds before his patients expire from lack of personal attention."

Schroder leaned forward on the couch, his hands braced on his knees. "Branson, I've got an old saying for you. You can't see the forest for the trees. You're too close to this case and you're gonna get kicked in the gut by one of your client friends."

"I have already had some experience with being, uh, hit in the gut. I shall risk surviving another such blow. Please continue, Sergeant."

Schroder's face was pinched like a bear with a bellyache, but he lit a cigarette and pulled a candy dish closer. Jenner closed his eyes. "Dr. Bailey, you were having an argument with Jim Steele in the living room of the Steele ranch when Amy Steele returned home. Is that correct?"

The doctor glanced at John Lloyd who nodded. "Yes, I was."

"What was the argument about?"

John Lloyd interrupted. "Next question, Sergeant."

Schroder took a deep breath. "What happened after Jim left the living room?"

"Please be more explicit, Sergeant," said John Lloyd. "Where did you go?"

John Lloyd made a casual gesture and the doctor answered. "I went into Alice Steele's bedroom to check on Christy. Amy had made some of her usual distasteful remarks and Christy was upset."

"Where in Alice Steele's room was Miss Deveraux?"

"She was lying on the bed crying."

''What did you do?''

''I went into Alice's bathroom for a wet cloth. I bathed her face and tried to comfort her.''

''Did you remove anything else from the bathroom?''

The doctor sat up straight, his rotund stomach shaking with indignation. ''John Lloyd told us what you suspect, and if you are accusing me of stealing Quindat with the idea of poisoning my godchild, you are wasting your time. As a physician, I can obtain many more potent drugs than Quindat.''

''But were there more potent drugs in the Steele household, Doctor?'' asked Schroder.

''I did not poison Amy,'' said the doctor firmly.

''Who came into the bedroom while you and your niece were there?''

Bailey glanced at John Lloyd and again the lawyer nodded. ''Alice may have looked in. I think Cammie was with her. But they didn't stay.''

''Did either of them go into the bathroom?''

''Not that I noticed.''

''Did Jim Steele come into the bedroom?''

The doctor raked his fingers through his hair until it stood on end. ''Do you think the man's a fool, Sergeant? His wife had already called my niece a filthy name. Do you think he'd come into the bedroom and give that psychotic woman another reason to abuse my niece?''

Jenner exchanged glances with Schroder. If Jim Steele had never gone into his mother's bedroom, then where had he obtained the Quindat for his wife's coffee? Jenner rubbed his stomach. It was just as he told Schroder: Jim Steele was going to walk on this one, and that gave him a bellyache. It didn't help that Steele's mouthpiece was looking so damn self-satisfied.

''Why did you and your niece go to the kitchen? Why take a crying woman to the kitchen?'' asked Schroder, his face and eyes as blank as a whitewashed wall.

''I wanted to get her a cup of coffee,'' replied the doctor.

''And where did you get the coffee?''

"From the fresh pot, the same one used to fill that thermos, and there was nothing wrong with it then."

"Who was in the kitchen when you got there?"

"Alice and Cammie."

"What did the four of you talk about?"

"Do not take advantage of my cooperativeness, Sergeant," said John Lloyd, holding up one hand. "I have not issued you a fishing license."

"Did you pour the coffee into the thermos?"

"I most certainly did not."

"Miss Deveraux, did you pour the coffee into the thermos?"

"She did not," interjected her uncle. "Why should she do a favor for Amy Steele?"

"Maybe so she could add a surprise to the coffee," said Schroder, flicking his ash into the candy dish. Jenner noticed John Lloyd flinching.

"I didn't!" cried Christy. "I didn't even know there was Quindat in the house, and if I had known, I couldn't have used it. I *couldn't* have. Not because I didn't hate her, and not because I didn't want her gone, but because . . ."

John Lloyd was out of his chair and at her side grasping her hand. "That's enough, Christy."

". . . I was terrified of her. I'm too cowardly to commit murder." Her shoulders slumped and Jenner saw her lower lip tremble. Of all the suspects, Christy Steele was the only one he believed. Not because she was a coward and afraid to lie—cowards lied more frequently than the brave—but because his gut instinct told him this woman was incapable of deliberately hurting anything. That didn't make her a coward; it made her compassionate. Schroder probably wouldn't agree with him.

He didn't. "In my experience, terror makes a very good motive for murder, Miss Deveraux. How do you stop being terrified? Murder the person responsible. I've seen it happen that way before."

Christy sat up, her odd-colored eyes flashing like gold in the sunlight. "It didn't happen this time. Another thing

I don't do, Sergeant, is lie.'' Jenner grinned. Just like he thought. She wasn't really cowardly. She just thought she was. Anybody who could snap back at Schroder was no coward.

Schroder rubbed his chin where Jenner could see a sandy-gray stubble. ''Dr. Bailey,'' he said, still looking at Christy. ''You prescribed Quindat for the Steele household? Why did they all need sleeping pills?''

''My God, man! There wasn't any ulterior motive. I wasn't planning on supplying everyone with a murder weapon. If I had, I would've found a better one. You saw Cammie's condition. She is in constant pain. She can't go outside in the sunshine without feeling discomfort. She is traumatized both physically and mentally. She requires a sedative to sleep. Alice has the same problem that many handicapped persons do: she has difficulty sleeping. I prescribed a milder dose for her. As for Jim, he was on the edge of a mental and physical breakdown. It was imperative that he rest. Even a chemically induced sleep was better than none at all. Medically and ethically, I had a very poor reason for prescribing Quindat for Amy . . .''

''What!'' Schroder's hoarse voice cracked on the word.

The white-haired little doctor pursed his lips. ''I said I had a very poor reason . . .''

Schroder's thick fingers beat a tattoo on his knees. ''Amy Steele had a bottle of Quindat?''

''That's what I just said, Sergeant,'' repeated the doctor. ''Are you hard of hearing? Many men develop a hearing impairment in their later years. I would be happy to recommend a specialist in Amarillo.''

Schroder's irritation was growing. ''I heard you! I want to be sure I understand you. Amy Steele had Quindat in her medicine cabinet?''

''I don't know where she kept it, but most people keep their prescription drugs in a medicine cabinet,'' said the doctor. ''*She* could've kept hers in a locket around her neck.''

Schroder looked at John Lloyd. ''Jim Steele was in his

wife's room while she was packing, just a step away from a supply of Quindat. Motive and means, Branson, and according to the testimony of his own family and friends, he was the only one with the opportunity. No one else was alone with that coffee. Only Jim Steele during that minute or two when he was out sight of those in the kitchen, and before his mother could see him coming down the hall from the dining room. It's the law of averages, Branson. Your client can't be innocent every time. I'm sorry for your sake that your luck ran out when the client was a friend.''

''For God's sake, do something, John Lloyd!'' cried Christy, twisting a sodden handkerchief into a knot. Jenner had never seen a woman who still looked beautiful with wet eyes and a runny nose.

''About what?'' asked the lawyer blandly, making a steeple of his fingers.

''About Jim! That man is going to arrest him.'' She gestured at Schroder.

John Lloyd studied her. ''Do I hear a note of concern in your voice?''

''Yes!''

Lydia scrambled out of her chair to embrace the smaller woman. ''That's the stupidest question I ever heard you ask, John Lloyd. Don't you have any soul at all? Can't you see she's upset?''

Dr. Bailey interrupted. ''Of course she is. Silly question, John Lloyd.''

Jenner couldn't see that being called stupid or silly made a dent in the lawyer's tough hide. Even Schroder's summation of the evidence didn't seem to faze him.

John Lloyd Branson still had that cat-who-ate-the-canary expression on his face when he spoke.

''While Miss Fairchild is often impetuous and emotional in expressing her opinions, I did not expect you to be equally impulsive in your remarks, Dr. Bailey. I have not in recent memory asked a stupid or silly question. I merely wished to ascertain Christy's state of mind.''

Lydia's blue eyes looked as turbulent as a hurricane

off the Gulf Coast. Jenner was glad that particular storm was directed at Branson. "You shouldn't have to ask, *Mr. Branson*," she said. "It should have been obvious even to a stiff-necked, hard-hearted lummox like you."

The insults seemed to bounce off John Lloyd like rubber balls off a brick wall. "That has been the difficulty with this situation, Miss Fairchild. The obvious has been a stumbling block in Sergeant Schroder's investigation, such a stumbling block that he has failed to account for the state of mind of all the participants. The answers to the who, when, where, and how have led him to the obvious, so he feels he may ignore the why, the motive, which evolves from the state of mind, because the why does not support the obvious. Jim Steele lacked a strong motive; therefore, we shall ignore motive altogether." He shifted his eyes to Schroder. "You and I have been both adversaries and partners in the past, Sergeant, and you have always begun with the strongest motive and worked backward to the perpetrator. Why have you changed your pattern? Why have you selected the one person with the weakest motive?"

Schroder stubbed out his cigarette. "You know that in seventy to eighty percent of domestic homicides, the husband or wife is guilty. As you say, we started with the obvious."

John Lloyd tapped his fingers against his chin. "Perhaps someone was anticipating that very event, Sergeant. Perhaps someone was depending on Jim Steele's state of mind being such that he would project an attitude of guilt. For whatever reason, that would predispose you to accepting the obvious without question."

Schroder frowned as he peered at the lawyer. "Who might that be, Branson? Who hated Jim Steele enough to bait a trap and then wait six months to spring it?"

"I believe the evildoer's intent was for immediate results. The mistaken identity of the victim and the assumption the wreck was a simple accident created an almost insurmountable obstacle. The magazine article and Amy's reappearance provided a solution. You initiated a police investigation, which was the villain's intent from the beginning. The discovery of the Quindat-laced coffee led back to Canadian and Jim Steele, the *obvious* suspect. But who is the reverse of the obvious, Sergeant? Who also possessed the means and opportunity, and whose state of mind provided the motive for this diabolical scheme? You have not posed those questions; therefore, I shall. Who would benefit from Jim Steele's being charged with attempted murder? Who had access to Quindat? Who was alone with the thermos of coffee without fear of interruption? Write down the answers to those three questions, and only one name appears three times.''

Schroder struggled to his feet. ''Branson, you're crazy.''

John Lloyd smiled and Jenner decided he'd never seen a more dangerous-looking expression on a man's face. ''Ask the questions, Schroder, and watch the reactions. Then begin your search for evidence in a new direction.''

Schroder reached for another cigarette and found an empty pack. ''Why did you wait until now to trot out this theory, Branson? Because you realize I'm about to ask for an arrest warrant, and you want to send me out on a wild-goose chase?''

The lawyer shook his head. ''I was fairly certain who was responsible, but I lacked enough facts to support my supposition. Dr. Bailey here provided the final fact.''

''What did I say?''

John Lloyd continued as if the doctor had not interrupted. ''In any event, you cannot obtain a warrant for Jim Steele's arrest.''

Schroder crumpled his empty cigarette package in his large hand, and Jenner had the feeling the investigator wished it were John Lloyd Branson's neck instead. ''What the hell are you talking about, Branson?''

The lawyer leaned back in his chair and crossed his legs. ''Your search warrant was invalid, Sergeant. I can't imagine how you managed to obtain it in the first place. You asked for a warrant on the basis of evidence eight months old, to search for more evidence, also eight months old. The Quindat you found was not the Quindat present eight months ago.''

"You son of a bitch! You knew that this afternoon! Why didn't you object then?"

John Lloyd removed one of his cigars from his pocket. ''I needed to know what evidence you had, Sergeant, and I could not wait for an arrest when you would be forced to disclose the state's case. I needed knowledge of where the danger lay now, so that I might reconstruct the crime and prevent my client from being arrested. Reading the search warrant and allowing you to execute it gave me that opportunity. It also provided me with badly needed information for tomorrow's alimony hearing. You must attend, by the way. It should provide you with a glimpse of the state of mind of the perpetrator that you will not get otherwise.''

"Damn it, John Lloyd!" shouted Lydia. "Who are you talking about?"

John Lloyd raised one eyebrow. "Amy Steele, of course."

CHAPTER
SEVENTEEN

"I WANT TO KNOW EVERYTHING, JOHN LLOYD," SAID Lydia as she handed her menu to the waiter. "Who knows? I might switch from law to psychology, and your thought processes would make a fantastic topic for a thesis."

"Please bring us coffee immediately," said John Lloyd to the waiter. "It has been an exhausting day and we are both in need of a stimulant."

"Yes, sir, Mr. Branson." He looked at Lydia and did a double take. "Did anyone ever tell you that you look like Mrs. Steele? The first one, that is?"

"A few people have mentioned it," said Lydia dryly. He turned back to John Lloyd. "Say, what's going on with Jim Steele? I heard the cops were talking to him. Mrs. Steele, the first Mrs. Steele, was telling me that he was guilty of something awful, and that I should go to the hearing tomorrow and watch. Is it going to be a good show, Mr. Branson?" The waiter was almost stuttering with excitement.

"Our coffee, please," said John Lloyd, giving the man

a look that sent him skittering back to the kitchen in mid-stutter.

Lydia braced her elbow on the table and rested her chin in her cupped hand. "Give, John Lloyd, before I die of curiosity."

He waved his hand in a negative gesture. "Not now, Miss Fairchild. Let us enjoy a pleasant interlude without referring to the subject. Discussing Amy Steele on an empty stomach is not conducive to a good appetite. Speaking of which, will you require my aid in cutting your meat? You may have some difficulty holding your utensils in your injured hand."

"I'll manage. I'm not a child."

"Thank you, Lennie," he said as the waiter poured their coffee. A cold look from John Lloyd was not quickly forgotten, thought Lydia as the waiter disappeared without a word. However, the regard he now favored her with could almost be called hot. If John Lloyd Branson were capable of being in that condition. "Believe me, Miss Fairchild," he said. "Only a blind fool would consider you a child, and I am neither. Shall we enjoy our dinner?" he added as the waiter silently placed their salads in front of them.

Lydia wasn't sure if the steak was really as delicious as she thought, or if she had been so hungry that grilled shoe leather would have sufficed. Even John Lloyd's having to cut her meat after all didn't disturb her peace of mind.

Her stomach was full, and John Lloyd hadn't made a single comment about the size of her appetite as most of her dates did. Of course, he wasn't really a date, but he was male, urbane, distinguished-looking, charming when he wanted to be, and best of all, he was taller than she. All things considered, he was a very pleasant companion.

She took a sip of coffee and looked around. The restaurant was pleasant, too. It sat on a hill overlooking a golf course on one side, and the river and town on the other. Canadian was such a pretty town, a sort of Brigadoon. One had the feeling that a thousand years from now it would exist more or less unchanged, untouched by the uglier aspects of modern civilization. She wondered at herself. A product of a big city, she should be bored. Instead, she felt challenged, alive. Was the town, or the man sitting across the table from her, responsible? It didn't matter. She fantasized herself the heroine in some romantic detective movie. She and the hero were enjoying some lighthearted banter before sallying forth to catch the murderer. In a moment John Lloyd would look up, smile, pour her another glass of champagne, and make some seductive, romantic remark.

He looked up, smiled, and poured her a cup of coffee. "Miss Fairchild, may I compliment you on the fragrance you are wearing. It is an improvement over your previous scent. I trust you discarded your shoes. While it might have been possible to clean them, they would have retained a certain odor in warm weather which might have occasioned you some embarrassment."

Lydia picked up her coffee cup. So much for romantic daydreams. "Are you insinuating that I stank?"

John Lloyd cut a piece of steak before answering. "Stepping in manure, then standing in a barn on a hot June day will usually result in a certain stench." He looked up and smiled at her. "You stank, Miss Fairchild. If I had more soul, which you accuse me of not having, I would say that even smelling of horse manure, you retained an earthy beauty that would tempt a man to dream of haystacks and the sensual pursuits popularly associated with those rural signs of a bountiful harvest."

"I think I'm allergic to hay," Lydia blurted.

"A condition that would doubtless prevent a painful interlude, Miss Fairchild. Provided one could locate a haystack in the Panhandle, it would consist of such an array of sand burrs, goatheads, and lesser unpleasant varieties of noxious weeds and grasses, that even the most hardy and desperate of souls would lose interest in any intimate behavior. Nevertheless, I am disappointed in your response."

Lydia set her cup down. "What did you expect me to

say? That you say the sweetest things? That you make my heart flutter?''

John Lloyd carefully wiped his mouth and laid his napkin by his plate. "A simple thank you would suffice.''

If she didn't know better she'd think her response genuinely bothered him. She smiled. What would the heroine do to reassure the hero in her imaginary movie? She reached across the table and rested her uninjured hand against his cheek. "Thank you, John Lloyd,'' she said in the seductive voice she had practiced so meticulously just in case she might someday find someone to use it on.

John Lloyd wasn't the someone. He captured her hand and held it firmly on the bale. "Miss Fairchild, you forget yourself.''

"You started it,'' she said, trying to free her hand. "You and your talk of haystacks.''

He clasped her hand between both of his. "I was speaking rhetorically, Miss Fairchild. Unlike Jim Steele, I do not allow physical desire to lead me into unsuitable liaison.''

"So now I'm unsuitable. Thanks a lot!''

"You misunderstand, Miss Fairchild. As I told you in the beginning, I am an unsuitable object for your romantic fantasies.''

"You're certainly no swashbuckling hero.''

"I pride myself on always being in control, and never taking any action not based on objective reasoning.''

She could feel her blood begin to boil—if such a thing were possible. "I'd like to see you lose control just once, John Lloyd. It'd be good for you, increase your heart rate, lower your blood pressure, work up a good, honest, emotional sweat.''

"A stress test will serve the same purpose,'' said John Lloyd dryly. "Now that we've finishing dining, and you've returned from whatever imaginary place you've been visiting the past hour, I'm prepared to satisfy your curiosity about my, er, thought processes.''

"How do you know I've been imagining anything?" she asked sharply.

"Your eyes were slightly unfocused, your face flushed, and there was an aura of romantic femininity about you. You were either involved in some daydream with ourselves as hero and heroine, or you were exhibiting symptoms of influenza. Your skin is not feverish," he added, rubbing his thumb over the top of her hand, "so I deduce you were daydreaming."

"Don't flatter yourself. And if you don't let go of my hand, I'll stab you with my fork."

He chuckled. "Now that you are threatening bodily harm, I know that your mind is fully rational. Shall we discuss the case?"

He hadn't released her hand and she decided not to stab him. Besides, her left hand was still too sore to hold a fork. "How can you be so sure that Amy doped her own coffee?"

"She had the greater opportunity, Miss Fairchild, and the greater motive. Jim Steele was going to divorce her. There would have been no large property settlement. She forged his name to the checks she cashed the day she left, the checks which emptied the bank accounts of the Bar-S Cattle Company and virtually left Alice Steele bankrupt. If Jim Steele were accused of attempted murder, she would have a stranglehold on him. If he and Alice agreed not to prosecute her for forgery, and signed over the ranch or part of it to her, she would have undoubtedly remembered that yes, she *had* added a sedative to her coffee. She had planned to drink it before retiring, and had completely forgotten to remove the thermos from her car before loaning the vehicle to whomever it was who had the misfortune to cross her path."

"You mean she planned this?" Lydia shuddered. "She is diabolical."

John Lloyd shook his head. "No, she is merely an opportunist. I believe the whole plan was an impulse, perhaps invented during that quarrel with Jim while she was packing. Then like a she-wolf, she went hunting for an innocent victim who might drink the coffee, drive the car, and wreck it. I do not believe she intended her prey to die, although I'm equally sure she did nothing to prevent it. It was immaterial to her. A blood test of the victim would disclose the presence of the sedative. A police investigation would discover the coffee and trace the car back to Canadian and Jim Steele. But fate intervened. The victim was misidentified and the police did not investigate. She was free to disappear with the quarter of a million dollars.''

Lydia interrupted. "Then why did she come back? Why risk having her whole scheme uncovered?''

John Lloyd squeezed her hand. "Think, Miss Fairchild. Disclosure was her ultimate goal, and she had failed! No one knew of the poisoned coffee, Jim Steele was not being investigated, he was now a wealthy man, and he was married to a woman she hated. The magazine article gave her an opportunity to rectify the situation. If she came back from the dead, she could force a police investigation, destroy all the Steeles, avenge herself on all those who had crossed her. The wealth she might very possibly gain is a by-product of her vengeance, not its primary aim.''

Lydia traced the rim of her glass with her forefinger. "I don't know, John Lloyd. It sounds so complicated.'' She looked up at him. "When did you first know it must be Amy?''

He freed one of his hands to pull out and light a cigar. "When I read the search warrant.''

"Come on, John Lloyd. I'm serious.''

"So am I, Miss Fairchild. Only Amy Steele has the character capable of doping the coffee. You might have wondered why I allowed my clients to answer Schroder's questions so freely. I allowed it because they were also answering mine. By the end of the interrogations, I knew only Jim and Amy had both the means and the opportunity. And only Amy had a motive.''

"Doesn't it worry you that Sergeant Schroder might

not be convinced? Or that he might not be able to find any evidence against Amy and still arrest Jim?''

"Not particularly. I am more concerned about the possibility of Jim Steele becoming a pauper than I am about his becoming a prisoner. However, now that I know what hold Amy has over Jim, I have taken steps to neutralize her. Also Schroder's search turned up more than Quindat.''

"What did you find? What are you planning, John Lloyd? You have that sneaky look on your face. It had better not involve me again, or I'll break a rib on your other side.''

John Lloyd released her and put his hand over his heart. "Miss Fairchild, you cut me to the quick.''

She looked at her freed hand and felt bereft. *He* didn't, she thought, looking at him. He'd just been holding hands to prevent her from striking him. "You don't have any quick,'' she grumbled.

"Quite the contrary, Miss Fairchild; but in view of your affinity for violence, I am keeping its location a secret.'' He took the bill from the waiter and got up. "To show you I do not hold a grudge for your lack of trust in my ability to behave ethically, I shall take you for a moonlight ride along the Canadian River.''

He pulled out her chair and she rose, grabbing her purse and smoothing her skirt. "There isn't any moonlight. It's still dusk.''

He guided her toward the cashier, and she was once again conscious of his height. He was almost a full head taller than she. "Miss Fairchild,'' he chided, "have you no soul? Can't we pretend it's moonlight and this is a romantic interlude?''

"Up your shaft, John Lloyd Branson,'' she sputtered, and slammed through the door, wishing it would close with a bang instead of a soft *whoosh*. Outside she took a deep breath. Two could play a teasing game, and as a woman, she'd bet she had more experience. She started to turn back toward the door. The loud crack that reverberated through the twilight evening was simultaneous with the burning force that struck her arm like the flick of whip and the round hole that appeared in the glass door she was about to open. Someone's throwing rocks, she thought, clapping her hand over her arm. She whirled around to look and heard again the loud crack and felt the sharp blow, this time low on her left side. She looked down and saw the crimson stain spreading on the bodice of her dress.

The next blow she felt was the ground as a heavy body slammed into her and rolled her over and over down the incline and into a hedge. "Goddamn it, Lydia! Are you all right?" John Lloyd's face loomed over her from a height of a few inches. He looks concerned, she thought. And worried. Almost like I mattered very, very much.

"What happened?" The burning sensation in her arm and side was increasing to an absolute inferno. "I hurt, John Lloyd. I've never hurt like this before."

He cursed again and rolled off her. "You've been shot, Lydia. Some bastard had the unmitigated audacity to shoot you."

"Oh, God!" It came out a whimper, and she hated whimpering.

"Lie still, Lydia. I'm going to check your wounds, see if I can stop the bleeding."

"John Lloyd, I'm scared."

He glanced at her and smiled. "You have my permission to be scared, Lydia. I'm your boss, and what I say goes." He ripped her sleeve off without touching her arm.

"You ruined my new dress!" She wished she could stop whimpering.

"I'll buy you another," he said, as he grasped the neck of her dress and ripped it to the waist.

"John Lloyd!" There, she thought dizzily. That wasn't a whimper; it was an indignant shout. She tried to cover her breasts with her arms and screamed as she lifted her left arm.

"Lie still!" He whipped off his jacket and laid it over her exposed chest. "Your modesty is restored. Now don't

move again," he ordered as he exposed the wound in her
side. "A flesh wound I think. The bullet went clear
through."

"Bullet! Oh, God!" she moaned. An incredible burst
of pain radiated from her side and she caught her breath.
"John Lloyd, please. I hurt."

He stripped off his vest and shirt, wadded up the latter
and placed it against her side. "I know you hurt, Lydia."
He brushed her hair away from her face. "I assume that
the sound of gunshots disturbed our fellow diners enough
to ensure that at least one of them will alert the local
constabulary, who will in turn summon medical aid. So
be still, little one."

She laughed and caught her breath at the pain. "Little
one? I'm five feet ten and one-half inches."

"Compared to me, you're small and dainty."

She reached up to touch his chest. "You're using contractions. "

He looked startled. "What?"

"*You're, I'm, don't.* You know, contractions. You
never use them."

He smiled. "I believe I mentioned before that you are
a disturbing influence." He grasped her hand and held
it.

"You saved my life, didn't you?" she asked, looking
at his naked chest. He definitely wasn't skinny; just lean.

"I can only surmise that had you stood upright for
another few seconds, even a poor marksman would have
succeeded in doing you some terminal injury."

"Does that mean that you saved my life?" she asked.
His face was indistinct, and she blinked. Was it the gathering darkness, or was she about to faint for the first time
in her life?

"Perhaps," he agreed.

"Just like a hero in a romantic movie." Her voice
broke in a gasp of pain. "Talk to me, John Lloyd, so I
won't notice the pain. Tell me about the haystack."

His face went blank. "Haystack?"

"You said I made you think of haystacks and sensual pursuits."

She wasn't sure, but she thought she could detect a flush of red in his face. "I was speaking rhetorically."

The pain in her arm was getting worse, spreading up to her shoulder and down to her hand. As for her side, it was one giant burning, shivering agony. "Please, John Lloyd, pretend. I won't tease you about it later, I promise. Cross my heart and hope to die."

"Don't say that!" he said sharply.

"I'm going to start screaming, John Lloyd, and I don't want to. Talk to me, please. What would you say if there was a haystack somewhere without stickers and we were in there together."

His face looked stiff, but his voice was the soft drawl she enjoyed so much. "I would tell you how beautiful you are."

"And?" she prompted.

He swallowed. "I would quote from the Song of Solomon."

His drawl seemed to wrap around her like a velvet cloak, and she felt the tears seep from her eyes and trickle down her face. The grass beneath her back was sun-warmed and the air indolent of earth and sage, cattle and dust, the wet smell of the river, and that indefinable odor of open spaces. She was lying on the ground, bleeding from two gunshot wounds, while a bare-chested man with a bad leg was quoting an ancient Hebrew love poem to her. Hollywood never thought of anything nearly as romantic. It was almost worth getting shot.

CHAPTER
EIGHTEEN

"WHAT HAVE YOU TO SAY FOR YOUR THEORY, BRANSON, now that your young lady got herself shot up? Ready to admit you were wrong, you stupid son of a bitch?" Schroder lumbered behind John Lloyd and the gurney carrying Lydia Fairchild, snapping at the lawyer's heels like a bulldog chasing a greyhound.

"Back off, Schroder," commanded Sheriff Taylor as he hurried along beside the lawyer. "You can chew on John Lloyd later. We better be finding out where everybody was, and look for that rifle. From the looks of the shells we picked up inside the restaurant, I'd say it was a .22. Good thing for Miss Fairchild, too. Anything bigger, and she'd been tore up something awful."

"You won't need to check on me, Sheriff," said Dr. Bailey, dressed in surgical greens and guiding the gurney into an examining room. "I was right here at the hospital making my evening rounds." He stuck his hand in Schroder's face.

"Oh, no, you don't. You're not coming in this examining room. You lawmen aren't going to gawk at my patient and get in my way.'' He turned back to the gurney. ''Miss Fairchild, let go of John Lloyd's hand.''

Lydia opened her eyes. ''No,'' she said weakly. ''He comes, or I go home. He's the only one who knows about haystacks.'' She closed her eyes again.

Jenner noticed John Lloyd flushing. Made the bastard look human, he thought. Of course it was hard to be too formal when you weren't wearing a shirt and had a fist-sized bruise over your ribs. Looked like the lawyer'd been in a fight. The other guy probably looked worse. Branson had a lean, mean build that you'd never guess from seeing him with his clothes on.

Bailey patted Lydia's shoulder gently. ''Just take it easy, little lady. If you want this overgrown ox, you can have him.'' He looked at John Lloyd. ''Why would anybody want to shoot this pretty little girl?'' he asked.

Lydia eyes popped open. ''Because I look like Amy Steele.''

The doctor looked shocked, then angry. ''That woman's worse than the plagues of Egypt. Every time she's around, somebody else gets hurt. Why don't you lock her up, Sergeant, so everybody'll be safe?''

Schroder shifted his weight from foot to foot. ''Maybe I should lock her up so she'll be safe from everybody else.''

''Look for someone with poor eyesight, Sergeant. That's the only way anybody could mistake this young lady for that female barracuda.'' With that comment, the doctor reared his back to peer through his trifocals at Schroder's face. ''That's a nasty scratch on your face. Stop by the desk and ask the duty nurse to put something on it.'' He pushed his glasses further up on his nose and followed the gurney into the examining room, closing the door in their faces.

''You look like you got throwed off your horse into a mesquite tree, Sergeant,'' said Taylor. ''What happened?''

Schroder grunted and stopped at a cigarette machine and searched through his pockets for the correct change.

He gave up and turned to Jenner. "Loan me some quarters."

Jenner thought about denying that he had any, but only for a moment. Schroder without cigarettes was worse than Schroder with cigarettes. He dropped three quarters on his outstretched hand. Paw was more like it, he thought as he watched the investigator add some change to the quarters, pull the lever, and fall on the pack of cigarettes like a starving dog on a beef steak. "Are we going out to the Steele ranch?" he asked, inhaling the last breath of unpolluted air he was likely to get.

"No. We're going back to the motel and find out why someone thought Amy Steele might be at that steak house. The sheriff can check on the Steeles."

"You better get a catcher's mask before you talk to that woman again, or you might get marked on the other side of your face," said Jenner with a grin.

"Did Amy Steele do that?" asked Taylor.

"She sure did," said Jenner still grinning. "She was already a little high-strung . . ."

"She was foaming like a mad dog," interrupted Schroder.

". . . because Schroder had just told her about the doped coffee being the probable cause of the wreck. She starting screaming that Jim Steele had tried to kill her because she was leaving him. Then Schroder kind of hinted that she might have done it herself. That's when the claws came out. Took her lawyer and me both to get her off. I've never heard language like that from a woman, not even the whores we bust on Amarillo Boulevard."

"You better get a tetanus shot," said Taylor. "That woman's scratch is more dangerous than sticking yourself in the foot with a pitchfork full of horse shit."

Schroder rolled his cigarette over to its traditional resting place in the corner of his mouth. "You just hightail it to that ranch and let me worry about Amy Steele. My bite's a lot more dangerous than her scratch. If I didn't hate murder so much, I'd turn my back and let the whole bunch of them take potshots at her until their aim improved. But we already got one dead and one wounded innocent bystander because they keep missing. By the way, I called Special Crimes and they'll be up here to investigate the crime scene and search for the rifle. Keep your boys posted at that restaurant and some down on the river about where we think the shots were fired.''

Sheriff Taylor pushed his hat back on his head. "Look here, Schroder. This ain't Amarillo. I don't have a couple hundred men I can call on. I'll do the best I can with the police chief's help, but I need somebody in the office. And the town still has to be patrolled.''

"You just keep people away from that riverbank," said Schroder and pushed open the hospital door. "Come on, Jenner. Let's go tell Amy Steele to stay away from open windows."

"Is Mrs. Steele in?" demanded Schroder of the desk clerk.

"Is Mrs. Steele expecting you?"

"She knows us.''

"I can't answer questions about our guests without instructions or some kind of identification."

Schroder pulled his I.D. card out of his shirt pocket. "Will that do?"

The clerk examined the card and passed it back.

"I have to be careful, you know. There's a lot of motel burglaries. Not in Canadian, of course, but you never know." He lowered his voice. "Can you tell me what's happening? I mean you're some kind of a policeman, aren't you? What are all the sirens and police cars? And I saw the ambulance go by."

"Is Mrs. Steele in?" asked Schroder again, leaning over the desk and staring the clerk in the face.

It was an unequal contest, thought Jenner. Schroder could stare a bobcat right out of a tree. The clerk swallowed. "I don't know. She has her own key and doesn't have to come through the lobby. She did leave word she'd be at the steak house in case anyone called."

"Did someone call?"

"Yes, about an hour ago. I rang her room but no one answered."

"Was the caller a male or female."

"I'm not sure, it was muffled, but I think it was a man. Or it could've been a woman with a deep voice. I just don't know."

"Would you recognize Jim Steele's voice over the phone?" asked Schroder.

"It couldn't have been Jim Steele. He'd already been by to talk to his wife before she went to eat. It must've been a short conversation because I saw him leave in his pickup about five minutes after he asked her room number. He was in a terrible hurry."

Schroder nodded. "I bet he was." He turned and grabbed Jenner's arm. "Let's go ask the little lady about her husband's visit."

"Can I call my wife first?" asked Jenner, pulling back.

"I had Special Crimes do it," grunted Schroder. "She's knows where you are, and not to set a place for you at the dinner table for a couple of days."

"That's not what I'm worried about," protested Jenner. "I want her to check the department health plan to see if I'm covered for human bites."

Schroder spared him one warning look. "I'm on a short fuse, Jenner, and I'm not in the mood for any of your smart-ass jokes."

"Who's joking, damn it?" he demanded, following Schroder to avoid having his arm pulled out of its socket. "Once Amy Steele finds out someone tried to kill her again while you were playing around with the idea that she might've set the car wreck up, she's going to be ready to gnaw on both of us. Then I'll bet she calls the papers, and when the Chief reads about it, he'll do a little gnawing of his own. I told you I didn't want anything to do with murder. I want to go back to traffic. The worst I can fuck up there is give the mayor a ticket."

"Shut up!" ordered Schroder, hammering on Amy Steele's door.

There was rattling of the safety chain and H. Curtis Rutherford stood in the doorway. Jenner noticed the lawyer's cheek was beginning to show a purple smudge from Amy Steele's right hook. He bet the next time that broad took after somebody with her claws out, Rutherford would know better than to get between her and her opponent.

"My client has nothing to say to you, Sergeant."

Schroder simply walked into him, and since the burly investigator outweighed the lawyer by at least fifty pounds, H. Curtis Rutherford did a quick two-step backward. "You can't come in here. I'll charge you with police brutality."

"And I'll charge your client with assault," Schroder replied, pushing past the man and lumbering over to the couch where Amy sat. A Chinese dragon writhed up the skirt and over the bodice of her slinky, crimson robe. A motel towel covered most of her wet hair. Jenner could detect a faint darkness at the roots. He almost smiled. He knew she was a bleached blonde. She sat smoking a cigarette and filing her nails. The dragon lady must have broken one off on Schroder's cheek, he decided.

Amy laid down her file and burst into tears. "Oh, Sergeant, I'm so sorry I lost my temper."

"When was Jim Steele here?" demanded Schroder.

Amy sniffed. "Just after you left. I refused to open the door. I made Curtis go out in the hall and talk to him." She looked up and Jenner thought someone ought to tell her that if a woman was going to cry for sympathy, she'd better squeeze out more than a couple of tears. Besides, crying made her look like hell. Her face was puffy and splotched under too much makeup. "I was afraid. After all, he tried to kill me. Then you were so cruel, accusing me of some unspeakable crime. If I turned up stabbed in the back, I suppose you'd say it was suicide. You're against me, all of you."

"Did you go to the steak house for dinner?"

"Yes. I was so tired of this room. I just needed to get around people."

"Did you see John Lloyd Branson and Miss Fairchild there?"

"Miss Fairchild? Oh, that young woman he *says* is his clerk. I guess everyone in this dinky town might believe that, but I don't. John Lloyd Branson gropes everything in skirts. He even tried it with me when I was married to Jim. I didn't respond, so he hates me. I'll bet she does, though. You should've seen her holding hands with him and hanging on to every word he said. And he was worse; he was just eating her up with those eyes of his. He didn't even notice I was there." She was clenching and unclenching her fists and Jenner made a note to warn Lydia to stay beyond the reach of Amy Steele's fingernails.

"You did see them, then," said Schroder dryly.

"And I lost my appetite. Poor Curtis had to ask for a doggie bag because he had to bring me back to the room. I lay down for a while. Seeing John Lloyd nauseated me." She rubbed her arms, and the slithering of the material against her skin reminded Jenner of the sound of a snake crawling through the grass. "What are all these questions? What are you accusing me of this time?"

Rutherford cleared his throat. "Yes, Sergeant, what is the object of this interrogation?"

"Lydia Fairchild was shot as she was leaving the restaurant."

"What does that have to do with my client?" demanded Rutherford.

"Why would anyone want to kill that woman?" asked Amy with a blank stare. Then the same ugly something that Jenner had noticed before stirred in her eyes. "It was supposed to be me, wasn't it? That's why you're asking if we were at the restaurant at the same time. That's why you want to know about Jim Steele." She jackknifed to her feet, clawing at her arms and chest. "That son of a bitch tried to kill me again. I want police protection, Sergeant. I demand it. He's a maniac and he won't stop until I'm dead. I'm not safe anywhere." She turned to Rutherford. "Curtis, you'll have to sleep in my room tonight and I'll take your room. He might try to murder me in my sleep.''

Rutherford looked distinctly uncomfortable. ''I hardly think we need to go that far, Amy. I'm sure you'll be perfectly safe with the door locked.''

''You're my lawyer!'' she screamed, grappling his arm.

He flung his other arm in front of his face. ''I'm not a bodyguard,'' he protested.

''I'll leave a man,'' said Schroder, opening the door. ''Sergeant Jenner will be right outside your door.''

CHAPTER
NINETEEN

"Where are we going, John Lloyd? Aren't we supposed to be in court?"

"*You* are supposed to be in bed, Miss Fairchild, not sitting in a courtroom all day."

"I feel fine. Dr. Bailey said the wounds were superficial. I got a good night's sleep, thanks to your tricking me into swallowing a sleeping pill, and I took some aspirin before we left. However, I didn't anticipate an auto tour around Canadian. Could you slow down? This may be a luxury car, but I can still feel the bumps." She caught her breath and felt the sweat break out on her forehead as he swerved around a corner. A spasm of pain swerved around her middle.

John Lloyd immediately slowed down. "Your being out of bed was against my better judgment, Miss Fairchild. You are pale, you have the most interesting mauve circles under your eyes, and you gasp and clutch your side with every breath. I should never have surrendered to your pleas."

"I didn't want to miss the best show in town," she

said, clutching her side. "Besides, I didn't plead; I blackmailed you."

"I was attempting to gloss over your devious methods."

"I wasn't devious; I was very straightforward. I just promised to give the next reporter who called an interview about how you tenderly nursed me through the night in your very own four-poster bed. The town ladies would have been scandalized, and your reputation as a Victorian gentleman would have been ruined."

"But all the gentlemen would have envied me. My reputation would have been enhanced. Yours, however, would have been exterminated. I chose not to allow your virtue to be questioned." His voice was sharp: John Lloyd Branson at his most dictatorial and proper.

"Chauvinist pig!" Lydia knew she should be outraged. At the same time she felt a curious softness in the vicinity of her heart at the notion that John Lloyd would protect her. Petite women like Christy Steele were constantly cosseted. Women as tall as the Lydia Ann Fairchilds of this world were expected to protect themselves.

John Lloyd glanced at her and she had the uncomfortable feeling that he could read her mind. "I cannot speak for every male of the species, Miss Fairchild, but as for myself, the instinct to safeguard a female is part of my genetic code, just as the desire for independence is part of yours."

"John Lloyd, I am a grown woman."

A faint pink tinted his cheekbones. His voice was as calm and slow as ever, so Lydia decided his heightened color must be the sun reflecting off the plush red interior of the car. "Miss Fairchild, even had I not already been aware of your sex and approximate physical maturity, your distressing lack of a foundation garment under the frock I so crudely removed from your body last night revealed that your anatomical structure could in no respect be that of a child."

Lydia felt herself blushing from the roots of her hair

down to those anatomical structures he was referring to. "I couldn't wear one with that dress."

He glanced at her chest. "What is your excuse today?"

She crossed her arms over her breasts. "I couldn't fasten my bra because my arm's too stiff. And what business is it of yours anyway?"

"I saved your life. According to ancient Chinese philosophy that makes me responsible for you."

Lydia touched his arm. "John Lloyd, I am not Chinese. My underwear, or lack of it, is my business. And you are *not* responsible for me."

"The discussion is closed, Miss Fairchild. Until this attack upon your person is solved to my satisfaction, you may consider yourself under my protection."

Lydia shuddered and felt pain spasm through her injured side. "Were you wrong about Amy, John Lloyd? Am I going to be sitting at the counsel table with the person who pulled the trigger and shot me? Is Jim Steele guilty?"

John Lloyd parked behind a large square three-story building made of the same ubiquitous red brick that surfaced many of Canadian's streets. There must have been a fire sale on that particular kind of brick around the turn of the century, Lydia thought. A square cupola with a domed top squatted above the building's front door, and she knew without being told that this was the county courthouse.

John Lloyd unbuckled his seat belt and twisted around to face her. "The answers to your questions are *no* and *yes*. No, I do not believe I was wrong about Amy, and yes, you will be sitting at the counsel table with the person who shot you."

"Oh, God, no!"

He leaned over and took her hand. "But the Hemphill County Courthouse only has one counsel table in the district courtroom, Miss Fairchild, and all of us will be sitting there: Amy, her attorney, the Steeles, Cammie, and Dr. Bailey. One of them is your assailant with your blood

still warm upon his hands. Whether that assailant is Jim
Steele I cannot answer."

He raised her hand to his lips and kissed it, releasing
it only to look at her, the expression in his eyes as merciless as an executioner's. "I promise you, Miss Fairchild, if he is guilty, nothing will save him from me."

She struggled for a deep breath. He sounded like an
Old Testament prophet invoking the wrath of God. Ex-
cept God would be kinder than John Lloyd Branson.
"Ease up, John Lloyd. Duels are out of style."

His smile never touched the hard glitter of his eyes.
"As you are so fond of pointing out, Miss Fairchild, so
am I."

Lydia twisted uncomfortably in the wooden armchair.
She glanced at her watch. It was still too soon to take
more aspirin, and she frankly wasn't sure how she was
going to survive until she could. Her arm was aching
abominably, and her side felt as if someone were press-
ing a hot iron against it. John Lloyd was definitely stuck
in his protective mode, she thought as she caught him
glancing at her yet again. He'd seated her at the end of
the long table between himself and Alice Steele. Jim and
Christy were seated on John Lloyd's left, with Cammie
and the physician taking the chairs next to where Amy
and H. Curtis Rutherford would sit—provided they ever
arrived. They were nearly an hour late.

Alice Steele leaned over and patted her hand, her turquoise blue eyes sympathetic and a little fearful. "None
of us shot you, Lydia; you can depend on that. For one
thing, we would've killed you. Someone was a lousy
shot."

Lydia stretched her lips in what she hoped would pass
as a smile, but whatever she was going to utter, and she
wasn't sure exactly what that was, remained unsaid as
Amy Steele made her entrance. And an entrance it was.
She paused in the doorway, her pale blue eyes sweeping
the courtroom. Counting the house, thought Lydia. Amy
couldn't complain that she didn't have an audience. Every

seat was full and people were standing along the walls. As Alice had said, reporters were thicker than ticks on a dog, but the general populace of Canadian was well represented, too. In fact, Lydia wondered how an impartial jury could ever been selected for the final hearing still two months ahead. There were enough locals in the courtroom to pass the word to those who couldn't get a seat. One would think this was a full-scale jury trial instead of a temporary hearing.

Her eyes went back to Amy. Jim Steele's first, or rather *only*, wife was dressed in a white suit with a crimson blouse and matching shoes. She should have been striking, but she wasn't. Her face seemed faintly swollen and her makeup was layered on. Lydia looked more closely and nearly laughed. Amy Steele had zits! Several red spots were discernible under the makeup. She turned to share her discovery with John Lloyd, but swallowed her words. John Lloyd was looking at Amy, his eyes absolutely blazing. A Spanish inquisitor might have borne such an expression just before he picked up the red-hot pinchers to persuade a heretic to recant.

Followed by Rutherford, Amy walked regally to the counsel table, stopping in front of John Lloyd. "Good morning, Lawyer Branson." Her eyes went to Lydia and she leaned over to whisper to John Lloyd. "And how is my understudy? Is she as good as I would have been, or just the best a cripple could do?"

Lydia gasped and searched her shocked mind for a retort, but John Lloyd was quicker. He rose to his feet with majestic grace. "Shut your filthy mouth about Lydia, or I shall not be responsible for my actions. Your very presence is an insult to her."

Amy flushed under her makeup until her skin was the same color as the painful-looking eruptions that marred it. Rutherford grabbed her arm and whispered something to her. She shook free of his hand and moved down the table to stand in front of Jim. "Still flaunting your tart in front of your wife and the community, I see," she said, sneering at Christy and not bothering to keep her voice low.

Jim rose to his feet with fists clenched, and Lydia was shocked to the depths of her feminist soul to realize that she was rooting for him to knock Amy on her butt. He didn't. "I gave my word that I wouldn't fight you if you left me and mine alone. Don't push."

Amy smiled. "Did I say that? I don't remember."

Rutherford took her arm with a general apologetic nod in Jim and John Lloyd's direction. "Amy, the judge is ready to enter. Let's sit down. Please."

With a smile to the spectators like the queen might give to the Coldstream Guard, she obeyed. Lydia noticed Rutherford surreptitiously blotting his forehead with a handkerchief color-coordinated to his navy blue suit. She suspected it wouldn't be the last time he broke out in a sweat.

It wasn't. The second occasion came more than two hours later after a myriad of financial statements and tax returns were introduced into evidence with Jim carefully identifying each one. John Lloyd gave Jim a cancelled check and turned to face the spectators. He tucked his thumbs into his vest pockets in his best country-lawyer style, a masquerade if Lydia ever saw one, but the reporters loved it. John Lloyd was good copy. The crowd was silent in hushed expectation.

"Jim," he drawled, "is that your signature on that check for one hundred thousand dollars drawn on the Bar-S expense account?"

Jim wiped his forehead, and Lydia wished she had the handkerchief franchise for the courtroom. "That's my name," he finally said.

"That wasn't my question. Is it your signature?"

A vein became visible in Jim's temple as his whole face tightened. "I refuse to answer."

John Lloyd leaned casually against the judge's bench. "You can take the Fifth Amendment only if you are the one to be incriminated by your answer. It does not apply if you are incriminating someone else. I ask you again: is that your signature?"

Jim looked at Amy and bit his lip. "No," he said in a low voice.

"Speak up, Jim. The court reporter cannot hear."

"I said no!"

John Lloyd smiled his friendly man-eating tiger smile. "Thank you." He handed Jim another check, this one for fifty thousand. "Is this your signature?"

Jim seemed resigned. "No."

"But it is your name?"

"Yes."

The questions continued until the stack of checks in front of Jim amounted to a quarter of a million dollars. John Lloyd straightened up to his full height. "Who signed your name to those checks?"

Jim was silent, his jaw working until the muscles stood out taut.

"Who signed your name?" John Lloyd thundered in his Old Testament voice.

"Amy did," he answered reluctantly.

Amy erupted from her chair—a bleached-blonde volcano. "You two-timing bastard! The deal's off!"

Judge Myers pounded his gavel. "Mr. Rutherford, you will caution your client against any more such comments, or I'll hold her in contempt of court."

Rutherford pulled Amy down and whispered in her ear. He wiped his forehead and stood up. "Your Honor, we object to this line of questioning. Witness is not an expert in handwriting."

John Lloyd turned to the judge. "Your Honor, I believe the answer to my next question will satisfy Counsel's objection."

Judge Myers considered this a moment. "I'll delay ruling at this time, Mr. Rutherford."

John Lloyd turned back to Jim. "Amy Steele had forged your name on other checks, had she not? Is that how you could recognize her forgery on these checks?"

"Your Honor," interjected Rutherford quickly. "We

wish to stipulate that the checks in evidence were signed by my client. She required funds with which to live on while putting her life back together after leaving the Steele household and her disastrous marriage."

John Lloyd's pale blond eyebrow rose. "Two hundred and fifty thousand dollars could put a lot of lives back together. In fact, it could support the average family for ten years."

Rutherford rose to his feet. "Objection, Your Honor. We are not here to decide on whether or not Mrs. Steele's lifestyle meets with Mr. Branson's approval."

"Mr. Rutherford, I believe Mr. Branson is within his rights to bring into evidence the amount of cash Mrs. Steele took when she left Mr. Steele. However"—the judge paused and looked at John Lloyd—"Mr. Branson is reminded not to make any judgmental statements about the defendant. That is the job of the court."

John Lloyd bowed. "Of course, Your Honor. Your witness," he said to Rutherford, returning to his seat.

"Why did you stop?" demanded Lydia. "You had them on the run."

"There is always the danger of asking one question too many, Miss Fairchild. We have shown that Amy Steele is a forger. That is enough. For now."

Rutherford rose from the counsel table. Impeccably dressed in his navy three-piece suit, hair perfectly styled, shoes highly polished, fingernails manicured, and voice unaccented. In a courtroom where even the judge wore boots under his judicial robes, Rutherford was decidedly out of place.

"Mr. Steele, how long have you known Christy Deveraux?"

John Lloyd was on his feet in an instant. "Objection, Your Honor. Counsel may only cross-examine on issues raised during direct examination."

"Sustained," said the judge.

"But this is a vital issue, Your Honor," protested Rutherford.

"It might be, son," said the judge. "But you're going to have figure out some other way to ask about it."

Rutherford sat down to a hissing argument from Amy. John Lloyd sat, then leaned over to Lydia. "That, Miss Fairchild, is an example of *not* asking one question too many. I did not want Jim questioned about a possible affair with Christy, so I simply didn't mention her name at all."

"You may call your next witness, Mr. Branson," said the judge.

John Lloyd waited until the courtroom was absolutely still. "I call Christina Deveraux Steele to the stand."

"Objection, Your Honor," said Rutherford, rising to his feet. "There is no such person as Christina Deveraux Steele," he said with a sardonic emphasis on the word *Steele*.

"My apologies to the court," John Lloyd drawled slowly. "A slip of the tongue on my part. When you get to be my age, it's difficult to change your ways of thinking. I have regarded this fine young woman as Christina Deveraux Steele for so many months, I find it hard to think of her otherwise."

Several spectators chuckled at John Lloyd's references to his age and senility. Personally, Lydia had never heard so many bald-faced lies in the space of so few words in her life. John Lloyd was never guilty of a slip of the tongue; he wasn't old; and he was too stubborn to change his way of thinking. Age had nothing to do with it.

"Your apologies are accepted, Mr. Branson," said the judge. "Young lady, you may take the stand. Please remember you're under oath as administered to all witnesses and interested parties at the beginning of these proceedings."

"Yes, Your Honor," said Christy, seating herself and smoothing her skirt over her knees. Lydia hoped Christy could survive her testimony without fainting. Her face was so white, her gold-colored eyes like two coins thrown against a bedsheet.

"Christy," asked John Lloyd, in his best courtly manner, "why did you marry Jim Steele?"

She looked at Jim. "Because I loved him."

"How long have you loved him?" John Lloyd asked gently.

Christy searched his face for a clue to what he wanted her to say. She swallowed. "All my life," she admitted.

"I am sure you told him frequently as a child that you loved him. Did you ever tell him as an adult?"

"Of course; he was my husband." Her voice was stronger.

"And before that, Christy?"

Lydia sat up straighter. What was he doing? He'd refused to question Jim about Christy because he didn't want to open the door to cross-examination about a possible affair. Now he was not only opening the door, he was inviting Rutherford in.

Christy licked her lips. "Yes, I did."

"And what did Mr. Steele reply to your declaration?"

"He said he was married and not to repeat such a thing again."

John Lloyd's voice seemed overly loud as he asked his next question. "Did Mr. Steele promise you he would get a divorce? Did he give you any hope for an eventual relationship?"

"No, he did not. We never spoke again unless someone else was present."

"Did you forget Jim Steele and form relationships with other men?"

Christy shook her head. "No, I didn't."

"You remained faithful to a man married to someone else, who didn't speak to you alone, with no hope of any kind of a relationship. Madam, either you are a fool, or Jim Steele is a very lucky man."

John Lloyd's voice was brisk as he turned to his next question. "Christy," he said, handing her a document. "Is this your signature on the partnership agreement forming the Bar-S Land and Cattle Company?"

"Yes, it is."

"Were you surprised that Alice Steele signed over a one-third share in her holdings to you?"

Christy nodded. "I was shocked."

"You realize that your share is independent of any claim you might have had under community property law?"

"Objection, Your Honor. The status of Miss Deveraux's share is one of the issues to be decided at this hearing." Rutherford was on his feet and looked triumphant. He ought to be, thought Lydia. John Lloyd had given him everything he needed to crucify Christy.

"We are aware of that, Your Honor. What I'm trying to elicit from Christy Deveraux is her understanding of her position."

"Overruled," said the judge.

John Lloyd waited until the courtroom was completely quiet. "Do you believe you are entitled to a share in the ranch now that your marriage is invalid?"

Christy looked shocked at his sharp tone. "I don't know," she said. "But Alice did give it to me personally, not just as Jim's wife."

"Then you intend to fight to keep your share of the ranch?"

"Yes!"

"If Alice Steele asked you to sign your share back to her, would you do so, Christy?"

Christy chewed on her lower lip. "I hope she wouldn't ask me."

"Would you sign your claim back to her if she asked you?" John Lloyd's voice was more insistent.

Lydia wanted to pull him back in his chair by his coattail. Or better yet, gag him. She gave in to the urge and jerked on his sleeve. "What are you trying to prove, John Lloyd?" she whispered. "That she's a grasping bitch? If so, you're doing a good job."

He gave her a single glance that promised her a gag of her own. "Be quiet and trust me."

"Witness is directed to answer the question," the judge interjected.

"I would hope Alice wouldn't ask me to if I explained my reasons," Christy said finally, twisting her skirt between her fingers.

"What are your reasons, Christy? What possible reason could a woman whose marriage is bigamous have that could convince Alice Steele to support your claims?" John Lloyd's voice was louder, commanding the attention of the courtroom. Lydia heard a chair creak behind her and knew Schroder the bloodhound was listening more intently than anyone.

Christy's voice was beginning to shake. "My reasons are personal and have no bearing on the divorce suit."

John Lloyd placed a small pill bottle on the table in front of him. Christy's eyes focused on it in recognition and her face went completely white. "Do you want me to make this easier for you?" John Lloyd asked.

Lydia leaned over and picked up the bottle. This must be the evidence John Lloyd appropriated while Schroder was searching the Steele house, the evidence he thought would help. My God, she thought as she read the label; no wonder Christy wanted to keep her share. And no wonder John Lloyd had followed this whole line of questioning. He wanted Jim to fight, and this just might do the trick.

John Lloyd's eyes were expressionless. He placed his hands flat on the counsel table and leaned over. "Christy, are you pregnant?"

CHAPTER
TWENTY

THE CRASH OF A CHAIR FALLING TO THE FLOOR WOKE
Jenner out of a sound sleep. "What happened?" he
asked, blinking his eyes and feeling like warmed-over
horse dung.

"She's pregnant," whispered Schroder.

"Amy Steele's pregnant?" asked Jenner, rubbing his
stiff neck.

"*Christy* Steele!" hissed Schroder, sounding as much
like a snake as someone with his hoarse voice could.
"Wake up and pay attention."

"I can't help it if I've got Amy Steele on the brain.
You ought to try guarding that broad. She was opening
that door all night long badgering me about something.
If Jim Steele had walked in with a sawed-off shotgun,
I'd have let him shoot her. I felt like it myself a couple
of times."

"Just shut up and listen."

"Christy, is the child Jim Steele's?" asked Branson
softly.

"The child is mine!" Jim Steele's voice was raw. He

197

stood with legs wide apart, head swinging from side to side, like a fighter waiting for the next challenger. It was the first time Jenner had seen him exhibit any life.

"Mr. Steele, I sympathize with your position, but I will not permit interruptions of any kind in this courtroom. Do you understand?" asked the judge.

Branson grasped Jim's arm, pulling him down to whisper fiercely to him. Jim twisted away and remained standing. "I apologize, Your Honor. I just don't want any doubt in anybody's mind." He picked up his chair and sat down.

Jenner leaned over to Schroder. "Who's arguing?" he whispered. "I mean, the second Mrs. Steele looks like a nice lady. Nobody's going to accuse her of slipping underneath somebody else's blanket."

"What else do you think Amy Steele will do?" Schroder asked. "Offer to knit her a pair of booties?"

"I forgot about her," admitted Jenner.

Schroder pointed his thumb at John Lloyd. "You can bet that bastard hasn't."

"You won't give up your share of the ranch because you are pregnant. Is that correct, Christy?" asked John Lloyd.

"Yes."

"I have no further questions. Your witness, Mr. Rutherford."

Rutherford rose to his feet, carefully smoothing his hair. What a prick, thought Jenner. "Miss Deveraux." He seemed to savor the unmarried form of address and repeated it. "Miss Deveraux, you've testified you're pregnant. How far along are you?"

"About six weeks. And I've been married almost two months," she added defensively, her voice wobbling. Jenner felt sorry for her. Hell of a situation for a lady to be in: pregnant and testifying in court for your husband so he can divorce his other wife.

"Do you have proof of this alleged pregnancy?"

"I've had my pregnancy confirmed by a doctor."

"Is the doctor in the courtroom?"

"Yes, he is." Her voice was shaking more noticeably.

"And who is that doctor, Miss Deveraux?"

"Dr. Bailey."

"The longtime family doctor of the Steeles who also happens to be your uncle, and who most definitely would not like to see the Steeles deprived of any of their land?"

"He is my uncle, yes." Even Christy's lips were white.

"Claiming pregnancy to force a marriage is the oldest ploy in the world. It's the basis for a thousand cheap romantic novels."

"I am pregnant!" she cried. "I am."

"You say you are. That's not quite the same thing, is it, Miss Deveraux? This court will not be deceived by a falsehood perpetrated by a woman who has already admitted she fell in love with a married man."

"I'm not a liar, Mr. Rutherford. And I loved Jim Steele before he was married. I just waited too long to tell him. I didn't try to break up his marriage, and I didn't chase him. And I certainly didn't force him into marrying me."

"I didn't ask for a dissertation, Miss Deveraux. I merely state that you have given this court no basis for believing you. You want to force your poor uncle into the position of supporting your claims. You want to give this poor, crippled woman the false hope of a grandchild only to obtain land you have no moral right to own. You want to trick this man into marriage after destroying his love for his real wife. What king of depraved creature are you?"

"That's enough, damn it!" yelled Jim Steele, kicking his chair over again.

"Objection, Your Honor!" said John Lloyd a second later.

Jenner had the feeling the lawyer had deliberately waited until Jim Steele exploded before objecting.

"Gentlemen, approach the bench, please," said the judge. His caution, voiced low, still carried past the counsel tables to the first few rows of spectators. "Mr. Rutherford, I don't know how you conduct yourself in

Dallas, but in Canadian, Texas, you will not abuse a witness in my court. Do I make myself clear?''

''Perfectly clear, Your Honor,'' said Rutherford, patting his forehead with his handkerchief.

The judge turned to John Lloyd. ''Mr. Branson, you control your client's outbursts. Is that clear?''

''Yes, Your Honor,'' drawled John Lloyd. ''But it may be difficult. Mr. Rutherford insulted the mother of my client's child, and we in Canadian do not consider that gentlemanly behavior.''

''I'm sure you'll manage,'' said the judge. ''Now if we may continue these proceedings?''

Rutherford returned to the counsel's table. ''I have no further questions of this witness, Your Honor. It's clear it would be a waste of the court's time.''

''I'll determine when this court's time is being wasted, Mr. Rutherford. Mr. Branson, call your next witness.''

''We rest our case, Your Honor,'' said John Lloyd.

''Mr. Rutherford, call your first witness.''

''I call Mrs. James Steele.''

Amy Steele stood up and walked to the witness stand, clutching a handkerchief in her hand. ''I'm ready, Mr. Rutherford.''

''Mrs. Steele, how long were you married to James Steele?''

''Five years.''

''Was your marriage a happy one, Mrs. Steele?''

''Jim and I were ecstatically happy the first year,'' Amy replied demurely.

''And the later years?''

''He was moody, always locking himself up in a room next to our bedroom that he called his office. He refused to let me in just because I'd damaged something on his computer by accident.'' Lydia nudged John Lloyd and whispered something. The lawyer nodded and turned his attention back to Amy.

''Why did you take separate bedrooms, Mrs. Steele?'' Rutherford asked gently.

''We were arguing one night. I don't remember over

what—a horse, I think—and he started jerking his clothes out of the closet. He told me he was moving into his office until he could build another wing onto the house. He said he had to think through our marriage. I accused him of having another woman. He looked at me strangely and told me if he ever wanted another, he knew just where to get one. That's when I started following him.''

''And what did you learn?''

''He was going to Dr. Bailey's house every Friday and Saturday night. Because *she* came home from college every weekend!'' Amy pointed to Christy. ''She was years younger, a child. It was obscene the way he chased after her. We would go to parties and he'd spend all evening watching her. He was obsessed with her. Then when she came back to Canadian to work, it got worse. 'I'm going to the library to do research, Amy,' he'd say, and he'd be gone for hours. When I learned she was the librarian, I realized what kind of research he was up to. He was researching what was under her skirts!''

''No!'' shouted Jim.

''Sit down, Mr. Steele,'' said the judge. ''This is your last warning. You may continue, Mr. Rutherford.''

''Why didn't you just divorce James Steele?'' asked Rutherford.

''I still loved him in spite of his treatment of me. I hoped that by letting time pass, with each of us away from the other, we could meet again and try to make our marriage work.'' Her voice broke on a sob.

She wiped her eyes and sniffed. ''I didn't realize Jim thought I was dead until I read of his marriage to Christy Deveraux. That woman destroyed my marriage, drove me into leaving Jim, and now is claiming property that should be mine in return for what I lived through. No one knows the hell of being an unloved, unwanted wife until you are one.'' Amy's voice broke. Hiding her face in her hands, she sobbed loudly. Jenner hoped she had an onion hidden in that handkerchief she was clutching. That was the only way the woman could generate any real tears.

He nudged Schroder. "How much of what she's saying do you buy?"

Schroder scratched a mosquito bite on his chin. "She believes everything she's saying, but that doesn't make it true. I think Jim Steele is going to walk out of this courtroom with his ranch and most of his money. Branson's already proved Amy Steele's a forger, and no telling what he'll prove when he gets a chance to cross-examine her. If Jim Steele hadn't got impatient and taken a potshot at Lydia Fairchild thinking she was Amy Steele, and trusted his lawyer instead, he'd have been all right on the attempted homicide charge, too. Our case was weak, and Branson would've persuaded the jury it was Amy if, and it's a big if, we could've gotten an arrest warrant. But James Steele won't walk on this shooting. I'm asking for another search warrant, and we're going to dig up his whole goddamn ranch until we find that rifle."

"You didn't find anything at the river?"

"Bunch of mosquitoes," answered Schroder, scratching his chest. "I think that woman's going to carry on all day. I haven't heard anything like it since a mouse got loose in the grand jury room."

"Mrs. Steele, do you think you can continue now?" Judge Myers asked.

Amy dabbed at her eyes, and took a shuddering breath. "I'll try, Your Honor."

"Mr. Rutherford, next question, please," said the judge.

Rutherford rose and faced the witness box. "Mrs. Steele, if you could relive your life, would you do anything differently?"

"I would never leave Jim," Amy declared, her face set in a pose of determination.

"Would you be willing to try a reconciliation, Mrs. Steele?"

"Oh, yes! I offered, even begged Jim for another chance to make our marriage work, but he filed for divorce anyway. Of course, I didn't know until yesterday that Miss Deveraux's claim to be pregnant had trapped him into ending our marriage.'' The look she gave Christy would have shriveled a mesquite tree at the root, a tree Jenner knew was impervious to all known methods of eradication.

''Then you would still continue in the marriage if such a choice were possible?''

''Yes, I would!''

''Your witness, Mr. Branson.'' Rutherford seated himself and picked up his yellow legal pad. His pen was poised over the blank sheets ready to take notes of Branson's cross-examination.

John Lloyd rose and patted his pockets, making a great show of looking for something. Finally, after much fumbling, he pulled out a crumbled envelope and casually glanced at it. He then folded it in half, then into quarters and tucked it back in his pocket. He smiled sheepishly at the judge and sat back down.

''Mrs. Steele, I believe you said Miss Deveraux trapped Jim into ending his marriage to you. Is that correct?'' John Lloyd's drawl was very evident, with a hint of satisfaction in its cadence. Jenner sat up a little straighter in anticipation.

''Yes, I said that.'' Amy was watchful, less relaxed.

''Yet we know from the evidence of our own eyes that James Steele was unaware of his impending fatherhood until yesterday in this courtroom. Tell me, Mrs. Steele, how did Christy Deveraux trap him?''

''Perhaps I was wrong about the pregnancy, but Jim was obsessed with her. Nothing I could say stopped him from filing for divorce.'' Amy admitted her mistake graciously.

''I believe you were pregnant at the time of your marriage to Jim Steele. Is that correct?''

Rutherford's objection muffled Christy's exclamation of shock. ''Your Honor, I object to this line of questioning. Mrs. Steele's condition at the time of her marriage is not an issue in this case.''

John Lloyd cleared his throat and spread his hands in

a gesture of innocence. "Your Honor, the issue of who trapped whom was brought up by the witness with her claims that Christy Deveraux trapped Jim Steele. I merely wish to show the entrapment was done by Amy Steele, and that her marriage was never a happy one."

"I think, Mr. Rutherford, since the issue of entrapment was raised by Mrs. Steele, then Mr. Branson has a right to attempt to refute it. Objection overruled. Witness is directed to answer the question."

"Yes, I was pregnant. I was young and foolish and defenseless against an older man." Amy's voice was pitiful.

"You were twenty-seven at the time. According to a photostatic copy of your birth certificate," he added.

"That's an invasion of privacy," she shouted.

"Obtaining copies of public records is not construed to be an invasion of privacy, Mrs. Steele," said Judge Myers.

"You were married a short six weeks after meeting Jim Steele for the first time?" asked John Lloyd.

"Yes, we had a short courtship," Amy replied, an ugly frown attacking her brow at the spectators' laughter.

"What happened to the baby you were carrying?" Jim Steele grabbed his arm and whispered furiously to him. Then Jim released the lawyer and buried his face in his hands.

"I miscarried. I am completely sterile as a result. It has been a great tragedy for me." Amy was watching Jim, her arms clenching restlessly on the arms of her chair.

"You were under the care of Dr. Bailey at the time of your miscarriage?"

"No, I was in New York at the time."

"How long after your marriage did this occur, Mrs. Steele?" asked John Lloyd, pulling the neatly folded envelope out of his pocket.

"I don't remember."

"You suffered a miscarriage, and you don't remember when?"

"No, I don't," Amy snapped.

"Wasn't it three weeks after your marriage?"

"Perhaps. I don't remember."

"Why were you in New York, Mrs. Steele?" asked John Lloyd, doodling on the back of his envelope.

"I went shopping," replied Amy, bitting off her words.

"Most of the women in Canadian are satisfied to go to Amarillo for their shopping," said John Lloyd wryly. "Did Jim go with you on this shopping spree?"

"No, he was working on another book and couldn't go."

"How many weeks along were you, Mrs. Steele?"

"About seven weeks, I think."

John Lloyd's eyes widened noticeably. "An expectant mother in the first trimester of pregnancy, when she is most vulnerable to miscarriage, and you did not attempt to persuade Jim to accompany you?"

Amy sat a little straighter, an expression stirring in the back of her eyes like a gator disturbing the mud in the bottom of a creek. "I was afraid to."

"You were afraid to ask Jim Steele, your husband of three weeks, who promised to love and cherish you, to accompany you on a shopping trip?"

"Yes!" She put her hands over her mouth and closed her eyes for the space of a breath. Her eyes opened and she looked at Jim, reaching toward him with her hands. It was the best parody of entreaty Jenner had seen since he'd watched a counterfeiter try to persuade a jury he was working on an engraving project for an art class at Amarillo College.

"Jim!" she cried. "I can't be quiet any longer. As much as I dislike Christy Steele, it's my moral duty to warn her." Her gaze returned to John Lloyd. "He struck me with his fist, knocked me down, told me he wished I was dead and my brat with me. He caused my miscarriage."

Pandemonium! Reporters scribbled furiously. Spectators gasped. The judge pounded the bench with his gavel.

Jim Steele leaped up. "That's not true! I never hit you. It was an accident!"

John Lloyd's voice rang out over the noise. "I am shocked! I am horrified!" He rose to his feet and faced the spectators. "Is there a man or woman with even a trace of human decency who is not repulsed by such an assault upon an expectant mother?" The crowd grew quiet and he turned back to face Amy. "James Steele caused your miscarriage. Is that correct?"

She nodded. "Yes."

"Which occurred in a strange city, in a strange hospital where there were no friends to comfort you?"

She touched the corners of her eyes with her handkerchief. "Yes."

"You used your insurance policy for the hospital bill. Is that correct?" he asked, his voice incisive with no trace of a drawl. Reporters struggling to be first out the door to call in their stories stopped, alerted by his change of tone and accent.

Amy's blue eyes narrowed. "No, I didn't know the name of the company, nor the policy number. I paid cash. I had some traveler's checks with me."

"You did get a copy of the bill for tax purposes, of course?"

Amy's hands fluttered up in a gesture of dismissal. "I did, but I'm afraid I lost it. It wasn't a large bill anyway."

"That is unfortunate. These days everyone needs every deduction possible." John Lloyd moved around the counsel table toward the witness box.

"I know it's too late to claim your deduction now, but I happen to have a copy of that hospital bill, Mrs. Steele. Is this your signature on that bill?" John Lloyd demanded, his spare frame seeming to loom over her although he had stepped back after giving her the paper.

Amy sat like stone, her pale eyes darting back to Rutherford, then around the courtroom. She licked her lips before speaking. "No."

John Lloyd pulled another document out of his pocket. "Your Honor, this is an affidavit from the records clerk of the hospital certifying the authenticity of this bill. We can, of course, bring him to Canadian as well as the physician mentioned on the bill if necessary, Mrs. Steele."

John Lloyd waited, but Amy sat staring at him. "Is this the hospital bill and is this your signature?"

"Yes, yes, yes!" she screamed. "That's my signature!"

John Lloyd smiled impassively and returned to the counsel table. "Now, Mrs. Steele, this hospital bill tells a very different story from yours. This bill is for the *voluntary* abortion of a three-month fetus, followed by a *voluntary* sterilization procedure. You had not even met James Steele three months prior to this abortion. You know all about trapping a man, don't you? You trapped James Steele into marriage because of a baby whom he did not father! I further charge you with deliberately provoking an argument so that you might fake an accidental fall, a fall Jim Steele blamed himself for causing. You convinced him to accept responsibility for a miscarriage which never occurred!"

Jim Steele staggered out of his chair like a bull who finally sees an opportunity to kill the matador torturing it. "You bitch! You tormented me for years with your lies. I could kill you for this!"

"You've already tried to kill me twice! I won't be safe until the sergeant over there arrests you." She pointed directly at Schroder.

More pandemonium!

Judge Myers pounded his gavel. "There will be order in this court, or I'll direct the bailiff to throw all of you out on your ears. And I dare a single reporter to mention a single word about freedom of the press." There was silence. "That's better." He swung his chair to face the witness stand. "Mrs. Steele, you accused your husband of trying to kill you. Do you have any basis for that accusation?''

''He tried to poison me! And last night he shot Mr. Branson's clerk because he thought he was shooting me! He's being investigated for attempted murder. Just ask Sergeant Schroder.''

''Which one of you gentlemen is Sergeant Schroder?'' asked the judge.

Schroder struggled to his feet. ''I am, Your Honor.'' Jenner noticed his shirttail was showing below his jacket.

''Are you investigating James Steele?''

''Yes, sir. Sergeant Jenner and I are members of the Special Crimes Unit of Potter, Randall, and Armstrong counties. James Steele is a suspect in a homicide that occurred in Potter County. Last evening Miss Lydia Fairchild received multiple gunshot wounds. We have reason to believe it was because she resembles Mrs. Amy Steele.''

''Your Honor, I object to these questions.'' John Lloyd's voice and manner were as calm as if his case hadn't just received a death blow. ''This is a hearing on temporary alimony, not a trial of James Steele for a crime for which he has not been charged. We have, however, shown that Mrs. Amy Steele is a liar and a thief. She, therefore, deserves no monetary support from the husband she has wronged. We respectively request the court to rule on this matter.''

''Mr. Branson, in view of the serious nature of this investigation, and the fact that it directly concerns this case, I shall take the matter of alimony under advisement for a period of ten days. It is entirely possible that these divorce proceedings may be delayed indefinitely pending the results of Sergeant Schroder's investigation.''

''Your Honor, might I remind the court that Christy Deveraux Steele's delivery cannot be delayed indefinitely? It would not be justice to force her unborn child to bear the stigma of illegitimacy because this court does not see fit to grant James Steele his divorce after the legally stipulated period of sixty days.''

Judge Myers looked at Christy. Jenner could feel the tension as the courtroom full of spectators waited. The judge expelled a deep breath. "This court stands adjourned."

"Your Honor," shouted Schroder over the voices of reporters as they descended upon the stunned tableau of figures at the counsel table. "Your Honor, Sergeant Jenner and myself request an appointment to discuss our findings and obtain certain legal documents necessary to our further investigation." Jenner found himself being dragged through the crowd toward the judge's bench.

"Your Honor." John Lloyd's deep voice brought an immediate hush. "Your Honor, I suggest that your talking to these officers might be construed as a conflict of interest in view of the fact that you are the presiding judge in the divorce case of James and Amy Steele."

Judge Myers looked from John Lloyd back to Schroder. "Sergeant Schroder, Mr. Branson is correct. I am presiding judge in a civil matter involving James Steele which has already begun. If I muddy the waters by issuing warrants and subpoenas in a criminal matter also involving James Steele, I may violate the legal canon of ethics at least morally, if not legally. If I excuse myself from the civil case, the appointment of another judge will further delay matters, and as John Lloyd pointed out, Christy Steele's condition has a time limit. I'm sorry, gentlemen, but you'll have to find another judge. And let me give you a friendly warning, Sergeant Schroder. John Lloyd Branson is a genius in criminal legal procedure. You'd better play it strictly by the rules, and you'd better have twice as much evidence as you think you need before you talk to any judge about a warrant."

John Lloyd bowed. "I am flattered, Your Honor."

Judge Myers grinned. "The hell you are, John Lloyd. You have to be modest to be flattered, and you've never been modest a day in your life."

"I stand corrected, Your Honor."

"Nobody's ever been able to that, either, John Lloyd," said the judge as he left for his chambers.

"All right, Branson, just what did you hope to gain by that little trick?" demanded Schroder.

"Time, Sergeant," said John Lloyd.

"Time for what, John Lloyd?" asked Lydia as he assisted her out of her chair.

"I'd like to hear your answer to that one, Counselor." Schroder's hoarse voice sounded like a shovel being scraped over concrete. It also sounded angry to Jenner's ears.

"Time to conduct an investigation of my own," replied Branson. "Time to apply deductive reasoning to this latest unpleasant incident."

Lydia turned to look at him with a little anger of her own. "You'd use a little stronger word than unpleasant if *you'd* ever been shot, John Lloyd."

"I have been shot, Miss Fairchild, and it was"—he hesitated—"unpleasant."

"Stick it in your ear, John Lloyd," she said under her breath, and Jenner winked at her. They had a lot in common, he thought; both their bosses spent a lot of time acting like horses' asses.

"And he's going to be shot again, Miss Fairchild, if he sticks that long nose where it doesn't belong," interrupted Schroder. "Because I'm going to blast it off personally if he sticks it in the middle of my investigation. Civilians have no business interfering with the police in the performance of their duty."

John Lloyd looked indignant. "I agree with you, Sergeant Schroder, and I would never contemplate interfering with your gathering of fingerprints, blood and saliva samples, and all the other oddments of physical evidence which you weigh and measure and analyze in your sterile laboratories. It is the interpretation of those oddments that interests me."

"Your interpretation was full of shit, Branson, and it nearly got Miss Fairchild here killed. If I'd arrested Jim

Steele last night instead of listening to you, she wouldn't have a hole in her side.''

''You are quite correct, Sergeant, but for the wrong reason,'' said John Lloyd, taking Lydia's elbow and guiding her toward the door where Jim Steele and his extended family waited.

CHAPTER
TWENTY-ONE

AMY STEELE STEPPED BETWEEN JOHN LLOYD AND THE door. "I've won, Mr. Branson. I've beaten you. Your legal maneuvering with the judge only postponed the inevitable. You threatened me with prison over what happened to that drab Cammie you wanted to marry unless I gave Jim a divorce. How do you feel now, John Lloyd? I'm giving him the divorce, but *he's* going to prison. I'll see to it. I'm going to get it all, or most of it anyway—the money, the ranch. Or maybe if they're nice to me, I'll just take possession of the house and half the money, and they can have the ranch. I always hated that ranch anyway. Of course, that cripple and her friend will have to move out."

Lydia dug her fingernails into her palms to keep from applying them to Amy's face. "That's their home. Where would they go?"

Amy shrugged her shoulders. "Let Alice Steele go to a nursing home. It's where she needs to be. And Cammie, too, if she can find one to admit her with that fright mask of a face."

John Lloyd raised his cane, his obsidian eyes filled

with a terrible rage. Lydia grabbed his arm. "You'd better get her out of here," she said to Rutherford. "Clear out of the courthouse, because I can't guarantee she won't have some scars of her own when I let go of John Lloyd."

"For God's sake, Amy, shut up!" The lawyer began pulling her toward the door.

Suddenly, Lydia saw Cammie's thin figure cowering against the wall, her hands covering her face, and realized the woman had overheard everything. She watched Alice spit on Amy as she paused by the older woman's wheelchair. Rutherford might look like a wimp but he had good reflexes, she thought, as the lawyer grabbed Amy's other arm before she could strike Alice. He herded her through the door and toward the staircase, with a crowd of reporters snapping at his heels.

"You may release me now, Miss Fairchild. I am in control again, although I cannot imagine why you would wish to save that woman from the sound thrashing she deserves." John Lloyd's drawl was back, but Lydia could still feel the tremors that shook his arm.

"Save her! I don't give a damn if you beat her to death, but you would look terrible in jailbird clothes, John Lloyd. I'll bet there's not a single tailor in the whole prison system."

John Lloyd gently disengaged her hand. "You are undoubtedly correct in your assumption, Miss´ Fairchild. Neither, I am sure, would the warden serve brandy after dinner. I am grateful for your intervention in saving me from such a deplorable environment." He straightened his tie and clasped her elbow. "Bailiff, we have need of your elevator for Mrs. Steele's chair. In fact, we shall all use the elevator and exit through the jail. I have no desire to face the gauntlet the press is preparing. The evening news will have to do without a quote from me."

Jim Steele directed a bitter look at him. "The judge was right; you've never been modest. The press isn't interested in you. It's Christy and me they want to flay."

John Lloyd raised his cane and poked Jim in the chest. "You, sir, will make no comments of any kind to the press. Your uncontrolled, unconsidered remarks have already caused enough damage.''

"What are you talking about?" demanded Jim, maneuvering his mother's chair into the elevator.

"Your outburst in the courtroom gave Amy an opportunity to cast the accusation of murder at you. That cost us a quick decision at this hearing.''

Jim held the elevator door open. "Damn it, John Lloyd. Don't use that pious tone with me. Not everyone is so goddamn cold as you. Sometimes I don't think you're even human.''

Lydia lay on the couch and contemplated John Lloyd's office. On this end of the room were a comfortable couch, two armchairs with hassocks, occasional tables, bookcases lining the walls, and what Lydia thought was a genuine Persian rug on the polished hardwood floor. On the other end of the room was the office proper: John Lloyd's rolltop desk, her own small table, bookcases, a door into the library. Every piece of the furnishings was an antique, beautifully polished and lovingly cared for. It was a perfect office for John Lloyd.

She rolled her head to one side to look at him. He sat in one of the armchairs, his feet crossed and resting on a hassock, his elbows propped on the arms with his fingers laced together across his chest. He had removed his coat, but not his Victorian formality; that was innate. She sighed. He fit this office, this town perfectly. She was the only incongruent thing in the room, a modern female with a brash veneer among all the solid oak.

"Yes, Miss Fairchild?" asked John Lloyd in his slowest drawl.

"I should be wearing a corset and having an attack of the vapors.''

He arched one eyebrow and rose out of the chair, using his good leg for leverage. "I believe corsets were a major cause of the vapors, Miss Fairchild. Something to do with being laced too tightly. However, I am certain you have a most interesting explanation for aspiring to wear such a garment.''

"I suddenly felt out of place," she confessed. She waved her good arm at the room. "All the antiques."

"One often feels disoriented when waking up in a strange place," he said, walking the few steps to the couch, his limp perceptible. Or maybe he was too tired to control it, she thought suddenly, as she noticed lines of strain around his mouth.

She eased over and patted the couch. "Sit down, John Lloyd. You look like an undertaker who just buried his best friend."

"An apt description, Miss Fairchild. You slept through the funeral, however." He sat down.

"Slept through what?" she asked. "I haven't been asleep."

"Actually your state was closer to unconsciousness. Dr. Bailey was quite concerned at one point. He was preparing to check your reflexes, but you began to snore and he decided no one who could snore like that was in danger of dying."

"I don't snore," she said indignantly. "And what was Bailey doing here?"

John Lloyd smoothed her hair back from her face and laid his hand on her forehead. "Everyone was here: the Steeles, Cammie, Dr. Bailey. Alice was proposing that they form a club: the Amy Steele Homicide Suspects Anonymous, the only qualification for membership being that you have a motive for murdering Amy Steele. Alice abandoned the idea when I pointed out that it would be necessary to rent the high school auditorium for meetings."

His hand was now against her cheek and stroking downward toward the side of her throat. She felt like a cat being petted and wished she could purr. "Why were they all here, John Lloyd? I thought Jim was so angry this afternoon that he'd either fire you or punch out your lights."

"A much more satisfactory state of affairs than his

self-immolation has been. I am in debt to your impulsiveness, Miss Fairchild. Had you not confronted him
with so much righteous indignation, I would never have
discovered the motive for his behavior. Once I knew of
Amy's pregnancy, it was a matter of a few phone calls
to uncover her misdeeds. And a chartered jet to fly the
evidence to Amarillo where Mrs. Dinwittie picked it up.
The expenses in this case will put a sizable dent in Jim
Steele's next royalty check.''

"And to quote somebody, you snatched victory from
the jaws of defeat.''

He picked up her hand. "I did nothing of the sort. To
resurrect another cliché, Miss Fairchild, the operation
was a success, but the patient died. I merely provided
Jim Steele with an excellent reason to murder Amy. Add
the results of my investigations while you were sleeping
to that fact, and it may prove impossible to persuade
Sergeant Schroder that Jim is innocent of last night's assault.''

"What did you find out?'' she asked, wondering why
Jim Steele had ever thought John Lloyd cold. The rancher
should see him holding her hand.

"None of my clients have an alibi. Dr. Bailey drove
by his office to look at some patients' medical history
before going to the hospital. Cammie went horseback riding. Christy read a book. Alice watched television in her
room. And Jim, my dear, stupid friend, went to Amy's
room, then drove around. He was thinking he said. I told
him he was incapable of that activity. I, however, am
not. But there are still mysteries. I lack the evidence I
need.''

His long fingers wrapped around Lydia's wrist and her
eyes closed. John Lloyd was sweet, a closet romantic.
She opened her eyes to watch him . . . taking her pulse?
"What are you doing?''

"Taking your pulse,'' he replied. "You looked flushed
when you awoke. How do you feel?''

"Like someone had slipped a hot coal into my side
and sewed the hole shut.'' Actually, she felt worse than

that, but disappointment didn't count as a physical symptom. Neither did anger, and she was beginning to feel very angry.

He placed his hand gently against her side, then touched her arm about her bandaged wound. "Feverish," he said with a frown. "I knew it was unwise to permit you to attend the hearing."

"You didn't permit me; I blackmailed you."

"Only because I allowed it."

"Then was all that talk about protecting my reputation just bull—?"

John Lloyd clapped his hand over her mouth. "Your fondness for profane expressions is most unbecoming, Miss Fairchild. I must insist you curtail your excessive usage of inappropriate phrases."

Lydia slapped his hand down. "You permit! You allow! You insist! You go to hell, John Lloyd. If I want to be dictated to, I'll move to Russia."

"I would not advise it, Miss Fairchild. You would clash with the authorities within the hour, and I do not believe *habeas corpus* is a cornerstone of their legal system. However beautiful you might look in a fur parka, the climate of Siberia has very little to recommend it."

"You are evading my question. Every time you get uptight and start acting like a male chauvinist, you're hiding something." She grabbed his tie and jerked on it, bringing his face to within inches of her own. His eyes were expressionless. Almost. Buried in their black depths was a hint of guilt. "You didn't care about my reputation at all, did you? You had some other motive." She felt disappointed all over again. Not only had he not been stroking her as a prelude to seduction, but he hadn't even been protecting her reputation as if she were a delicate Victorian lady who matched his furniture.

"I was concerned about your reputation, but I was more concerned about your safety," he admitted.

"My safety," she echoed.

"I would find it less difficult to explain, Miss Fairchild, if you would let go of my tie. I am in danger of losing the oxygen supply to my brain."

She opened her fingers. "I'm sorry, John Lloyd. Are you all right?"

He loosened his tie and took several deep breaths before sitting up. "I believe so, but for future reference, choking someone is the easiest method of committing murder. Within twenty seconds, the victim is unconscious; within forty seconds, the brain is dead. The body lives a maximum of four minutes before dying."

"But I've read about drowning victims surviving four minutes without oxygen, and without brain damage."

"It is not the oxygen, Miss Fairchild; it is the sudden loss of blood sugar to the brain. Blood-sugar loss is more quickly and surely fatal than loss of oxygen. Individuals are strangled by accident quite frequently because few people understand the physical process involved. And contrary to popular belief, very little strength is required. Only enough to constrict the throat for twenty seconds. The fear of being unable to breathe is so great that the victim seldom fights his attacker effectively. The organism's first instinct is to fight for air. That is why most strangulation victims have scratch marks on their throats. They are endeavoring to release the pressure of the murderer's hands or the rope or whatever means is being used to relieve them of their lives. If you are ever so attacked and you have the use of your hands, a right hook into the assailant's diaphragm, or better still, into his throat, is an excellent defense. I believe you are aware of an effective target for your knees and feet."

"What if my hands aren't free?"

"Then you are dead, Miss Fairchild," he replied.

"How do you know all this, John Lloyd?"

"An attorney who defends clients suspected of murder had best have some familiarity with forensic pathology. I also have a working knowledge of fingerprints, serology, hair and fiber comparison, and ballistics. They are all part of those oddments Schroder and I were discussing. I specialize in murder, Miss Fairchild. I must understand its mechanics and the traces it leaves behind.''

"And?'' prodded Lydia.

He raised an eyebrow.

"Tell me the rest of it. This little dissertation on murder isn't to further my education. It has something to do with why you let me attend the hearing. I know you, John Lloyd.''

"I am beginning to believe you do, Miss Fairchild, and I find it most disconcerting. The truth is I did not want to leave you unprotected. While I failed most miserably to prevent the first attack, I am determined to protect you against a second attempt. I can do that most easily if I keep you with me.''

"How? By throwing yourself between me and a bullet? Don't you dare! I won't have it, do you understand? I won't''—she fumbled for a word—''*permit* it!''

"If it is necessary to shield you, I shall do so. However''—he leaned over and reached in his briefcase—''I believe this and a watchful eye will be more effective.''

"Oh, my God, it's a gun!'' Gritting her teeth against the pain in her side, she struggled to a sitting position. "John Lloyd, that is a gun!''

"You have identified the object correctly, Miss Fairchild. Congratulations. To be specific, it is a .45 centerfire caliber Colt Single-Action Army revolver, 1873 model.''

"I knew it had to be an antique! I knew it!''

"It is quite a valuable antique,'' he agreed. "And quite deadly. It must be cocked between shots, but since I seldom have to fire more than once, that is not too much of a disadvantage.''

"This isn't happening to me,'' said Lydia, shaking her head. "I'm in the middle of the Texas Panhandle, in a town with a WCTU chapter, and working for a man who looks like a tinhorn gambler, talks like a pompous English professor, and carries a gun in his briefcase.''

"I do not resemble a tinhorn gambler.''

"Quit changing the subject! You were carrying a gun!''

"For one who nearly committed murder by strangulation not five minutes ago, and who regularly physically retaliates for imagined slights, your attitude toward a weapon puzzles me. You are overreacting, Miss Fairchild."

"That gun is an overreaction! It's not *me* someone wants to kill; it's Amy."

John Lloyd slipped the gun back in the briefcase. "That is the obvious explanation."

Lydia felt a chill that had nothing to do with her feverish wounds. "What other explanation is there?"

He stood up and raked his fingers through his blond hair. "That you were the intended victim."

CHAPTER
TWENTY-TWO

LARRY JENNER FELT DIRTY—FROM HIS MOUTH, WHICH
had not touched a toothbrush for over thirty-six hours, to
his boots, which had lost their shine sometime yesterday
afternoon. His beard had grown from a five o'clock
shadow into a fashionable stubble that itched. His uniform shirt was splotched with perspiration stains; the
knife-edge crease in his pants looked more like a serrated
blade; his undershorts felt welded to him; and the less
said the better about the condition of his socks after two
days without removing his boots. His eyes were red and
his head ached from lack of sleep. His stomach felt
queasy from too many meals either missed or eaten in
the front seat of a car. He wanted a shower, a decent
night's sleep, and a chance to breathe clean air instead
of recycling Schroder's cigarette smoke.

He glanced at Schroder and felt his resentment take a
quantum leap from mild to severe. There were some ad-
vantages to looking like you slept in your clothes. Schroder appeared exactly the same as at eight o'clock
yesterday morning, if you discounted Amy Steele's claw
marks and several mosquito bites. Bad meals and lack of

sleep didn't seem to bother him. Looking at it logically, Jenner decided the investigator could live off his stored bulk for a month, and all that nicotine in his system probably kept him from sleeping under any circumstances. Or maybe he hibernated between cases and lived off sleep stored up during an investigation. Whatever the source of Schroder's stamina, it kept him lumbering through the investigation while Jenner could feel his own ass dragging.

He opened the car door and dredged up enough energy to put both feet on the brick pavement and pull himself into an upright position. He braced himself against the fender and locked his knees in order to stay that way, and looked up and down the street. God, it was so late nobody was still out except carloads of Canadian's teenagers. "Schroder, he's not going to be in his office. It's after midnight. He's in bed asleep."

"He doesn't sleep during a case."

"That makes two of you," muttered Jenner, unlocking his knees and stumbling after the investigator. "Schroder, when are we going back to Amarillo?"

"Tonight."

"Thank God! I can sleep in my own bed instead of leaning against a motel door or sitting in a courtroom." He took a deep breath and wrinkled his nose. "I smell so bad my wife'll make me hose off in the backyard before she'll let me in the shower."

"Tell her to bring a clean uniform to Special Crimes."

Jenner felt his stomach drop to the vicinity of his knees. "What the hell for?"

"Because you're not going home. We're gonna draw up a search warrant *and* an arrest warrant, then get one of the assistant D.A.'s out of bed to check them. I want all the *i's* dotted and *t's* crossed. I don't want to leave Branson an opening. Give that man a one-inch-high tunnel and he'll drive a Mack truck through it."

Schroder stopped on the sidewalk and lit a cigarette. "After the assistant D.A. tells me I got foolproof warrants, we'll get a judge out of bed to sign them. That's kind of a risky business—judges don't like to be rousted out of bed like they were snot-nosed graduates with a brand new membership card in the bar association—but I know a couple that'll jump at the chance after I tell them Branson's the attorney of record. Branson was responsible for getting a couple of their verdicts reversed on appeal on the basis of judicial error. Makes a judge real unhappy to have a case shoved back in his face.''

''So why are we going to talk to Branson?''

''Public relations, son. Ordinarily, I'd serve the warrant and haul Jim Steele to jail, but Branson likes to surrender his clients and save them the public embarrassment of being handcuffed and taken to jail in a patrol car.''

''I thought you were mad as hell at Branson. Why are you worrying about what he likes?''

Schroder sighed and ground his cigarette under his heel. ''Son, you don't ever tease a sleeping tiger, 'cause he just might wake up and take a chunk out of your behind. Besides, Branson was doing his job. You might say he was doing a trial run on his defense, and it's a good one. He nearly convinced me Amy Steele set up the whole thing.'' He stopped at a heavy wooden door. ''This is it.''

''This is what?'' asked Jenner.

''Branson's office.''

''This is a drugstore!'' said Jenner, looking in the windows adjacent to the door. ''Branson has his office in a drugstore?''

Schroder pulled open the door to reveal a small foyer with an elevator and wide flight of stairs. ''Branson has his office on the second floor,'' he said as he started up the steps.

Jenner grabbed the banister and began hauling himself up a step at a time. ''John Lloyd Branson doesn't live in the twentieth century. Lawyers have offices in bank buildings, insurance buildings, highrises, never over a drugstore! I bet he still signs his name with a quill pen.''

He followed Schroder through a door at the top of the stairs, the old-fashioned variety with opaque wavy glass at the top and a solid wooden bottom. "I'll give you ten-to-one odds he has a stovepipe hat he keeps for special occasions. He probably even has buttons on his fly; a zipper'd be too modern for him."

"Shut up," said Schroder, walking through a reception area—furnished in antiques, Jenner noticed—and knocking on another door.

John Lloyd Branson opened the door and, stepping to one side, gestured them in like a butler at an English manor house. "Sergeants, come in. I've been expecting you."

"I'll have a warrant for your client's arrest by tomorrow morning, Branson. I'm doing you the courtesy of informing you. Do you wish to surrender him, or would you prefer me to bring him in?" Schroder stood in the middle of the room like an immovable object.

"Please, sit down, gentlemen," said John Lloyd, limping back to the couch and sinking down beside Lydia Fairchild. "It is quite late, or quite early, depending on one's point of view. In either case, it has been a fatiguing twenty-four hours, and I see no point in standing during what will be a lengthy discussion."

Schroder's brows drew together in one of his frowns. "Don't sit down, Jenner," he said. "We don't have anything to talk with Mr. Branson about."

Jenner stopped himself with a hair's breadth between his posterior and the seat of the first comfortable-looking chair he'd seen since coming to Canadian.

John Lloyd leaned back and stretched out his long legs, crossing them at the ankles. "You don't consider arresting my client on insufficient evidence worth discussing, Sergeant Schroder?" Jenner closed the gap between posterior and chair. Branson's question was guaranteed to send Schroder into at least a five-minute tirade.

Schroder's brows drew a fraction closer together. "I've got all the evidence I need, Branson. I have motive, means, and opportunity on the spiked coffee, and I have motive and opportunity on the assault on Miss Fairchild. I don't have the gun yet, but I'll have a search warrant in the morning, and I suspect I'll find it somewhere on Jim Steele's ranch."

"Hey, Schroder! You shouldn't have told him that!" said Jenner.

Schroder didn't look away from John Lloyd. "Don't worry, son. John Lloyd Branson wouldn't remove evidence if it meant sending his own mother to Huntsville. Would you, Branson?"

John Lloyd shook his head. "I trust my mother would never have found herself in such a situation, but had it occurred, no, I would not have violated my principles. If I might ask one question, Sergeant, I might prevent you from obtaining warrants against the wrong individual. How did the assailant happen to be waiting for Miss Fairchild to step out the door of the restaurant?"

"A phone call, Branson, a simple phone call. Amy Steele left word at the desk that she'd be at the restaurant. What he didn't know was that she'd seen you there and left without eating."

"Of course, I see how it was done now. Had I been more observant last night, this conversation could have taken place shortly after the incident." He turned his head to look at his clerk. "I underestimated my opponent and placed you in danger, Miss Fairchild. My apologies."

Lydia looked puzzled. "You're not clairvoyant, John Lloyd. You couldn't anticipate what Jim Steele was planning."

He waved away her comment. "I am not speaking of Jim Steele. I am speaking of his wife."

"Christy!" exclaimed Lydia in horror.

"The little pregnant lady!" exclaimed Jenner with equal horror.

"Sergeant Jenner, I will excuse your ignorance, not knowing you well enough to judge whether or not you are capable of rational thinking. However, Miss Fairchild, you are quite intelligent. It should be obvious to you that I am not speaking of Christy Steele, whom I suspect would be unable to step on a cockroach, not to mention attempting murder. I refer to Jim's legal wife, Amy Steele.''

"You're crazy as hell, Branson . . . ," began Schroder.

"Am I?" interrupted John Lloyd. "Ask yourself who had the most to gain if Amy Steele were the victim of a murder attempt? The answer is: Amy Steele. Her plan to have Jim arrested was a failure. You, Sergeant Schroder, were asking questions about her own involvement in the drugging of the coffee. Something must be done to convince you that her life was truly in danger. How better to accomplish that goal than another homicide attempt? I'm sure in the few minutes between your leaving her and Jim's arrival at the motel, she had formulated and discarded many plans. But Jim Steele came to her door, and he came bearing arms.''

"He had a gun?" asked Lydia. "He was planning to kill her?"

"If you would allow me to finish my explanation, Miss Fairchild, I should greatly appreciate it. Sergeant Schroder will be appreciative as he will be spending the rest of what is left of this night proving my theory.''

"You're full of crap, Branson," said Schroder, turning toward the door. "Come on, Jenner. I'm not going to listen to any more of this two-bit Perry Mason's fairy stories.''

"One moment, Sergeant. Are you afraid to face your own prejudice? You came to Canadian believing Jim Steele was guilty and you have steadfastly refused to consider any other alternative. Ask yourself why. Is it because of the statistical probability of the spouse's guilt and the evidence against Jim Steele? Or is it because he failed to mourn his wife as you believe a wife should be mourned, no matter how unworthy that wife may be?''

Schroder whirled around and started for the lawyer, his hands clenched into fists the size of small hams. "Shut up, Branson!''

John Lloyd pushed himself up and took a defensive stance as Lydia thrust her body in front of him. Jenner discovered energy he didn't know he had and leaped up to grab Schroder's arms. "Cool it, Sergeant! The Chief'll have your ass!"

The investigator shrugged off Jenner's grip and shook his head as if to clear it. John Lloyd in the meantime caught Lydia before she sagged to her knees. She was clutching her side. Carefully avoiding her wound, he deposited her on the couch. "Miss Fairchild," he said. "I believe I said something earlier about my not imposing my body between you and harm. The reverse is also true. I insist you curb your heroic impulses. At least until your wounds heal." He turned to Schroder and extended his hand. "Sergeant, I apologize for my remarks."

Schroder stuck his hands in his pockets. "You hit below the belt, Branson."

The lawyer nodded and sank back onto the couch. "It was necessary, Sergeant. I had to stop you. It seems I've spent the last two days forcing those for whom I have affection or respect to face their delusions in the coldest possible manner. I shall continue to do so if necessary. Will you listen to my reconstruction of the crime?"

Schroder sat down. "Tell me," he said.

Branson seemed to relax. "As I said . . . ," he continued, with just a trace of a drawl, and Jenner had the oddest notion that he was hearing John Lloyd's real voice. "When Jim Steele knocked on her door, Amy realized that chance had given her a weapon. Leaving her attorney to argue with Jim, she slipped out her patio door and around to Jim's pickup. Like many ranchers, he carries rifles in a gun rack in his pickup. It was the work of a moment to steal one and slip back into her room and hide the gun. She now had the motive and the means; only the opportunity was lacking. Leaving word at the desk as to her whereabouts, she and her lawyer went out to eat. Chance again worked in her favor. Miss Fairchild and I were dining at the same restaurant. Realizing the superficial resemblance between herself and Miss Fairchild provided an opportunity to stage an attempted homicide, she left quickly and returned to her motel. Making some excuse, she locked herself in her room. She went out her patio door again with the gun and drove in her rented car to the river. There she waited for Miss Fairchild to emerge.''

"That is the damnedest story I ever heard, Branson. It's crazier than your theory about the coffee. You've got no proof at all. Save it for the jury. Maybe you can convince them.'' Schroder got up and turned toward the door again.

"I suggest you check the tires on Amy Steele's rented car, Sergeant.''

Schroder stopped and turned around. "Why?''

"There is mud on her tires, Sergeant. River bottom mud. I also suggest you look closely at her face.''

"Mosquito bites!'' said Lydia suddenly. "Those weren't zits on her face! They were mosquito bites!''

John Lloyd reached over and patted her hand. "Exactly, Miss Fairchild. She was bitten by mosquitoes while waiting by the river for her opportunity to shoot you.''

He rose to his feet. "I put to you, Sergeant, that Amy Steele has no logical reason for having mud on her tires. She is not the type to indulge in recreational driving by the river. I further put to you that Amy Steele would not suffer mosquito bites by choice. But she had no choice. In order to set up the alleged attempt on her life it was necessary that she take advantage of what might be her only opportunity. She had to stay on the river in a place of concealment, and that resulted in her being repeatedly bitten by mosquitoes.''

"But what about the phone call from Jim Steele?'' asked Jenner.

John Lloyd shrugged. "It is possible that someone else made that call, but it is most logical to assume that Amy Steele made it herself to further throw suspicion on Jim Steele.''

Schroder was silent and Jenner mulled over the lawyer's theory. "She didn't have anything wrong with her face when we talked to her yesterday morning, Schroder.

But last night, her face was a mess and she kept scratching her arms.''

Schroder lumbered toward the door. "I'm going to take a look at those tires, Branson. That's all I can promise.''

John Lloyd picked up his coat and briefcase. "Miss Fairchild and I will accompany you, Sergeant. I have an understandably human desire to be in at the kill.''

Schroder opened his mouth, then closed it. "All right, Branson, you can come. But keep the hell out of my way.''

"But of course, Sergeant," agreed the attorney, helping Lydia Fairchild off the couch.

Jenner took the stairs two at a time. Sometime in the last five minutes he'd lost his fatigue. "Do you think he's right, Schroder? Could that bitch have set this one up, too?''

Schroder lit a cigarette without missing a step and without answering. He hit the door at a run and beat Jenner to the car. Jenner barely had a chance to get one leg in when the investigator backed up and drove off up the street. "Goddamn it, Schroder, take it easy. The woman's not going anywhere.''

"Do me a favor, Jenner, and shut up.''

Jenner closed his mouth and concentrated on hanging on instead. Before his sinuses had a chance to stop up from Schroder's cigarette, the investigator was turning in at the motel. He stopped with a screech of tires, grabbed a flashlight from underneath the glove compartment, and was out of the car before Jenner could unfasten his seat belt.

A black Continental pulled up as Jenner was scrambling out of the car. The tall figure of John Lloyd Branson emerged. "Sergeant Jenner, Amy Steele is driving a dark green Mercury Marquis, this year's model. The license number is NAD 880.''

Schroder walked out of the motel. "Did you check the guest registration card, Branson?''

"I called the car rental agencies in Amarillo, Sergeant.

It's amazing what a convincing cover story and a sincere voice can obtain in the way of information.''

Schroder grunted and started checking cars in the vicinity of Amy Steele's room. He frowned and motioned at Jenner. "Get the other flashlight out of the glove compartment and take the other side of the parking lot. Check every goddamned car.''

Jenner hurried back to the car, and closing his eyes, reached for a flashlight. He had a feeling that if he could see what was actually in the glove compartment, he'd never have the courage to stick his hand in it. Clicking on the flashlight, he started checking cars. Ten minutes later he joined Schroder, Branson, Lydia Fairchild by the attorney's Continental. "Nothing, Schroder. That car's not in the parking lot, and it's not on the street.''

"She's not checked out, but she's not answering her door and neither is that lawyer of hers,'' said the investigator. "I pounded on her door until a couple of other guests cussed me out.''

"Where can she be?'' asked Lydia. "It's nearly three in the morning.''

"What about it, Branson? Have I got enough probable cause to get the desk clerk to use his pass key?''

"Very dubious probable cause, Sergeant. However, in the event of any legal complications, I shall defend you and Special Crimes. At no charge,'' he added.

"Nothing like this has ever happened at the Cottonwood Inn Motel,'' said the desk clerk when Jenner had escorted him to Amy's room. "I'll just have to tell Mrs. Steele to leave. I can't have the police coming around all the time. Gives the place a bad reputation.'' He unlocked the door and stepped back. "Nothing like this has ever happened,'' he repeated.

Schroder was first in the room. He flicked on the light and saw—nothing. The bed was made, clothes were tossed on chairs and on the floor. He checked the bathroom. He knelt down and picked up a pair of flat-heeled shoes. He examined them carefully, then looked over Jenner's shoulder at John Lloyd. "Mud,'' he said.

"Legally you may take them, Sergeant. They were in plain view."

"I know my job," snapped Schroder. "Open the lawyer's room," he ordered the desk clerk.

"I don't know what the owner's going to say about all this," said the clerk, opening Rutherford's door.

Jenner was the first through the door and decided the room looked just like the person: everything in place. Even his shaving gear was lined up in precision order. "Nothing here," he told Schroder.

Schroder waved the desk clerk away and looked at John Lloyd. "Any ideas, Branson?"

"Perhaps they have gone to Amarillo for the evening." He rubbed his eyes and looked back at Schroder. "But that would be illogical. Amy knows you are ready to arrest Jim. I do not think she would leave until she sees him in jail. And she has no friends to visit in Canadian."

"This is your town, Branson. Where can she go until three o'clock in the morning?"

Branson had white lines bracketing his mouth. "I don't know, Sergeant, but I know where my destination is."

"Where?"

"Miss Fairchild and I are going to the Bar-S. All of my clients are out there on my instructions. Primarily so that they might alibi each other," he said ruefully. "I intend to gather them in the living room for the rest of the night, or however long until Amy Steele condescends to show herself."

"You just keep that big black vehicle of yours at the legal speed limit, Branson, because I'm going to follow you out there. I'm curious as to whether one of your clients might know anything about Amy Steele's whereabouts." He hustled everyone out of Rutherford's room and closed the door. Still holding Amy's shoes, he followed John Lloyd and Lydia out to the parking lot.

"Where the hell do you think they are, Schroder?" Jenner asked, as the investigator started his car and followed John Lloyd.

"Damned if I know, but Branson's worried as hell," Schroder said, rolling his cigarette into the corner of his mouth.

"Don't follow so damn close, Schroder!" yelled Jenner as he peered through the windshield to see the taillights of John Lloyd's car barely a yard in front of their hood.

"You're nervous, son. You ought to watch that."

Jenner closed his eyes and braced himself. "Why do you think Branson's scared?" he asked, not really interested, but the answer might take his mind off the very likely possibility of running up the tailpipe of John Lloyd's Continental.

"I didn't say scared—I've never seen the man scared—I said worried. Running out to round up his clients like they were a bunch of steers is the act of a worried man."

"Damn it, Schroder, he's turning! Slow down!"

"Did anybody every tell you not to backseat drive?" asked Schroder, turning onto the graveled ranch road after John Lloyd.

Jenner shut his eyes again.

CHAPTER
TWENTY-THREE

"IF THAT MAN WERE ANY CLOSER, I COULD LEAN OUT the window and kiss him," said Lydia, looking at the side mirror.

"I do not think he would turn into a prince, Miss Fairchild."

"Maybe he'd turn into a frog. That would be an improvement. John Lloyd, what's wrong?"

"Why should you think something is wrong, Miss Fairchild? Have I perhaps turned into a frog?"

"No jokes, please. I'm tired, hungry, my side hurts, and I want a straight answer. I saw your face when the desk clerk unlocked Amy's room. You were surprised. Did you expect to find her dead?"

"We are developing an almost symbiotic relationship, Miss Fairchild, and I confess to feeling some tribulation."

She unfastened her seat belt and slid close enough to touch his arm. "Please, John Lloyd. Don't close me out with one of your polysyllabic statements that even a philosophy major couldn't decipher."

His fingers tightened on the steering wheel. "A symbiotic relationship, Miss Fairchild, is one in which two or more organisms form a dependence on one another, often to the detriment of one of the organisms. A close relationship with me would be detrimental to you. However, I am having more difficulty remembering that unpleasant fact, particularly when you demonstrate a perceptiveness of my innermost thoughts.''

''If that means you're a bad influence, let me worry about that. Even you admit I'm a big girl. Now answer me before I have to get physical again.''

She could see his frown and sense his reluctance and knew if he decided not to share his thoughts with her, there was nothing she could do about it. John Lloyd would definitely be impervious to a wheedling female. She wasn't sure how to wheedle anyway. She'd never cared to share anyone's thoughts badly enough to learn. Until now.

John Lloyd sighed. ''I would not have been surprised to find Amy dead. Evil feeds upon itself, Miss Fairchild, and in spite of all my efforts, evil is increasing. With each passing incident, the motives for murder are spreading like a stone thrown in a pond. Soon, each participant will have a sufficiently strong motive and, at that point when motive, means, and opportunity meet, murder will occur. My only hope to avoid that situation is to keep my clients under my watchful eye so none will have the opportunity. And pray that Sergeant Schroder can find enough evidence to support my reconstruction and arrest Amy Steele. Once the source of evil is isolated, then Jim Steele and his family can reclaim their lives.''

''Are you saying those people you have been defending so hard are capable of murder?''

''Every human is capable of murder, Miss Fairchild. To think otherwise is to cling to a childish illusion.''

''You are incredibly cynical, John Lloyd.'' She scooted back across the seat.

''It is the price of wisdom, Miss Fairchild.''

''Then I don't want to be wise.'' Her voice trailed off

as she peered ahead. "John Lloyd, there's a car parked up there."

He slammed on his brakes and stopped just short of the car. The door on the driver's side stood open, and Lydia stared at it. "That's odd," she said. "The dome light is out."

"It's Amy Steele's car," John Lloyd said, leaning over to retrieve a flashlight from the glove compartment. "Stay here, Miss Fairchild." He opened his door and climbed out awkwardly.

Lydia opened her own door and slid out, wincing at the pain in her side. "When are you going to stop giving me orders, John Lloyd?" she asked, catching up to him as he focused the light on the driver's side of the green Mercury. Before John Lloyd blocked her line of vision, she had time to see the thin ribbon of blood that traced its way out of Rutherford's left nostril and the boneless way his left leg hung out of the car. "Was it a wreck? Is he badly hurt?" she asked, trying to remember the rudiments of first aid she learned one summer.

"He is dead, Miss Fairchild." Just then Schroder and Jenner came running up, the light from their flashlights making bobbing patterns in the darkness. "Rutherford," he said to Schroder, jerking his head toward the Mercury.

"But he can't be," said Lydia with disbelief.

"Blunt instrument of some kind," said Schroder, straightening up. "Caved in the back of his skull. Amy Steele's not in the car."

"Christ!" screamed Jenner. "She's over here."

Lydia whirled and stumbled around the car, ignoring John Lloyd's repeated order for her to stop. Jenner knelt on the ground, the powerful flashlight throwing a circle of light around Amy's body, glinting off the pale blue marbles that had been living eyes. She looked so obscene lying there on her side with her skirt hiked up past her thighs and her tongue protruding from her purple face.

Lydia turned away and walked numbly into John Lloyd's arms. She grabbed him around the waist and held on tightly, feeling the pain in her swollen hand and wounded arm recede to the back of her mind in the face of this new horror.

She looked up. "John Lloyd, I think I'm about to have a case of the vapors." She barely had time to notice the shock on his face before she closed her eyes and let the darkness take her.

CHAPTER
TWENTY-FOUR

JENNER LOOKED UP IN TIME TO SEE LYDIA CRUMPLE AND John Lloyd catch her sagging body. Looking at Amy Steele's corpse was enough to make a cop want to faint, much less a young woman who didn't see stiffs every day. Given the physical resemblance between the two women, Lydia Fairchild must have felt she was looking at her own body. He wasn't surprised at her fainting. What did surprise him was the four-letter word he thought he heard John Lloyd Branson utter as he picked up Lydia's limp body. He wasn't used to hearing the lawyer use any words with only four letters, much less that particular one.

"Schroder, the car door," said John Lloyd, limping slowly toward the Continental. As Schroder jerked open the door, the lawyer sat down heavily on the seat, still holding Lydia on his lap. Jenner saw Schroder raise his eyebrows at John Lloyd's actions. Leave it to Schroder to expect Branson to toss Lydia on the car seat like a sack of flour, Jenner thought. The man had no appreciation for what it might be like to have a lapful of Lydia Fairchild.

Branson didn't either, Jenner decided a few seconds later as he watched John Lloyd lightly slap Lydia's face. "Hey," he protested. "That's no way to treat a lady."

John Lloyd looked up at him. "You are correct, Sergeant," he said. "There is another way." He took a cigar out of his pocket, lit it, and proceeded to blow smoke in her face.

It worked. Lydia regained consciousness with a coughing fit. She opened her eyes, fanned the air in front of her face, and glared at John Lloyd. "That stinks," she said clearly.

"My apologies, Miss Fairchild. I was forced to improvise. However, if you intend having the vapors very frequently, I shall obtain a supply of smelling salts."

She rested her head against his shoulder. "Don't bother. I don't intend to faint again because I don't intend to look at any more dead people. Not dead like that anyway. Why were her hands tied to one foot like that?"

Schroder cleared his throat and Jenner was treated to the sight of the burly investigator fumbling for words. It was obvious he didn't like discussing murder with civilians. "I think she was tied up like a steer."

"Wrong age bovine, Sergeant Schroder," said John Lloyd. "Her hands and one ankle were tied together in front of her body similar to the procedure used when roping a calf for branding. Cowboys throw a loop around a calf's neck, wrap the end of the rope around their saddle horn, leap off their horse and force the calf to the ground, then tie the animal's feet together. A skilled roper on a good horse can complete the whole procedure in under thirty seconds. Of course, the cowboy doesn't ordinarily choke the calf to death first."

"Oh, God!" Lydia cried and burrowed her face into his shoulder again.

Jenner felt like burying his head somewhere, too. Did Branson have to be so graphic? His word pictures were enough to make a strong man puke.

"Jim Steele a good roper, Branson?" asked Schroder. "Or will you try to convince me that Amy Steele knocked

Rutherford in the head, then roped and tied herself, choking in the process?''

John Lloyd eased Lydia off his lap and stood up. "If you have a radio in your vehicle, perhaps you'd like to call the sheriff's department and have them call the Special Crimes Unit. I shall require more light than what our flashlights will provide.''

"Just what the hell are you planning, Branson?'' demanded Schroder.

"Before Miss Fairchild's attack of the vapors, I noticed some hoofprints by the body. To correctly interpret the meaning of those prints, I shall require light. Unless you are an expert in reading track, Sergeant.''

"I suppose *you* are?'' asked Schroder.

"I was fascinated by the skill when I was a child,'' said John Lloyd. "I have acquired some expertise since that time.''

"Is there any subject you *don't* have a little expertise in, Branson?''

"I am a very poor musician, Sergeant.''

"First time I ever heard you admit you were poor at anything. Secure the scene, Jenner, while I see if I can raise the sheriff's department,'' said Schroder, moving toward his car.

"Secure it? How? And who am I supposed to guard it against? Jackrabbits?''

"Just don't mess up the tracks,'' said Schroder over his shoulder. "I want to hear what kind of story our so-called expert makes out of them.''

The road was lined with cars before sunrise. The Hemphill County Sheriff's Department was there in force, as well as the big van belonging to Special Crimes and several investigators' vehicles. Portable lights made working the scene as hot and uncomfortable as working on a stage. It was a stage, Jenner realized. Each actor had a specific role. One Special Crimes investigator sketched the scene, locating each hoofprint, footprint, piece of paper, and any other miscellaneous physical evidence. A photographer took pictures from several different angles, with a log being kept of what each photograph was. An officer numbered, labeled, and initialed each piece of evidence and also kept a written log of each item. Jenner had the feeling that if he stood in one place long enough, someone would photograph, number, label, and initial him, then stuff him in a plastic bag and put him in the Special Crimes van.

But the actor playing the principal role was John Lloyd Branson. He began with Amy's body. He examined the knot on the rope around the victim's neck, then the method of tying the ankle and hands. Schroder, for once without a cigarette in his mouth, leaned over him. "Well?" he demanded.

John Lloyd put both hands on the knee of his good leg and pushed himself up. His face looked drawn. "The knot on the strangulation weapon is the so-called hangman's knot, which, as you can imagine, is not the average cowboy's choice for roping a calf. The inference is that the person meeting Amy Steele came prepared to murder her. The rope around her limbs is tied in the usual way. By the scratch marks on the throat, I would infer that she was tied after death. Otherwise, her hands would not have been free to claw at the rope."

"We'll see what the pathologist says, Branson, but I think I can detect some bleeding from rope burns around her ankle," said Schroder. "That argues that she was still alive when she was tied. You know what that means."

John Lloyd nodded. "If she was still alive when she was tied, then the charge is capital murder—and the penalty is life imprisonment or death by lethal injection."

"I think the D.A. will ask for the death penalty, Branson. Let's face it, this is a pretty heinous crime. Steele should've just shot her. Then it would've been plain murder and he might've gotten parole in time to see his kid graduate from high school. But by killing her with all the fancy touches, treating her like she was no more than a calf fit for slaughter, that's not going to set well with a jury. The D.A. will bring up those other two attempts during the punishment phase of the trial, and the jury will vote Jim Steele a meeting with the needle.''

John Lloyd's eyes resembled two burning coals. ''Jim Steele was innocent of those incidents. I proved Amy Steele was responsible. There was even some of your precious trace evidence on the second incident in the form of those muddy shoes and the mosquito bites.''

''She sure as hell wasn't responsible for this, was she?'' Schroder asked, waving his arm at the corpse. ''You know the old saying, Branson, third time lucky? Jim Steele finally got lucky on this third attempt.''

''Would you like me to look at the hoofprints now?'' asked John Lloyd, his face expressionless.

''You're not going to admit you were wrong, are you, Branson? Hell, it doesn't matter, not now. Tell me your story about the tracks.''

''Follow me in single file, please, so you will not destroy a print.''

Jenner noticed the lawyer's drawl had taken another vacation. That meant someone was in trouble, because Branson without a drawl was a dangerous man.

''There are scuffle marks, broken grass, displaced pebbles—which means Amy Steele was roped here and undoubtedly pulled off her feet. She floundered for a few seconds attempting to free herself, then became unconscious. Some of the marks are the result of the murderer's tugging the arms and leg into position. There are no hoofprints because the horse was some distance away. Due to the rocky nature of the ground, there are no identifiable footprints either.''

''Where was the horse?'' asked Jenner, more to erase the image of a woman being jerked off her feet by means of a rope around her neck, than because he had any real interest in knowing.

John Lloyd rubbed his forehead as if he were in pain. ''The hoofprints should be between the body and the car. I believe the murderer dispatched Rutherford first, then chased Amy down by horseback.''

"Why do you say that?" asked Schroder.

"Because the car door was open and one foot was dangling outside. I believe someone walked up and Rutherford opened the door and started to get out when he was struck. Amy saw what happened and ran from the car, seemingly a bad decision unless you consider that she could not close the door on the driver's side in time to keep out whoever was the murderer. Her alternatives were few: stay in the car and wait, or get out of the car and run. She chose to run."

He stopped and pointed to the ground. "Here are the hoofprints. The rider roped Amy and turned the horse to the left to jerk the rope tight. Now let us backtrack the horse." He walked toward the Mercury, slightly bent over, his black eyes searching the ground. "Here is where the horse left the road. We will now walk along the edge of the road to discover from whence the horse came. In other words, where was the murderer waiting?"

"Behind this big boulder?" guessed Schroder.

"Cammie's rock," said John Lloyd softly.

"What's that mean? Is it a favorite place of Cammie Armstrong's?" asked Schroder.

"No, it's not her favorite place at all. It is the site of the wreck that scarred her. It means nothing, Sergeant, except that it is the only landmark between the highway and the ranch headquarters. It is the logical place for the murderer to arrange to meet Amy."

"You got pictures of all this?" Schroder abruptly asked the photographer.

"Yes, Sergeant. And sketches, too," answered the photographer. "You want some molds of those tracks?"

"Might as well," answered Schroder. "I don't think a horse can testify, but I don't want to overlook a damn thing. If there's so much as a rusty tin can anywhere in the area, I want a picture of it, and then I want it processed and put in the van. You got all that?"

"We hear you," answered the photographer, and Jenner suspected the man wanted to kick Schroder's butt for telling him how to do his job. "And we've done it. I've got pictures of beer cans, gum wrappers, folded up pieces of cellophane that I guess came from candy, and some rubbers. Looks like a bunch of teenagers had an orgy out here."

"Where'd you find the stuff?" demanded Schroder, glaring at the police photographer.

"Beer cans and the rubbers were in front of that big rock, the cellophane about ten feet from the body, and the gum wrappers by the road."

"I hope you didn't touch any of them," said Schroder. "The department fingerprint specialist can raise prints on damn near anything."

"Give us some credit, Sergeant," the photographer complained. "We know what we're doing."

"I just don't want any mistakes on this one. It's capital murder, son; one mistake, and the murderer could walk." He turned to John Lloyd. "All right, Branson. Where did that damn horse come from?"

John Lloyd was hunkered down staring at the ground. He stumbled as he got up, and Schroder grabbed his arm to steady him. "The horseman waited here, behind the rock. You can make out the blurred hoofprints of an animal restlessly shifting his weight. I am afraid your men will find even more miscellaneous clutter. In addition to shielding a murderer from view, this side of the boulder is also a favored trysting place for lovers." He stuck his hands in his pockets. "As for the fingerprints, I must inform you that you are hoping for the unlikely. A good horseman always wears gloves."

"I appreciate the information, Branson, but it's not the information I asked for. Where did the horse come from?"

"You are standing on Bar-S property, Sergeant, and have been on Bar-S property since turning off the highway. I am hardly so foolish as to suggest that the horse came from anywhere but the Bar-S headquarters four miles away."

"And the rider?"

CHAPTER
TWENTY-FIVE

"WHAT'S HAPPENING NOW?" LYDIA ASKED SHERIFF Taylor, her back to the crime scene.

"One of Schroder's men is carrying another white sheet. I expect they're getting ready to take Amy's body."

Lydia swallowed. Rutherford's body had already been removed, also in a white sheet. She hadn't watched that removal either. "Why a white sheet?" she asked.

The sheriff rubbed his jaw. "I don't know. Maybe in case something falls off the body it'll show up against the white."

She swallowed again. "I wish I hadn't asked. Why aren't you down there? It's your county."

"I looked at the body. Bodies," he said, correcting himself. "I made my presence known, marked my territory, you might say, then I left. Schroder and his bunch are the experts. I'm just a sheriff of a not very populous county. I take care of fights, track down a burglar every now and then, sometimes even pick up a juvenile who's got in trouble. I've even had a killing every once in a while, but it's usually easy to decide who's guilty. Gen-

erally, they come apart and tell me all about it because
there's nothing cold-blooded about it, you see. It's just
that somebody got too mad and grabbed up the first thing
handy and let his victim have it. Like Mrs. Dinwittie,
John Lloyd's secretary. She just snapped one night. But
this kind of thing is over my head. Nobody's going to
come forward and confess. He's going to have to be
tracked down, and for that you need someone like Schroder and his bunch with all their microscopes and chemi-
cals and lasers and whatever else kind of fancy equipment
they use. The old-fashioned detective who sits in his office and traps culprits just by using his brain is as out of
date as a buggy whip."

"But John Lloyd used sheer deduction to determine
that Amy drugged her own coffee and shot me."

"Amy did what?" asked the sheriff.

Lydia explained and the sheriff slapped his knee.
"Sounds like the kind of back-shooting thing Amy Steele
would do. I never could match up Jim Steele or any of
the rest of them with poisoning somebody's coffee. But
all that's water under the bridge, 'cause Amy didn't do
this."

His voice stopped abruptly and Lydia glanced over her
shoulder to see him staring at the crime scene. "What's
happening? What are you looking at, Sheriff?"

"They found something on the end of that rope."

"Yes. Amy's neck," said Lydia, thinking that if she
was to the point of making macabre jokes, she wasn't far
from hysteria, and hysteria was worse than the vapors.

"The other end, the one that would be wrapped around
the saddle horn. I'm going to check this out," he said,
straightening his Stetson and pulling up his pants. Like
an old western sheriff getting ready for a shoot-out with
the bad guy, thought Lydia.

"Wait a minute! I'm going, too," she said, holding
her side as she ran after him.

"Amy's body's still there," he said without breaking
stride.

"I'll just look at the rope."

Schroder was standing nose to nose with John Lloyd. "All good riders wear gloves, do they? Then what's this on the rope? Ketchup? Or maybe your murderer had a nosebleed? In a pig's eye, Branson! Take a look through the magnifying glass. There's blood on that rope, and a little hide, too. Enough to send to the FBI lab. Somebody let the rope slip and got himself burned."

"Hey, Sergeant Schroder." An attractive woman in her late thirties who looked like everyone's idea of an executive secretary—except secretaries didn't wear .357's strapped to their hips, thought Lydia hysterically—was examining the rope. The woman continued. "There's some fibers caught in the hemp about eighteen inches from the blood smear."

Schroder crouched down and looked. "Blue, aren't they?" he asked the female officer. She nodded, and Schroder bounced up like a beach ball with legs. "We got him, Branson. I'm going to strip every piece of blue fabric out of that ranch house, including the curtains and the upholstery, if I have to, until I can match those fibers."

"Fibers are not positive evidence, Sergeant," said John Lloyd. "They are not in the same classification as fingerprints."

"I've got warrants to search the property for the gun used to shoot Miss Fairchild, and to arrest Jim Steele. You going to make me get one for all the fabric, or are you going to advise your clients to let me look?"

The sun was now well above the horizon, and its rays illuminated every line in John Lloyd's face. And there were lines, Lydia thought, lines she hadn't noticed yesterday. His voice, however, was as sharp and decisive as ever. "I do not condone capital murder, Sergeant. I will erect no legal barricades between the guilty and justice. The guilty person must render an accounting and meet society's bill with payment in kind. I ask twenty-four hours to assist in preparing the accounting."

"No deals, Branson," replied Schroder, and walked

away, motioning several of the Special Crimes officers
to follow.

"If thy right hand offend thee, cut it off," quoted Lydia softly. "These people are your friends, and you're
talking about them as if they were strangers. How can
you be so cold, John Lloyd?"

"Are you suggesting that I deliberately shield a murderer, Miss Fairchild?" he asked.

"Of course not! But you don't need to promise Schroder you'll serve up Jim Steele's head on a platter, either.
Payment in kind! Are you planning to execute him yourself?"

Without answering he turned and limped toward the
Continental. Overtaking his uneven stride, she grabbed
his arm. "Why don't you answer me? Because you can't?
Defending Jim Steele grates on you, doesn't it? Jim Steele
is a fool, you said. Jim Steele is incapable of thinking!
Maybe so, but he's a man, and he makes mistakes."

"Reducing this foul deed to the level of a mistake requires more romantic wishful thinking than I believed
even you capable of, Miss Fairchild."

"That isn't what I meant, and you know it, John Lloyd
Branson! I mean he's an ordinary man with all the weaknesses of a man. And he's your *client*; you've sworn an
oath to defend him no matter what kind of a person he
is. But you don't even care. He didn't meet your almighty standards, so he's not worthy of you. Why don't
you offer to strap him down to that gurney on death row?
Or would you rather push the plunger for the lethal injection?"

He still said nothing, his black eyes absolutely expressionless. He freed his arm from her grip.

"Damn you, answer me!" she cried.

"Our symbiotic relationship seems to be failing, Miss
Fairchild, and I must confess to being relieved. I would
not burden you with experiencing my feelings on this
matter." He opened her door and reached for her hand
to help her in the car.

She ignored the open door and climbed in the backseat instead. "You have no feelings, John Lloyd!"

"I cannot permit a murderer to escape retribution, Miss Fairchild."

"Even God promises mercy, John Lloyd."

"So do I, Miss Fairchild, but not in a manner of which you will approve."

CHAPTER
TWENTY-SIX

JENNER FELT AS IF HE WERE TRAPPED IN AN OLD WEST-
ern movie. When he and Schroder drove up to the ranch
house leading a caravan of Special Crimes officers, he
expected to see rifle barrels sticking out of every avail-
able window. The women would be crouching behind
their men to reload rifles as they were emptied. Horses
would be saddled and waiting at the back door in case
the Branson gang had to make a run for it. Branson gang?
Why not the Steele gang? Because, he thought, John
Lloyd Branson was the perfect outlaw chieftain. He was
smart, tough, hard, and, Jenner suspected, ruthless. Besides, he'd been giving the orders all along. But someone
in that house had been challenging his authority. Someone went behind his back and murdered Amy. That
someone was either brave or stupid, because in Jenner's
experience, men like John Lloyd Branson were dangerous men to cross. Someone twisted the tiger's tail, and
the beast was in a rage.

"You going to tell them to come out with their hands
up?" he asked Schroder as the investigator heaved himself out of the car.

Schroder flashed him a look that would have blistered an elephant's hide. "You think this is a damn posse?"

"Yeah. 1980s version."

"You're full of shit, Jenner," he said as he started toward the house.

Jenner looked around at the Special Crimes officers climbing out of the big van and from several cars, and at the deputies spilling out of Hemphill County Sheriff's Department vehicles to gather in a loose semicircle facing the house. The door opened, and there was a barrage of snapping sounds as lawmen of whatever jurisdiction unfastened holster flaps to rest their hands on the .357's they all wore. Branson stepped out, followed by Jim Steele—the outlaw chieftain and his lieutenant. Hands tightened around pistol grips. Branson stepped down from the porch, followed by Steele. They stopped in the middle of the yard.

"Sure feels like the shoot-out at O.K. Corral," said Jenner, keeping step with Schroder. His own holster was fastened. He hadn't shot anyone in the line of duty yet and he didn't intend to start with a bedeviled creature like Jim Steele.

Other than another blistering look, Schroder ignored him. He stopped a few feet from John Lloyd. "Mr. James Steele," he said, but looked directly at Branson. Schroder knew who called the shots in the Branson gang.

"I am James Steele." Poor devil sounded numb, Jenner thought.

"Mr. Steele," continued Schroder, still looking at John Lloyd. "I have a warrant to search your property and personal effects for a .22 caliber rifle suspected of having been used to shoot Miss Lydia Fairchild at about eight-thirty in the evening of June fifteenth of this year. This warrant is duly signed by the judge of the 251st District Court of the State of Texas. This is your copy, sir." John Lloyd stretched out his hand and the investigator gave him the document.

"You may execute your warrant, Sergeant Schroder," John Lloyd said. He and Jim Steele retraced their steps and disappeared into the house, closing the door behind them.

Flaps were snapped down over guns, and the officers gathered around Schroder who divided them into search groups. "You all heard me. We're looking for a .22 caliber rifle. If one of you Hemphill County deputies finds it, *don't* touch it! Call me or Sergeant Jenner here." The groups dispersed to the barn, the toolshed, the pump house, the old bunkhouse now used for storage, the stables, all the many outbuildings found on a working ranch.

"We got them surrounded," said Jenner as he followed Schroder up to the door of the house.

"I think losing a little sleep has affected your mind," observed Schroder as he knocked on the door.

"A little sleep! Try two nights' worth. I'm so tired I don't know what I'm doing."

"I noticed that. You're going to have to toughen up if you're going work in Special Crimes."

"I'm *not* going to work in Special Crimes! I'd rather resign from the department and be a security guard at a bank. At least I'd be around a little higher class of people."

"I doubt that many farmers and ranchers laboring to meet interest payments would agree that bankers constitute a higher class of people, Sergeant Jenner," said John Lloyd as he opened the door in time to overhear Jenner's comment.

"They beat the hell out of dead bodies," retorted Jenner, thinking that John Lloyd looked about half dead himself. The skin over his cheekbones had a gray tinge, and his eyes were red-rimmed and sunken.

Nobody else in the house looked much better, he observed as he and Schroder entered the living room. Everybody sat or stood with all the animation of a zombie. Jim Steele leaned against the fireplace as if he were afraid his legs wouldn't support him. Dr. Bailey and Christy sat motionless on one couch. Cammie huddled by the hall door, one hand covering her scarred cheek.

Even Lydia, sitting at the gaming table, looked more like
a raddled saloon girl than a professional woman.

Only Alice Steele, whose face resembled a parchment-
covered skull, showed any sign of life. Her turquoise
eyes glittered with defiance as she greeted Schroder from
her wheelchair. "John Lloyd tells me you're going to
search the house again, only this time you're taking our
clothes. Are we going to stripped naked and whipped
down the street for everyone to spit at, Sergeant?"

Schroder looked uncomfortable. "No, ma'am," he
said, making an effort to sound reassuring. "We just need
everything blue—pants and shirts and such. None of your
silk dresses."

Alice made a snorting sound. "Silk dresses and I don't
go together." She looked over her shoulder at her son.
"I guess you'll be working the ranch in your bare behind, Jim. He's"—she jerked her thumb at Schroder—
"going to take all your Levi's. You going to strip Cammie's shirt right off her back? It's blue. And what about
my daughter-in-law? Can she plead her belly like women
in the family way used to do, or will you take her clothes,
too?"

Jenner thought that Schroder ought to recruit Alice
Steele into Special Crimes. She was tougher than anyone
in the room. Except maybe John Lloyd.

"Mother, please," said Jim Steele. "He's just doing
his job."

"His job is to put us all in jail," snapped Alice. "But
nothing says we have to cooperate with him."

"Hear, hear!" shouted Lydia, standing up.

"Sit down, Miss Fairchild!" John Lloyd's voice
snapped out. "This is not a campus demonstration. You
will not interfere again."

Schroder's face was red up to his hairline. "Mrs.
Steele, we will have to have any blue clothes any of you
are wearing. It would be more pleasant if you would cooperate."

"Pleasant! You're not a guest and this isn't Sunday

dinner. Why should I make things pleasant for you?'' demanded Alice.

Jenner noticed Schroder had that impassive expression on his face that all cops have when dealing with obstreperous civilians. ''I wasn't talking about myself, ma'am. I get paid to do unpleasant jobs. I just wanted to make it easy on you. But I'll have the clothes one way or the other.''

This was it, Jenner thought: two gunmen facing each other at high noon. Would Alice Steele back down, or would Schroder have to use the very real power that he could command? John Lloyd's voice broke the impasse. ''Alice, I can delay this confrontation, perhaps for several days, but ultimately you will lose. In the interest of justice and of a final resolution, submit now with what dignity you can muster. To force the issue would only lead to more tragedy. Trust me in this matter.''

Jenner shivered as though someone had walked across his grave. Something was very wrong. The standard legal tactic was to promise cooperation while maneuvering to avoid it. It was a well-understood ritual between the police and the attorney. To see John Lloyd almost bludgeoning his clients into cooperation was like watching a dog pass by a fireplug without wetting it down.

Schroder frowned and studied the lawyer before finally speaking. ''Mr. Branson gave you some good advice, ma'am. If you'll excuse us now, Sergeant Jenner and I will begin our search.''

''I thought you were in a hurry for our clothes,'' said Alice.

''When Sergeant Ortega arrives, she will accompany the ladies while they change.''

''You mean we have to do a striptease for one of you?'' asked Alice.

''No! I won't let anyone see me!'' screamed Cammie. ''I won't let anybody look at me and pretend my scars don't make them sick.'' She wrapped her arms around her body and crouched down against the wall like an animal expecting a beating.

Christy and Dr. Bailey both jumped off the couch as if someone had tied a string through the top of their heads and jerked. Alice turned her wheelchair and rolled toward the huddled woman. Jim pushed through to kneel by Cammie and shield her from Schroder's eyes. Lydia hesitantly rose and walked toward the group. Only John Lloyd didn't move from his place by the window.

"Cammie!" His voice cut through the comforting sounds the others were making and Cammie's ruined face peered over Jim's shoulder at the lawyer. "Cammie," he continued in a softer voice. "I will not let anyone see you. Insofar as it is in my power, I will protect your dignity. Do you understand?"

She nodded, and John Lloyd turned to Schroder. "Special arrangements will have to be made, Sergeant. I will not have her shamed before others."

Schroder's face looked as kind as Jenner had ever seen it. "We'll arrange something, ma'am. Don't you worry." He jerked his head toward Jim Steele's bedroom. "Come on, Jenner."

"Poor damn woman," said Jenner in a low voice as he and the investigator left the room. "I don't blame her, Schroder. It's bad enough to look like that without somebody staring like you were a freak in a sideshow. And Alice Steele, too. I got a feeling she hates being crippled. The idea of some stranger watching her change clothes must make her sick at her stomach. Why are you pushing them so hard? Surely you don't suspect a crippled old lady and a woman whose body is so burned and scarred, she could barely hold a rope?"

Schroder grunted as he checked a gun cabinet in the hall. "If Alice Steele decided to murder Amy, she'd do it—even if she had to crawl on and off that horse."

"And Christy Steele," continued Jenner, getting madder the longer he thought about it. "She's a nice, sweet little lady."

"Worst murderer I ever arrested was a seventeen-year-old schoolgirl with the kindest face I ever saw. She shot her mother, father, and two brothers, then fixed herself breakfast and went to class. Don't let a sweet face fool you."

The police photographer burst through the front door followed by an exhausted-looking Sheriff Taylor. "Sergeant Schroder! We found the rifle, or anyway we found a .22 with two rounds fired. Jones is bringing it up. He's already printed it."

"And?" demanded Schroder.

"No fingerprints, just a few smudges on the barrel and stock. He raised some prints on the bullets, though."

"Where did you find it?"

"In the gun rack of a pickup. Registration in the glove compartment said James Steele."

Sheriff Taylor pushed his hat to the back of his head. "It's Jim's pickup, all right."

A lanky man in horn-rim glasses that magnified his eyes to owllike proportions came through the door carrying a rifle. "This is it, Sergeant. I'm pretty sure this is it. We'll have ballistics check it."

"But no prints?" asked Schroder, taking the rifle.

"Nary a one. If I didn't know better, I'd say somebody wiped it clean," said Jones.

Schroder sighted along the rifle barrel, then held the gun across his body. "I want that pickup gone over thoroughly. I want it vacuumed. Any mud you find should be compared to the soil samples we collected at the riverbank. Check for leaves, grasses, weeds, anything that matches up to the vegetation samples from the river."

Jones shook his head. "No mud in that truck. And it hasn't been cleared lately, either. Got dust an inch thick on the dashboard. There's some horse manure on the gas pedal. Want a sample of that?"

"Dust that truck inside and out," ordered Schroder. "I want every print lifted."

Jones nodded. "Sure, Sergeant," he said as he and the photographer left.

"Branson was right, wasn't he?" asked Jenner. "That's what you're thinking, isn't it? No mud in the truck and no mosquito bites. No prints on the gun except on the bullets. It all adds up, Schroder. Amy Steele set up her own shooting. What does that do to your case against Jim Steele?''

"I'd like to hear that myself, Schroder," said Sheriff Taylor.

"Not a damn thing. I got a gun that I have reason to believe was used in a shooting. That gun was found in the suspect's vehicle, and I'm betting the fingerprints on the bullets in that gun belong to the suspect. A pickup will go places a car won't, like a muddy riverbank. Maybe he never got out of that truck. Maybe he shot Lydia Fairchild from inside that truck. Not much chance of getting mud on your boots, or mosquito bites on your face, if you sit in a vehicle with the windows rolled up. Besides, there's something both of you are forgetting.''

"What?" asked Jenner.

"If Amy Steele stole the rifle, how did she get it back to the truck? He admits driving around most the evening of the shooting. She sure didn't flag him down to return his rifle. And you guarded her door all that night and you said she checked on you every few minutes. The hearing lasted most of the day yesterday, and she was dead by three o'clock this morning. Branson's real persuasive, but his story's got a hole in it as big as a .22 caliber rifle.''

CHAPTER
TWENTY-SEVEN

LYDIA RESTED HER HEAD ON THE GAMING TABLE, CUSH-
ioned on her one good arm. The other felt too swollen
and ached too badly for her to even think about raising
it high enough to rest on the table. In fact, she ached all
over and her face felt hot and dry. She wondered if she
should tell Dr. Bailey.

After raising her head to speak to him, she abruptly
changed her mind. Everybody in the room looked worse
than she felt. The physician himself could have passed
for a shrunken old gnome. He was mechanically patting
Christy's hand as though someone had wound him up
and he hadn't yet run down. Jim Steele was holding her
other hand against his face as if it were a talisman
against disaster, while Christy rested her head against
his shoulder. Lydia could see her lips moving as she
spoke softly to the man she'd loved all her life. Jim
bent his head suddenly and pressed it against her hair.
His shoulders jerked spasmodically as if he were
crying. Lydia felt her own eyes blur with tears.

She turned her head to hide her tears and saw that she
wasn't the only one crying. Cammie sat huddled on the

chair nearest the door, watching Jim and Christy and making no attempt to blot the tears that ran down her cheeks. Alice sat in her wheelchair.

John Lloyd prowled the room, his uneven gait causing an irregular thudding sound as his boots hit the wooden floor. He looked stern and lonely as he paced. Only once had he stopped, and Lydia felt ashamed every time she thought about it, and she was thinking about it far too much. John Lloyd had knelt and taken Cammie in his arms, kissing her briefly on her unblemished cheek. His lips had moved to her ear and Lydia thought she saw him whisper something before he released Cammie and rose awkwardly to his feet. He squeezed her hand, then turned his back and walked away to begin his pacing again. It was a poignant scene, one to touch a romantic heart. Yet all Lydia had felt was envy.

Suddenly, John Lloyd stopped pacing and looked toward the door. Lydia sat up as Schroder walked in clutching a rifle. "Oh, no," she whispered and looked at John Lloyd.

Schroder stopped by the table. Jenner and a very pale Sheriff Taylor flanked him on either side. "James Steele," said Schroder, and Lydia trembled at the way his hoarse voice seemed to reach every corner of the room. "James Steele, is this your rifle?"

Jim gently released Christy and rose to his feet. He walked toward Schroder, staring at the rifle the investigator held. He stopped a few feet away and raised his eyes to look at Schroder. "Yes, it's mine."

"Where did you discover the gun?" asked John Lloyd, coming up to Jim's side.

"In the gun rack in his pickup," replied Sheriff Taylor.

John Lloyd rubbed the faint blond stubble on his chin. "Not hidden in the barn rafters, nor under hay bales, but out in plain view?"

"That's right, Branson," said Schroder impatiently and turned his attention back to Jim.

"Where were you between midnight and three o'clock this morning, Steele?" Lydia noticed the investigator had dropped the formal address.

"Asleep in his bed like the rest of us," answered Alice, her hands wrapped like claws around the arms of her wheelchair.

"He was sleeping in your room with you, ma'am?" asked Schroder, swinging his large head toward Alice.

"No! But he was asleep all the same. Just ask his wife."

Schroder, his brows drawn together in a frown, turned his head and looked at Christy. "Mrs. Steele?"

Christy cleared her throat to answer, but Jim interrupted. "I slept in the old bunkhouse. Christy will be the target of enough gossip without my sleeping with her before we marry again."

"Your sense of propriety is commendable," remarked John Lloyd. "But in this instance, quite stupid."

"The bunkhouse close to the barn?" asked Schroder.

"That's the only bunkhouse there is," snapped Jim.

"The barn where I believe you keep horses?"

"There are a couple being stabled there. A few more are in the corral next to the barn, and the rest are in the pasture south of the house."

"Did you take a little ride this morning between midnight and three, maybe down to that big boulder between here and the highway?"

Jim looked wildly around the room. "I—I had trouble sleeping. I rode around for a while."

"Stop!" It was the first time Lydia had ever heard John Lloyd shout. "I cannot permit this."

"But you don't know!" began Jim.

"I know everything," interrupted John Lloyd. "And I understand what you do not."

"Let me see your hands and wrists, Steele," said Schroder, taking a step toward him.

John Lloyd grabbed Jim's hands and held them behind the rancher's back. "You may not do a body search without a warrant, Schroder," he warned. "If you do so, any evidence uncovered will not be admissible in court.''

''What are you playing at, Branson? You practically demanded I confiscate your clients' clothes, and believe me, a fiber comparison is going to put a noose around Jim Steele's neck just as quickly as my finding a rope burn. Plus I'll get there eventually anyway. We'll match the blood and tissue on that rope to his, and that'll be the icing on the cake.''

''I will not permit a body search,'' repeated John Lloyd. ''Not on Jim, nor on any of the others.''

''You're just dragging this out, Branson, so I'll bring it to an end myself.'' He pulled a document out of his pocket. ''James Steele, I have a warrant for your arrest on suspicion of homicide.''

There were gasps and the sounds of sobbing from Christy as Schroder held out the warrant toward John Lloyd. The lawyer ignored it and shoved Jim Steele gently toward the couch. ''Comfort your wife,'' he said.

He turned back to Schroder. ''It is indeed time to bring this to an end so that the healing of the wounds left by Amy may begin, and the self-guilt that has been an impediment to justice be expiated. I suggest you gentlemen sit down. The explanation is lengthy and complex.''

Schroder, Jenner, and the sheriff joined Lydia at the table, Schroder with a suspicious look on his face. ''If this is another one of your fairy stories, Branson, I'll arrest you for interfering with a police officer.''

''You are free to do so if, at the end of my discourse, you disbelieve me. Then we will all be forced to wait for the results of those analyses you depend upon so heavily.'' He hesitated a moment, looking across the room. ''I have the murderer's written confession in my briefcase.''

Lydia gasped and Schroder leaped from his chair as if a spring had suddenly unwound. ''Jenner, find that briefcase.''

John Lloyd held up his hand. ''No!'' he said sharply.

"I am voluntarily offering the written confession. If you take it by force, without a warrant, then the confession will be inadmissible in court, just as if it were a spoken confession obtained under duress. Do not let your impatience be your undoing. I will have my way in this."

"He's got you over a barrel, Schroder," remarked Sheriff Taylor with a speculative look. "I know things about John Lloyd that you don't, and I suspect that he's going to pay kind of a high price of his own before this is over. This is still my county, and I say let him alone."

"You may regret your generosity, Sheriff Taylor," warned John Lloyd. "Cammie," he said, his eyes never leaving Schroder's. "My briefcase is either in the dining room or the kitchen. Everything is in there. Hurry, please; the sergeant is impatient."

Cammie hesitated a moment, her eyes going to each person in turn. Lydia couldn't stand any more. She jumped up. "I'll find it, John Lloyd. You're a bastard to ask Cammie to be the Judas against one of her own. Can't you see she doesn't want to be responsible?"

John Lloyd moved to Lydia's side, almost graceful in his rapidity, and pushed her down in her chair. He ignored her gasp of pain as her injured arm struck the edge of the table. "You will not interfere in something you do not understand." His hand moved up to cup her chin. "Lydia," he said, "I should regret treating you harshly in order to gain your cooperation, but I shall do so if I must. Will you trust me?"

She nodded. "Yes, John Lloyd," she replied. He looked both surprised and relieved at her meekness. Maybe later she'd tell him that she complied not because he ordered her to, but because he called her Lydia.

He released her and stood up. "Sergeant Schroder, I should first like to relieve your mind concerning the rifle."

"Don't tell me you can explain that away, Branson."

"Don't you think it suspicious that the rifle was not hidden, Sergeant?" asked John Lloyd, his attention on the other end of the room. He must be waiting for Cammie, Lydia thought.

The room was silent as everyone waited for Schroder's reply. "I just thought he was stupid. He had to guess we'd look for it."

"Amy guessed it certainly, and returned the rifle to its original place for two reasons: so Jim would not miss it and become suspicious, and so you could find it easily."

Schroder pushed his chair back. "Come on, Branson. Give me credit for not being dumb. Amy couldn't have returned that gun. She didn't have an opportunity. Either she was watched, or Jim Steele was in that truck right up to when she was killed."

John Lloyd smiled, and Lydia shivered. It was the most unpleasant smile she'd ever seen. "Yesterday at ten o'clock, the Steeles, with Cammie and Dr. Bailey, were seated at the counsel table at the courthouse. If my powers of observation are not faulty, I believe you and Sergeant Jenner were seated directly behind them. Amy Steele did not arrive until nearly eleven o'clock, an hour late. An hour was more than enough time to drive out here, replace the rifle, and return to town for the hearing."

Schroder's expression was almost ludicrous. He pulled a cigarette out of his pocket and lit it, puffing until his head was haloed by a blue vapor. "I'll wait to see what the lab finds," he said. "Maybe you're right and maybe not. But I'm more interested in who roped and tied Amy Steele. Let's hear your story and see this confession."

John Lloyd moved over to the window and looked out in silence. After a few seconds his shoulders slumped and he turned around to face Schroder. "You made several false assumptions about the crime and the criminal. Coupled with your belief in Jim Steele's guilt, those assump-

tions led you to an erroneous conclusion. I do not claim
that I am a superior detective to you; only that my methods are different and, in this case, faster. Your own scientific investigations would have eventually arrived at
what I have suspected when viewing Amy's body, and
known conclusively since shortly after dawn."

"Which is?" asked Schroder.

"The identity of the murderer," replied John Lloyd.

Schroder sat back down and chuckled. "Now I know
you're full of crap, Branson. You eyeball a corpse and
follow a few hoofprints and right away you know who
the murderer is. Who do you think you are, Sherlock
Holmes? What about the blood and tissue on the rope?
And the fibers? Did you conveniently forget those pieces
of evidence? Or were you planning to prevent a body
search of Jim Steele long enough for his rope burn to
heal?"

"That was not the motive at all," replied John Lloyd.
"Because, you see, Jim Steele has no rope burn or any
other kind of injury to heal. Because you found blood on
the rope, you falsely assumed that it was Jim's based on
your false assumption that he killed Amy. That assumption is not unreasonable or illogical, because given the
proper circumstances, he is quite capable of murder. *But
not that way.* This particular method of strangulation and
subsequent mistreatment of the body requires both extreme hatred and a warped sense of justice. A hangman's
knot was used, implying her death was an execution. Her
hands and one foot were tied together, implying that she
was worth nothing more than an animal. Jim Steele simply did not possess the necessary hatred to strangle, then
bind her."

John Lloyd limped from he window to the table. He
laid his hand on Lydia's shoulder. "Your basic false
assumption—from which all others sprang—was that
because roping skills were required, Jim Steele was the
only logical suspect. That is untrue. Every person in
this room except yourself, Sergeant Jenner, and Miss
Fairchild, is an expert roper. Everyone in this room,

again excluding aforementioned individuals, either lived on, or spent a great deal of time at, this ranch. We all have ranching skills which include roping and horseback riding. I had an unfair advantage over you, Sergeant Schroder, in that I knew every participant, their strengths and weaknesses. Thus I eliminated no one from my deliberations on the basis of sex or physical infirmity."

Alice shifted her torso forward in her wheelchair. "John Lloyd, that is almost a compliment. I like the idea I'm still full of spunk and vinegar, but I'm not crazy about your thinking I might be a geriatric murderer."

John Lloyd smiled. "You do not possess the outraged sense of justice this crime required." He looked down at Schroder, sitting like an unkempt Buddha at the gaming table, and Lydia felt his hand tremble. "At the time I viewed the body, I knew that hatred and justice were the two motives. I also knew who possessed those two motives. By the time the sun rose, I had uncovered the kind of material evidence you would require as proof. But again, I had the unfair advantage of knowing personal habits which you did not. The fibers and bloodstains are also the kinds of objective evidence you can analyze and measure and examine. Without the results of any of your scientific tests, I knew who most certainly left blood on that rope. All ropers wear gloves, Sergeant, and so did the murderer. The injury suffered by the roper was high on the inside of the murderer's left wrist, not the palm as you falsely assumed. It resulted not because the murderer failed to wear gloves, but because the murderer handled the rope very awkwardly and the skin on the wrist was very thin."

John Lloyd took several objects from his pocket and threw them on the table in front of Schroder. "Your people found several of these near where the murderer waited on horseback, and one nearer the body. I found these particular samples when I arrived here. They were in the very ashtray you have been using."

Lydia looked at the cellophane neatly folded into accordion pleats and looked up at John Lloyd. ''Oh, God, no!''

His eyes were remote as he returned her glance. ''Cellophane wrappers, not from candy, but from a particular brand of beef jerky eaten only by Cammie Armstrong.''

Schroder cursed and, jumping to his feet, started running toward the door nearest the dining room. ''Goddamn you, Branson! You deliberately aided a felon in escaping.''

''No, I did not!'' stated John Lloyd. ''She will be waiting for you about three miles from the house under a very old, very large cottonwood tree near a bend in the river.'' He sank down in a chair by Lydia.

''Sheriff, we'll take your car! Which way, Branson?''

''It is accessible only by horseback,'' replied John Lloyd. ''I am sure Jim will provide you with horses.''

''The hell I will!'' Jim was on his feet looking angrily at John Lloyd. ''You can throw her to these wolves, but I'll be damned if I'll help them track her down.''

John Lloyd raised his head and Lydia sensed that it required every bit of energy he possessed. ''She committed capital murder, Jim. There is no escape from that fact. The needs of justice must be met. She realized that and accepted it.''

There was a peculiar note to John Lloyd's voice, and Lydia felt chilled. And very afraid. She kicked back her chair in her haste to rise. ''John Lloyd, your briefcase! Your gun was in your briefcase! We've got to find her!''

He grabbed her wrist. ''Do not interfere, Miss Fairchild!''

She clawed at his hand. ''Don't you understand, John Lloyd? She'll kill herself!''

Schroder slammed his fist into the wall. There was the sound of cracking plaster. ''You planned this, you son of a bitch! She's going to take the easy way out!''

''Is she, Sergeant? It has frequently puzzled me that so many take the view that self-death is the easy way. It

has always seemed to me to be the ultimate expression
of loneliness and desperation.''

"Why did you let her do it, John Lloyd?" demanded
Jim.

His eyes closed for a second before he replied, his
voice distant. "She asked me for mercy."

"Christ!" exclaimed Jenner. "I don't think much of
your mercy."

"She would have had to stand trial. She would have
been exposed in public to morbid, prying eyes. Her mutilation would have been Defense Exhibit Number One.
She would have spent years in prison, years of being the
object of pity or derision of the other prisoners; years of
no privacy where her scars could be stared at by anyone
caring to look; years of living in a small cell where no
sunshine ever reached. That—or death by her own hand
in a place where she was happy."

"Damn you, John Lloyd!" yelled Jim. "She had another choice. Schroder was ready to arrest me. Why
didn't you let him? The blood on the rope wouldn't
have matched mine! They would've had to release me.
But it would've given Cammie time to get away somewhere safe. And, God knows, she was justified in killing Amy."

"It was not for Amy's murder that I allowed her the
mercy of making a choice. It was for Rutherford's.
There was no justification for his murder. He had not
harmed her, and she did not hate him. She killed him
so there would be no witnesses, a murder strictly for
self-gain. There is no escaping the consequences of
such an act. With the single blow which ended his life,
she also ended her own. She recognized the horror of
what she had done and accepted the horror of what she
might yet do. Taking her own life was both an atone-
ment and the preservation of her own decency."

"What the hell are you talking about, John Lloyd?"
demanded Jim.

"You were also a witness, Jim. You saw her leave on
horseback last night, and she knew it."

"Cammie wouldn't have killed me!" said Jim in disbelief.

"She was a woman who understood herself well, and she was very much afraid that she might kill you." He stood up. "Sergeant Schroder, she will be waiting."

EPILOGUE

"JOHN LLOYD, I CAME TO SAY GOODBYE."

Lydia stopped in the middle of his office and waited
for some response from the silent man who stood looking
out his window at the town two stories below. She had
often found him at the window in the two months since
Cammie's suicide. What did he see? she wondered. The
shops, the red brick streets lined with parked cars and
pickups, the turrets and porches and clapboard exteriors
of the old Victorian houses, the ancient cottonwoods that
lined the banks of the Canadian River and shed their
leaves into its muddy waters? Or did he see another cottonwood, on another bend of the river, shedding its leaves
on blood-soaked ground?

And there had been blood, a lot of it, to hear Sergeant
Jenner describe the scene. Poor man! He seemed to have
as great an aversion to corpses and blood as she did. She
wondered what he was doing working on the Special
Crimes Unit.

Sergeant Jenner would have to fend for himself, she
thought, dismissing him from her mind. She was more

concerned with the man standing in front of her, the one so resolutely ignoring her.

"Do you want to borrow a shovel?" she asked.

The blond head turned until he was looking at her over his shoulder. "Once again I fail to understand your meaning, Miss Fairchild. I am constantly amazed that a woman with your command of the English language can be so obscure."

"Blow it out your ear, John Lloyd. You know perfectly well what I'm talking about. If you want to dig yourself a grave next to Cammie, I'll loan you a shovel." That comment cracked his shell, she thought with a quiver of excitement. At least he turned all the way around to face her, and his eyes showed more life than she'd seen them express in the last two months.

"I'll permit no more such insensitive comments from a callow young woman."

Better and better, she thought. "He moves, he speaks, he uses contractions," she mocked.

Blood rushed into his pale cheeks until Lydia thought he looked as if he'd borrowed Mrs. Dinwittie's rouge. "That is enough, Miss Fairchild," he said through lips that barely moved.

She verbally pushed him again. "One of the local stores is having a fabric sale. They're all sold out of sackcloth and ashes, but maybe you can buy some black crepe to drape around the office. And I'm sure the local funeral home can provide a black mourning band for your arm."

He grabbed her shoulders. "Shut up, Miss Fairchild!"

Almost there, she thought and gave him another push. "John Lloyd! I'm shocked by your rudeness to a lady."

He shook her once, hard, and she heard her own teeth snap together. Maybe she'd pushed him too far. "You are no lady, Miss Fairchild! You are a rude, brash, exasperating, irritating, ill-mannered young woman who seems to delight in provoking me."

"You forgot infuriating," she reminded him.

"Infuriating," he echoed.

"And you are an arrogant, conceited, uncompromising, stiff-necked, stubborn man who delights in tempting me."

He jerked his hands off her shoulders with all the rapidity of a man recoiling from a hot stove. "I do not recall making any overt sexual advances to you, Miss Fairchild."

"Other than a certain hot gleam in your eyes when you stripped my dress off under the guise of checking my wounds, you have been the model of propriety," she agreed.

"The hot gleam was an expression of appreciation for the beauty of the female form. In a strictly abstract sense, of course."

She wondered if he realized he was blushing. "A little honest-to-God lust would be more flattering to my ego, but what can I expect from a man who makes love in the dark?"

"I do not make love in the dark!" he bellowed, his face red up to the hairline.

"John Lloyd," she chided. "Lower your voice. Whatever will Mrs. Dinwittie think?"

"Perhaps that I am beating you. Which is a definite possibility in the very near future. I do not take kindly to insinuations that I would stoop to sexual temptations of innocent young women under my protection."

Lydia opened her eyes as wide as possible. "You misinterpreted my remark, John Lloyd. You don't tempt me to make love; you tempt me to kick you in the buns!"

He blinked, and she had the feeling she had at long last struck him speechless. "Buns?"

"Derriere, if you prefer. Throwing cold water on you might have the same effect. Kneeing you in the groin definitely would."

"What are you talking about, Miss Fairchild?" he demanded, his eyes black and most emphatically alive.

"Shocking you out of the guilt trip you've been on."

"Tread softly, Miss Fairchild," he warned.

"Women with feet as big as mine can't tread softly."

She put her hands on his shoulders. "You could not set aside the principles of a lifetime in order to save Cammie. It would have been a useless gesture. She was dead already. All that was kind and pure about Cammie Armstrong died in that car wreck. Only hate survived, the kind of hate that grows until it contaminates everything it touches. She told me that she had no human decency left. You gave her back her decency, John Lloyd, when you allowed her to commit a sacrificial act. She didn't kill herself to atone for murder. She killed herself to save not only Jim's life, but yours as well."

"My life?" he asked.

"She blamed you both: Jim for not punishing Amy, and you for being the cause of Amy's hurting her. You spurned Amy in favor of Cammie. That made Cammie a target of her spite. Eventually Cammie's hatred would have grown to the point of killing you both. I think she realized that and, from her memories of the rainbow days, dredged up enough love for both of you to prevent it. Don't despise her gift of love by wishing you hadn't given her the opportunity to express it."

She swallowed and spread her hands apart. "That's all I have to say, John Lloyd. Except goodbye. Classes start next week, and I have to leave. I can't say it hasn't been interesting. I'll be the only woman in my class who ever survived a murder attempt."

She looked up at him only to see him gazing out the window again. She'd like to board up that damn window. But he'd just find another window and continue being a martyr. God, she hated martyrs. She turned and walked toward the door.

"Miss Fairchild?" His voice was soft with just a suggestion of a drawl.

"What?" she asked without turning around.

"Thank you," he said.

"You're welcome." She took another step toward the door.

"Miss Fairchild?" The drawl sounded stronger.

She stopped again. "Yes?"

"I received a most interesting phone call this morning. A client of mine discovered an almost nude body in the middle of his wheat field."

"Almost nude?"

"The victim was wearing one pink and one yellow sock. Sergeant Schroder has advanced the most asinine theory for the deceased's apparent lack of style." His drawl was back to normal, soft and thick as molasses.

She took another step. "I'm sure you'll straighten out Sergeant Schroder."

"Lydia!"

She whirled around. "Yes, John Lloyd?" Her voice sounded breathless even to her own ears.

"The case should be coming to trial in about nine months. It occurs to me that you will be seeking employment in about that same length of time." He fiddled with his watch chain. "Would you prefer a rolltop desk similar to mine, or something more modern?"

About the Author

D. R. Meredith is the author of three critically acclaimed mystery novels featuring Sheriff Charles Matthews: *The Sheriff and the Panhandle Murders* (1984), *The Sheriff and the Branding Iron Murders* (1985), and *The Sheriff and the Folsom Man Murders* (1987). The first two in the series won the coveted Oppie Award, sponsored by the Southwestern Booksellers' Association, as Best Mystery Novel in their respective years. Ms. Meredith has completed a sequel to *Murder By Impulse: Murder By Deception*.

Attention Mystery and Suspense Fans

Do you want to complete your collection of mystery and suspense stories by some of your favorite authors? John D. MacDonald, Helen MacInnes, Dick Francis, Amanda Cross, Ruth Rendell, Alistar MacLean, Erle Stanley Gardner, Cornell Woolrich, among many others, are included in Ballantine/Fawcett's new Mystery Brochure.

For your FREE Mystery Brochure, fill in the coupon below and mail it to: